COPPERSUN 265

Fifty Years Later,
the Nightmares Continue

JOE WALKER

i

Although inspired by actual events, this book a work of fiction. The names, characters, and places were produced from the author's imagination. Any resemblance to locales, entities, or persons, living or dead is entirely coincidental.

For Kimmy Ann

DEDICATED TO:

Military Combat Veterans
First Responders
Breast Cancer Survivors
Sexual Assault Victims

The Common Denominator?
Post-Traumatic Stress

PREFACE

CopperSun 265 recounts the journey of a 70-year-old veteran whose life was indelibly marked by the Special Operations he carried out during the Vietnam War.

As a member of a covert "snatch and grab" fireteam, Joe Tyler participated in several enemy engagements deep inside North Vietnam. Joe Tyler survived the war only to face a new enemy, one even more relentless.

Over the last five decades, as the horrors of combat continue to fester inside, post-traumatic stress has rotted his brain.

"For the past 50 years, the memories of my combat sins are revived several times a month. They make random appearances through sudden flashbacks and sporadic nightmares." Joe Tyler as said to his psychologist in 2018.

With the Vietnam war ramping up in the early 1960s, the United States government reinstated the military draft of WWII. Between 1964 and 1973, 2.2 million men over the age of 18 were drafted into the United States Army. Most every American male was either eligible or knew someone qualified to join the "war on communism."

The other branches of the military countered by offering a variety of new enlistment incentives to fill their own quotas. The US Navy instituted an enlistment program to all high school students eligible to graduate at the end of their Spring semester. As a bonus, the enlistees received credit for active duty while they were still in high school. More importantly, they were guaranteed to enter the training school of their choice after completing recruit training.

After seeing Richard Widmark in the 1951 film, "The Frogmen" on late-night TV, Joe had dreamt of becoming a member of an elite Underwater Demolition Team, aka, Navy Frogmen. Leveraging the Navy's guaranteed training offer for Basic Underwater Demolition (BUD) training after boot-camp, Joe convinced his parents to co-sign his initial enlistment. What neither the recruiter, Joe, nor his parents knew at the time was that in January of 1962, President Kennedy had secretly ordered the Navy to begin guerilla warfare training after BUD training had been completed.

When he arrived in Coronado to begin his Basic Underwater Demolition training, Joe discovered his beloved Frogmen had secretly morphed into something called SEALs; the acronym representing their new combat roles: At Sea, the Air, and on Land.

After successfully completing Basic Conditioning, Hell Week, Underwater Demolition, SEAL Qual-School, and finally, Survival, Evasion, Resistance & Escape Training, Joe qualified for Advanced Warfare Training. At AWT, the Navy Lieutenant that commanded the base had hand-picked each trainee and assigned specializations for everyone's training. In Joe's case, his specialization would be Snatch and Grab Operations, which is military for "kidnapping."

Finally, after 78 weeks of training, Petty Officer Joe Tyler's 19th birthday, he began two combat tours as a Covert Mission Specialist, escorting CIA operatives in and out of North Vietnam.

In 1976, several years after active military duty, Joe, along with over one million other men and women, was diagnosed as being "shell-shocked" and suffering from "acute combat fatigue," the same prognosis all combat veterans have received since the War of Independence in 1776.

Each person was given the same prognosis: 'Future-life-events' would ultimately replace the horrific memories witnessed in combat. Their projections were wrong.

It was toward the end of the 1980s before Joe was identified has suffering from something called "Post-Traumatic Stress Disorder." He, and many others were told that with professional therapy he could receive through the Veterans Administration he should be able to live a healthy life.

Or not.

Once he began his involvement in covert operations, his military records and subsequent DD-214 (military discharge papers) were "cleansed." This essentially meant that all his military paperwork reflected a myth; one that he would have to memorize and repeat over, and over again for the rest of his life. Like all Special Operations people today, the early Navy SEALs had to sign a 100-year agreement to never tell any part of his actual duties, unless given permission to do so, for the remainder of his entire life.

When it came to obtaining services from the Veterans Administration this agreement proved to be problematic. For example, Joe was not eligible to receive medical benefits relating to such things as PTSD, Agent Orange, etc. Why? Because he could not prove that he was anywhere near the areas of defoliating or ever served in a combat role.

Talking to a civilian psychologist was nearly impossible. His 100-year agreement with the government forbade him to discuss anything about his actual military life. Therefore, Joe spent the next 50 years attempting to get help from well-meaning religious leaders, pharmacists (licensed or not), liquor store proprietors, and bartenders. Predictably, the daily flashbacks and weekly nightmares and that he had since 1968, continued.

Finally, in 2014, the Department of Navy government told him his Top-Secret military life had been recently downgraded to Secret. Over the next four years, Joe attempted to track down various tidbits of information that confirmed dates, places, and events as he remembered them. He was astonished to find vast quantities of formerly Top-Secret information on the internet. Google, Wikipedia, Military Archives, and the

4

librarians at the Department of Defense became his "go-to" sources.

In the Fall of 2018, Joe Tyler met Dr. Renae Mack, a Psychologist trained in EMDR Therapy. Thanks to the combined efforts of Dr. Mack's therapy, along with her counseling and careful monitoring of the latest prescription efforts from a psychiatric team, at age 71, Joe Tyler had broken free from the PTSD bonds.

CHAPTER ONE
Kent, Ohio - May 4, 1970

WHY NOT JUST KILL MYSELF?
Petty Officer Joseph E. Tyler, US Navy (Retired)

Night arrives.
Peaceful. Beautiful. Dangerous.
Each night brings its own brand of terror.
It is where the nightmares are replayed,
Over and over, every night.
And always in slow motion.
Always, as in, for the rest of my life.
Question: Who decides how long I can live?
The tortured souls of those that I have killed
Tell me that I should be the one to
Decide the time of my death.
And that time is drawing near!
Better I choose how, and when,
Than being surprised by an NVA tracker.
Or maybe someone from
today's Ohio National Guard,
Who today killed four innocents -
All were young students on the mall.

CHAPTER TWO
August 15, 1968

Joe Tyler stopped killing people on August 15, 1968.

Four weeks after the historic Tet Offensive of February 1968, Navy Petty Officer Joe Tyler was transferred from the Forward Operations Base located adjacent to Quang Tri. His new assignment sent him south, to Landing Zone Betty - a large military base located near the central coastal town of Phan Thiet.

After reporting to Lieutenant Commander Gallagher, Joe was assigned to an American advisory team near Xã Hàm Minh. The current advisers were comprised of five seasoned Army Green Beret Special Forces, whose duties focused on training platoons of elite South Vietnamese Rangers. Petty Officer Tyler, having spent the past 16 months as the point-man of a Navy SEAL Special Ops team, fit their training requirements perfectly.

Several months later, in mid-August, their training duties were completed. The six American advisors - five Green Berets and Joe - were ordered back to LZ Betty to await their next deployment. After the South Vietnamese Rangers departed, the six Americans were able to get a ride in the back of an Army transport convoy part of the way, but, as the trucks approached the coastline turn-off near Xā Thuàn Quy, The Special Operations advisors were once again on their own.

The Green Beret squad leader, a career oriented First Sergeant, studied the map and estimated they were still 12 miles south of the main base at LZ Betty. He glanced at his radioman and pointed to their location. Without being asked, the squad's radioman requested a bird (helicopter) to return them to the base. However, they were advised that the geography between them and the Base was actively "hot," and nothing could be made available for the next day or two.

The First Sergeant glanced at the map and quickly decided the squad would walk the final distance. Tyler, as the squad's point-man, came over and together, he and the First Sergeant studied the terrain between them and LZ Betty. Joe selected two terrain markers to use as location checkpoints.

With thoughts of sitting at a table, eating freshly cooked food, a hot shower, and sleeping on a bed running through their minds, the warriors quickly grabbed their gear and saddled up. Besides, asking these elite jungle warriors to hike alongside a white sandy beach that sat adjacent to a beautiful, turquoise ocean, was like asking them to take a carefree vacation in the Bahamas.

Several hours into their walk, they heard a firefight break-out a few hundred yards ahead of them. The Viet Cong's initial burst of machine-gun fire was followed by the whoomph, whoomph, whoomph of three enemy mortars being launched., At the sound of the enemy M-82s heading in their general direction, each member of the squad instinctively dropped to the ground. The First Sergeant crawled forward and tapped Joe three times on his left foot. This was an indication for Joe as the squad's point man, to move toward the fighting.

The other Green Berets, separated by 25-foot intervals, followed the First Sergeant's lead, and crawled forward. Once Joe drew even with the American platoon's front line, it took only a few seconds to surmise what was happening before him quickly. Using hand gestures, Joe signaled the other men in their squad to get small; combat language meaning to stop, stay low, and merge with your surroundings.

The First Sergeant made his way beside him and studied the situation. Before deciding as to what his squad should do to support the Marines, the Sergeant asked Joe where he thought the enemy was positioned.

"Looks like a jarhead platoon managed to get themselves trapped by a VC company. It looks like Charlie split his guys into three kill-zones." As Joe spoke, he used his Stoner 63A rifle to point in the general direction of the two flanking fire zones. The Green Beret Sergeant's own assumption of the enemy positions was in total agreement with his point-man.

With no time to lose, the sergeant ordered Joe and one of his men to set up a counter-flanking kill-zone, along the beach and to the northeast of the Marine platoon. Two other Green Berets were ordered to set up another flanking fire zone to the southwest. The four men quickly departed as the sergeant, and the radioman headed toward the center of the platoon to find the Marine leader.

Joe, along with his Green Beret counterpart, had no sooner established a strong offensive position when a black-pajamaed VC soldier suddenly broke from the dense jungle underbrush. The enemy soldier began running hard, away from the American's location and appeared to be carrying several mortar rounds against his chest. Pushing the Stoner 63A tight against his shoulder, Joe centered the gun's sights between the shoulder blades of the fleeing figure. Slowing his breathing, he gently squeezed the trigger. Twice.

The first bullet struck the enemy soldier in the back of the neck, precisely where the spinal cord and brain attached; the Viet Cong's body momentarily locked in an upright position. A quarter-second later, Joe's second-round penetrated the middle of the enemy soldier's back, causing the now lifeless body to tumble into the sandy beach.

A few minutes later, with the assistance of the cannons from a nearby Navy destroyer, the enemy attack dissolved. Any enemy soldiers not killed or severely wounded, quickly disappeared into the hillside.

Once the all-clear signal sounded, Joe cautiously walked down the white sandy beach to secure the enemy mortar rounds. Holding his MK-22 pistol in his right hand, he slowly approached the enemy soldier's body.

Because his first-round had entered at the back of the soldier's skull, Joe assumed that the Viet Cong soldier's facial features would be obliterated. The Navy SEALs Stoner 63A was infamous for making a small hole when the bullet penetrated a human body. Upon exiting, the tumbling projectile would leave a cavity the size of a man's fist. Such was the case with the VC soldier lying in front of him.

The second round had entered the middle of soldier's back, several inches below the first shot. Using the heel of his left foot, Joe slowly rolled the body onto its back and discovered the black-clad soldier was female. After two years of combat experience, Petty Officer Tyler was acutely aware that thousands of Vietnamese women were combat soldiers. Because of this, he was only mildly surprised by finding the soldier was female.

The Stoner carbine had lived up to its reputation. Where her face should have been was now a jelled mass of blood, bone, and brain matter. However, what he saw next was so horrifying that it caused bile to fill his throat, his body to collapse to the ground and his digestive system to explode in uncontrollable spasms.

The female soldier was not carrying mortar rounds. In fact, even in death, what she had held so protectively in her arms was something of significantly more importance.

CHAPTER THREE
August 16, 1968

Every night Joe Tyler remained on Vietnam soil, he found it difficult, if not impossible, to sleep. When he would eventually drift off, spirits and other apparitions of those he had killed would appear. The worst nightmare, of course, was his last kill; "The Dream" as he came to call it.

Today, five decades later, The Dream continues to make random appearances several times each month. The last fifteen or twenty years, The Dream is sometimes pre-empted by either of two additional combat experiences: "The Old Man," his first up-close and personal killing of another human being in 1966. The third major nightmare, Joe called "The Hotel" because it took place on the third floor of a blown-out building during the Tet Offensive in 1968.

After being slightly wounded, Joe angrily took revenge and assassinated three NVA soldiers. Because of their location in the building, Joe had deemed them responsible for firing the round that subsequently put a neat little hole above his left shoulder blade, two inches from his spine.

For the past fifty years, Joe always refers to the nightmare trifecta as the Frightful Three. To be sure, there are other nightmares based on Joe's other combat

12

events. Just like the Frightful Three, the cameo dreams have unique environmental characteristics such as the sights, sounds, and stench that accurately reflect the time and place where the original took place. Why they show-up is a good question. Joe's best guess is they are triggered by something he saw, felt, smelled, or heard in the previous 24 hours.

Not that it matters. To be sure, there are more benign military nightmares that occasionally appear, but they are centered on a variety of non-life-threatening themes. For example, being chased inside a crowded shopping mall by large Vietnam jungle-rats, or the torment of unintentionally giving his military commanders the wrong information on enemy troop movements.

And then there is the somewhat hilarious dream of his mother calling him on an old-style rotary phone, to complain that two Navy Shore Patrol officers are waiting outside, on her front porch. They tell her that they need the keys to a gunboat. They add that Joe said he left them in his mother's kitchen.

"The only keys on the counter are the ones to your dad's work truck. Should I give them to the Navy guys?"

Beginning with his falling asleep the night of the August 15, 1968, The Dream opens with a warm day that finds Joe having a somewhat brisk, yet peaceful walk over milky white sand covered beach. The air is irresistibly clean and fresh. The trade winds drift softly from a beautiful, turquoise ocean on his right, while palm trees gently sway some twenty yards to his left.

Within The Dream's opening, Joe is a tourist enjoying a vacation on a remote, South Pacific island. As he strolls along the beach, the waves are breaking into the sand in front of him. With every step he takes, Joe becomes more entrenched with a profound, intense sensation of tranquility and inner peace.

He wanders aimlessly; his attention is never more than the next wave as it ends ending its long ocean voyage. Other than an occasional seashell arriving within a wave, nothing occurs to break the tranquility.

A short distance behind him, and to his left, he hears the soft cacophony of children enjoying another of nature's perfect days. Although Joe never turns to see the children, he is acutely aware of them and their enjoyment of life; some are chasing one another in an endless game of tag, others laughing as they throw and hit brightly colored beachballs high into the dazzling blue sky.

They are Vietnamese children, none different from their peers in every other country on the planet. All are sweet, innocent young girls between the ages of seven or eight. They are kids - just being kids. Enjoying being alive. As he continues his walk, his feet begin to feel heavy, giving him the sensation of being completely body weary.

A short time later, Joe looks down at his feet. The beach flip-flops that he put on at the beginning of his hike, have strangely morphed into tattered combat boots.

14

Likewise, his specially purchased vacation-colored tan khakis and light-blue t-shirt have mysteriously become military apparel: Full-body, tiger-striped, camouflaged clothing.

The once white, soft, sandy beach has become gray, brittle, and roughly textured. Each step begins to make a crunching sound. What he cannot notice, but within The Dream, he is always somehow acutely aware is the fact that he is not leaving footprints in the sand.

The sky, too, has changed - from azure blue to thick, dark, gray clouds that merge with the similarly colored sand below his feet, making it impossible to discern which is heaven and which is earth. Occasionally, a single bolt of lightning flashes across the sky, dancing from cloud to cloud in such a way as to lead him somewhere.

A light rain begins. While each droplet begins the downward fall clear and pure, when the moisture meets the sand, it leaves a strange, slimy, blood-red stain.

Joe pauses, studies it with the right toe of his combat boot and decides it − it is what?

Thick. Yeah, that is it. And slimy. Walking more cautiously now, Joe arrives at a puddle of creamy blood. Hesitating, he slowly lifts his head and eyes forward.

A few feet away is the lifeless body of a young woman. She is lying on her left side with her back toward him and dressed in Viet Cong black pajamas. Military instincts tell him to pause, kneel, and while doing so, slowly make a 360-degree evaluation for possible danger. Despite his training and years of experience, Joe kneels by placing most of his weight on his right knee. He begins examining the body without first securing his position, something he would never do in Vietnam.

His knee becomes damp as his worn-out tiger-striped trousers begin soaking in blood from the puddle beneath him. Somewhere far in the distance, Joe hears a human voice that sounds just like his own, yelling loudly to his brother warriors, "the blood is still warm."

Joe begins searching for the wound, hoping to stop the blood flow until the medics arrive. He gently leans his right forearm on her right bicep and shoulder as his left hand slowly, reverently, reaches toward her head. A half-inch before touching her, his hand freezes in mid-air: he is mesmerized by her beautiful long, jet-black, silky hair. He stares at her, his hand frozen in mid-air, hovering not more than a half-inch above her head. Joe tilts his own head slightly to the right and, as he stares at her, she is no longer a Vietnamese soldier nor a peasant girl from some village.

To him, she is an angel sent from Paradise and represents the purest, the most beautiful entity that heaven has ever produced. From somewhere deep in The Dream, the name "Olivia" rises into his mind. In fact, for the next fifty years later, the name Olivia always appears in The Dream.

For the life of him, he cannot figure out why. Somewhere, deep inside, he knows it is a name he should remember.

Using both hands now, he softly almost reverently turns her face toward him. Her thin, dark eyebrows appear symmetrically balanced above a flawlessly sculptured nose. The presentation is finalized by lips that are soft, naturally pink, and curved to perfection.

Who is she?

What happened to her?

Within his sleep induced dream, Joe shakes his head, desperately trying to clear his thoughts. Hurrying now, in order to save her life, he must find her wound. When he turns her head to the side, he sees a circular opening about the size of an American quarter in the back of her head. The wound is low and appears to be the area that connects her brain to her spine.

Joe stares as a thick goo of jelled slime slowly oozes from the orifice and drips into the scarlet puddle beneath him.

The thought occurs to him as he remembers he has seen, smelled, and yes, even tasted, worse. Examining the injury more closely, Joe decides his shirt will have to serve as the compression pack to stop the flow of the brain matter and bodily fluids. As he begins removing his shirt, the sound of an infant's muffled weeping causes him to stop. He pulls the shirt back down and frantically begins searching the sand surrounding them, desperately trying to identify the child's location.

Not seeing the child, his confusion grows. The child's cries are close-by, but where?

Finally, his eyes drift to where the woman's arms are folded in front of her chest. Gently, he pulls at the dead mother's arms and there, to his horror, is a baby girl not more than five or six months old. The blanket her mother had wrapped around her in a failed attempt to protect her is drenched in dark red blood.

Joe's body becomes motionless, a stare froze on his face. His vision is focused on a savagely torn, tiny body. A deep voice rises from the endless blackness of inner space and begins to scold him.

"You are a murderer! Your unquenchable thirst for yet another adrenaline rush from killing another human has caused this little girl's body to be ripped apart."

Gradually, Joe realizes that a pitch-black abyss has replaced the serenity of his once idyllic island beach. Fighting to regain his senses, he again hears his own voice cry out, pleading for understanding. "Wait! This is not right. She was not carrying a baby! She did not have a face! I never saw a face. This cannot be her. Her face was destroyed. It's not the person I shot at!"

Upon hearing his plea, the mother's angelic face turns sharply toward him. Joe begins pushing backward in a futile attempt to put distance between her and himself.

His feet and hands dig into the bloody sand and, as he does, his once beautiful Daughter of Heaven mutates to that of a haggard witch.

Sitting upright, she stares back, but now her black, steely eyes pierce through him to consume his soul.

Gradually, together they begin dancing and spinning, moving to the cadence of Satan's Waltz.

The tormented faces of others Joe has killed begin to appear, assemble, and start floating around them, moving faster and faster in the opposite direction.

Joe begins to feel disoriented and out-of-control until suddenly, everything stops: The music. The dancing. The faces of others that he has killed stop spinning, too.

Slowly, they float above him, each smiling now, yet agitated with anticipation. After a few moments, the hag's boney arms rise-up and her equally boney hands hold the tiny, skeletal remains of the baby girl.

"You killed my baby! You MURDERED my little girl!"

Joe recoils and using all his strength attempts to push away. No matter how hard he tries, there is no relief from the mother's apparition, and, at that moment, he realizes there is no escaping the memory of what he has done.

The witch begins to levitate and float upward and, as she gains height, thrusts the remains of the baby girl into the air.

Her fully emaciated body continues to hover in the darkness, she slowly lowers the body and again, presents the remnants to Joe.

The mother shrieks at him, and when she does, the child's body disintegrates into a fine grain and accumulates in her cupped hands. The night-hag holds the grain inches from his face. For the first time in his life, Joe is afraid.

Sensing his fear, she gently blows the finely powdered contents toward him. The dust stings his eyes and clogs his nostrils, cutting off his breath.

Desperate now, self-preservation forces him to open his mouth and gulps precious air into his lungs. When he does, the child's dusty remains choke him, forcing him to taste the death of the baby he has killed.

Joe's body begins to twist violently. Reaching deep inside, he uses every ounce of his remaining strength to escape. No matter how hard he tries he cannot move; a monstrous, evil being with superior claw-strength has snuck up behind him and violently pushes against him. The gargoyle tightly grasps his biceps and forcibly pulls him backward and forcing him down, further, and further into an abyss from which he cannot escape.

In the far, far distance, Joe hears a voice calling him. It is a human male voice. The voice becomes clearer and more distinctive every second.

As the voice speaks, Joe's nightmare slowly loosens its dominance over him. As he attempts to open his eyes, but his eyelids are heavy and very pasty.

Gradually, he becomes aware that the darkness that has enveloped him in the spirit-filled world has faded away, giving way to morning in the real world. While his body remains constrained, his breathing is no longer labored.

Slowly, steadily, real-life returns and, as his eyes begin to focus, he recognizes a familiar, yet seriously concerned, face. The Green Beret radioman releases his grip on Joe's shoulders, then leans back to give him space.

"Hey there squid-man, you had me worried. Are you okay?"

"Huh?" Joe barely manages to garble out a few words. "Uh, yeah. Roger that."

"Well, saddle-up, bitch. Our debriefs are in the chow hall. Sarge says he wants an accurate report of each guy's KIA, so the friggin' Marines don't take all the credit for killing everyone."

CHAPTER FOUR
2018

Joe's 70th birthday had come and gone.

Number 71 is now only a few months away and the Spirit-of-Old-Age not only glares at him, but also reminds him every time he looks at a calendar that chronologically, he has become an old man. Joe has become the old guy every 35-year-old complains about. Worse, every 18-year-old feels human beings his age should be euthanized so that they, tomorrow's leaders, can begin to fix everything his generation screwed-up.

Fifty years ago, at age 21, Joe was transferred from fulltime active military duty and become a member of the Naval Inactive Reserves. In other words, in case of a future war, the military would offer him as a hostage. In all that time, he has never admitted to anyone that he thinks about his combat life at least once a day, every day, day in and day out. And at least once each day, sometimes more often, he finds himself zoning out and transported back in time when he was a member of a super-secret CIA Navy SEAL team.

His mental flashbacks came-on without warning, initiated by an infinite variety of obscure triggers: A smell, a sudden movement, a voice, a shadow or, music recorded from the 1960s or early '70s. The triggers are unique and impossible to explain.

Yesterday was a good example. As Joe drove by some open farmland, he saw two large pieces of damaged and rusted machinery standing alone in an open field. Instantly, his mind brought up a memory from 1967. Joe vividly recalled being on a Search and Rescue mission with three other SEALs, finding their targeted American fighter jet in the middle of a large rice-paddy. The tail number confirmed that the plane was the Navy F-8 Crusader they had been looking for the past three days.

The wreckage of the downed plane sat almost precisely in the center of a 12-acre farm. As Joe slowly scanned the area around the wreck, his instincts began firing on all cylinders: There were no civilians were working in the paddies.

An enemy ambush had been set.

As if being in North Vietnam was not dangerous enough, crossing several wide-open rice-paddies in the daylight to look for a pilot who might, or might not be in the wrecked aircraft, was near suicidal. He slowly backed into the dense jungle and got with the other three members of his fireteam. Together, the team would figure out a strategy of how they were going to get someone to the wreckage. He knew "that someone" was going to be himself. Why? 1) he was the youngest. 2) he had the lowest in rank on the SEAL team. 3) Out of the four positions on the team, the point man was the most expendable.

As mental flashbacks often due, this one had transported Joe to North Vietnam circa 1968, back to the midday heat and humidity, just as if he was there. Even though the late morning temperature was 60 degrees, and he was driving 30 mph (in a 45-mph zone) with all the windows down, his entire body was covered in sweat, drenching his underwear, socks, and t-shirt.

Of course, Joe was not in Vietnam. On that Monday he was driving his 2013 Chevrolet Avalanche west on State Highway 14 through Volga, South Dakota. Just as his brain fully returned to the driving task at hand, a young lady passed him on the left, honked her horn, then yelled something about nursing homes being available.

Five days later, Friday. August 31, 2018, marked a significant anniversary for Joe Tyler — it had been exactly 50 years since he last set foot on Vietnam soil. The day began like most others. He awoke abruptly, precisely at 5:30 AM.

Thanks to Thursday night's epic version of The Dream nightmare, when the real world jumped into focus, his body was shivering, his lungs gulping for breath, and he was sitting up.

The good news was that he found himself sitting upright in a familiar bed, within his own home, on the open plains of central South Dakota. Swinging his legs over the side of the mattress, Joe sat upright, placed the

24

palms of both hands on his lower back and arches backward. As he makes his first attempt at standing upright and hears the familiar crescendo of bones cracking and rubbing together.

Without looking down, he slides his feet into the slippers that await him, then reaches to the nightstand on his left and grabs the water glass that has also been expecting him. Finishing whatever liquid that remained from the night before, he makes a half-hearted attempt to stretch out. Nowadays, his enemy is arthritis. Each morning the pain assaults his body, then continuously provides random minor annoyances throughout the day.

The horrific nightmares, along with flashbacks of his combat life, remain. As he stumbles toward the bathroom, for at least the ten-thousandths time he hears himself say, "I gotta do something about this."

CHAPTER FIVE
1947 - 1957

At 6:30 PM, Thursday, November 27, 1947, Geraldine Bernice Tyler, after finishing the last bite of warm, fresh-from-the-oven apple pie, excused herself from Thanksgiving dinner. With brother-in-law Lehman at the wheel of his 14-year-old 1933 Chevrolet sedan, Geraldine Bernice Gardener-Tyler, and husband William Thompson Tyler II, arrived at the Emergency Room of Saint Joseph's Hospital just in time to give birth to their third child.

Because they had not decided on a name before his birth, his parents gave him the name "Joseph," taken from the name of the hospital of his birth. His father wanted no, make that demanded that his second son's middle name would be "Emergency," reflecting the name of the St. Joseph's hospital ward where their son was born.

Then again, his father had been drinking all day.

The nurse charged with filling out the birth certificate, refused the father's request and simply wrote down an E, without adding a period, and assumed the family would complete the name before the infant he left the hospital. The nurse's assumption proved incorrect. For the rest of his life, Joseph E. Tyler had to explain that the capital 'E' was in fact, his entire middle name and not an initial, hence no period required after the first and only letter.

Sister Karen Elizabeth Tyler was born nearly three years earlier on January of 1945, while his older brother, William (Bill) Thompson Tyler III, was born October 1946, 13 months to the day before his birth.

Between a couple of miscarriages and a stillbirth, years later, his mother had two additional sons: Hal was born in 1956, followed by Kennedy Jameson Tyler in 1963.

The year of Joe's birth, the Number One major news story in America, and most every newspaper in the world in 1947, was the reported crash of an interstellar spacecraft near Roswell, New Mexico.

That story of the aliens was uncovered by sister Karen when she was a sophomore at Warren G. Harding High School. For the next two school years, and several years after, whenever the opportunity arose, Karen would eagerly offer an explanation that the birth of her younger brother, and the finding of an alien spacecraft was in fact, not a coincidence.

In truth, the two seemingly unrelated events were the same story!

Her advice to anyone who would listen (and many who would not) was straight forward: brother Joe was an alien. People should treat everything he said or did with the utmost suspicion. After all, he was part of the advance group of aliens sent to Earth to plant nuclear bombs deep into the core of the Earth.

Before the two younger brothers' arrivals, Karen, Bill, and Joe grew up in the Ridge Hill Projects, which was located on the southeast side of town, adjacent to the north side of Niles Road. Their apartment was attached to several other, identically constructed and sat together in a nearly straight row. Tarpaper siding, designed to resemble brown bricks, covered the plywood siding. Asbestos insulation filled the walls.

Each unit had a coal-fired, pot-belly stove that separated the kitchen from the living room. There were three small bedrooms and one bathroom that contained a toilet, pedestal sink, and bathtub, all three of which were made of cast-iron. Twelve feet outside the front kitchen door was a coal bin located adjacent to an alley and leaned precariously.

The apartments were occupied entirely by blue-collar workers, most of whom were employed in one of the three steel mills located a half mile south of them.

The three siblings grew up in one of many 800-square foot apartments, each one of eight units-built side-by-side, on thin concrete slabs. Karen had a room to herself, while Bill and he slept in homemade bunk beds in an adjoining room.

A swamp bordered the southeast side of the projects. A wide drainage ditch ran behind and paralleled to an eastern strip of units, approximately 40 feet behind the Tyler's back door. Because the trench was connected to the swamp, after every heavy rain, cotton-mouth snakes would make themselves known to the children playing in the units adjoining backyards. Opposite the ditch sat several acres of dense woods. The trees were adjacent to an 80-foot hill on the east side. Atop the hill and running north-south, was Ridge Drive.

Within his youthful, active imagination, the small ravine, and adjacent wooded hillside became his version of a Pacific island jungle. As a kid, he would often spend the summer pretending he was a Marine in the forests of a Pacific island. In his make-believe fantasies, he Tyler the fearless, brave sergeant that led their patrol on secret missions. By far, his favorite fantasy game was leading his men on search and rescue missions.

As a seven-year-old, he quickly figured out a way to make the game harder on himself, to make it fair for his imaginary enemy soldiers. After entering the woods, he would walk-in precisely 25 steps, then throw a rubber baseball in some random direction. Where the ball came to rest became the location of the "American pilot" who had been shot down by the Japanese Zeroes. Their squad's mission was to save the pilot before the Japanese soldiers found him.

He would start the search by going back to the culvert and follow it to the other end of the woods. From there, he would walk through his "jungle" and locate the pilot, careful not to be spotted by the enemy patrols.

Sundays were always his favorite day of the week. Typically, the family spent the day with uncles, aunts, and cousins at his grandparents' house on Haymaker Street.

When they returned home in the evening, the family would gather around the radio in their tiny living room and listen to shows like Jack Benny, Red Skelton, along with Amos and Andy. Karen, brother Bill and he would be in their pajamas, sitting cross-legged on a wool Army blanket in the middle of the family room floor, eating freshly- popped, popcorn and drinking homemade lemonade.

Frances E. Willard Elementary School was a three-story, red brick building that had been built just before World War Two began. Regardless of the weather, Karen, Bill, and he walked to school each day, which was slightly more than a one-mile walk from their apartment.

Joe remembered little about attending Willard. However, there was an event he has stuck with him forever. At the time, Bill was in the fourth grade and him in the third. One spring afternoon as they walked home from school, three bullies pushed Bill into a mud puddle. He attempted to come to Bill's rescue and promptly got his butt whipped.

Because their school clothes had been muddied and torn, Bill and he thought for sure they were in big trouble when they got home. Instead, their dad praised them for standing together as brothers and not backing down to the bullies. In fact, their dad took them both next door to his

Uncle Charlie's apartment, then to other neighbors, to retell their adventure, over and over again. Thinking back, Bill was always bigger and stronger than him; he probably could have handled the situation if Joe had not interfered.

Ah yes - the memory of the first of several black eyes and cut lips received at the hands of someone bigger than himself. Years later, sometime in Joe's late 20s, he wondered if he may have missed getting the fear gene; or did he just lack the common sense to avoid confrontation?

Compounding that issue was the fact that he always recovered from his encounters. And, because he seemed to be able to take whatever punishment anyone placed upon him, he has never intimidated by anyone's size or stature.

Before he began attending fourth grade, the family moved to a house on the southwest side of Warren. Compared to their apartment, their new home was luxurious. It had two stories, gas heat, hot water, a dirt driveway, and a front porch that had a wooden swing, held up by two, squeaky chains.

The summer before the school year started, his father, along with a couple of his dad's brothers, built a giant lean-to that somewhat resembled a one-and-a-half car garage.

Joe's first memory from attending Horace Mann Elementary school was coming home from school one afternoon with yet another blackened eye and swollen lip. His dad and Uncle took him to the side of the house where they cleansed his face with the garden hose, hoping that his mom would not figure out he had been in yet, another fight.

Because both his father and Uncle had more than a couple of beers that afternoon and, as the three of them set on the steps of the back porch, the older men swapped stories about the times they came home from Dickey Avenue Elementary School, their clothes torn, faces lacerated, lips cut and bodies bruised.

To be sure, he has no memory of the moral principle the story was supposed to deliver, he did remember his Uncle telling him, "Never allow a bully to threaten you, or anyone else for that matter. Stand up for others, especially family and friends. Most important, win or lose, never talk about what you have done - especially if you won."

He could not swear those were his Uncle's exact words; the meaning, though, stuck with him the rest of his life.

The following summer, as he was riding his bicycle on the sidewalk out front of Horace Mann Elementary School. Two boys from another class waved him down and when he stopped, the heavier of the two, Jamie, asked him to join everyone for a pick-up baseball game later that afternoon.

While standing there holding on to his bike and talking with Jamie, the second guy, Larry, slowly, worked his way behind him.

Like everyone else in the sixth grade (including the girls), the two boys were a lot bigger than he. Suddenly, Larry grabbed his arms and pulled them tight behind him. Having been forced to release his grip on the bike, it slid to the sidewalk. As it was falling, the chain guard ripped his jeans and caused a deep scratch in his right calf.

With Larry propping him up from behind, Jamie stood in front of him, both hands clenched into tight fists, his face within inches of his. The look on Jamie's face was like that of a spider that had just caught his favorite morsel in his web. And now it was dinner time.

Having been on the losing end of many confrontations, he was not afraid. Joe knew he would recover from whatever was about to happen, so he just glared at Jamie, daring him to take his best shot. Jamie did just that.

Out of habit, his face became tense as he prepared to take the hit. Instead, Jamie's tight fist landed hard in the center his solar plexus. The blow took him by surprise, as did the additional punches to his midsection.

Feeling that he could not, and probably would never breathe again, he doubled over. As he did, Larry let go of him and he sank to his knees. Wanting to get his shot in too, Larry kicked him then stomped hard on his back.

As he laid there, gasping, and gulping what air he could, the two older boys turned away, and laughing, patted each other on the back as they began walking across the broad front school lawn.

Gradually, he started to breathe somewhat normally again. After wiping the tears from his eyes, he got to his feet and, slightly shaken, rode home. During the short, half-mile ride home, he remembered his dad telling him that when fighting someone bigger and stronger, find something to equalize the situation.

Using the garden hose on the side of the house, he rinsed his face and cleaned the blood from his leg. Refreshed by the cold water coming out of the hose, holding his stomach, walked down the driveway to the garage. When he entered through the always-open garage door, he immediately spotted his dad's large pipe-wrench - a gift delivered from the "Gods of Get-Even."

Carrying the wrench in both hands, he limped through their back yard, across the school's asphalt basketball court and heavily graveled playground. His instincts told him his two abusers would soon be passing by the back wall and would not expect the ambush he had in mind for them.

Less than 30-seconds later, he heard his two assailants laughing as they approached his position. Holding the pipe-wrench in a two-handed, baseball bat-type grip, he prepared to unleash vengeance upon them both.

Larry had the misfortune to be the person walking nearest to him. When he swung the wrench, the blow connected into Larry's stomach, causing him to double-up and slowly sink into a fetal position on the cement. On his way to the ground, Larry had vomited what food was in his upper digestive system; simultaneously, his lower bowels discharged the previously digested food from his rectum.

Witnessing what had just happened to his friend, Jamie looked at Joe. His eyes grew wide as Joe began slowly, pulling back the wrench in preparation for the next victim. As Joe held the wrench back, he hesitated to further enjoy the fear radiating from Jamie's face.

Suddenly, Jamie took off running through the grassy field behind the schoolyard. For a second, Joe thought about chasing after him.

However, Larry continued to lie on the sidewalk and was struggling to breathe normally. Joe knelt beside him and, after making sure he had not broken any of Larry's ribs, helped him sit upright and relax so he would be able to breathe somewhat normally.

Once Joe was confident that Larry would be okay, he slowly helped him to his feet. Placing Larry's right arm over his shoulder, Joe helped him walk through the playground then through Joe's backyard, until the two of them reached the garden hose. Joe helped Larry clean-up, even assisting Larry to rinse out both his dirty jeans and soiled underwear.

Larry put on his wet clothes, and they both sat on the back-porch steps. Sitting in the sun helped the wet clothes begin to dry and provided Larry additional time to regain his bearings. They sat side-by-side for several minutes, looking straight ahead into the neighbor's back yard; neither saying a word to the other.

After several minutes, Larry finally spoke.

"Thanks for helping me."

Joe's reply was to shrug his shoulders as he continued studying the freshly mowed grass on the neighbor's lawn. They sat for several more minutes until Larry stood up, stretched, and then, without saying another word, began his journey home.

As Joe watched him saunter-off, he started feeling proud of himself. After getting beat-up by two bigger, older guys he did not just sit and cry, nor did he feel sorry for himself. Instead, he got on his bike and formulated a plan to make sure it never happened again.

The adrenaline rush that slowly grew inside him as he visualized what he needed to do, then grew in intensity as he successfully executed the ambush, was nothing short of amazing.

High school life was a constant blur to Joe. He never seemed to know what everybody else knew. Who was dating whom, who liked whom, what everyone thought about someone else. For the most part, Joe was usually unaware about some high school event that was coming up that he should attend. Thank goodness his sister Karen was two years older than him and made sure he was in the right place at the right time.

Another problem he had was never bringing a book home to study or do homework. Karen and Bill were always studying and somewhat transfixed on their grades. Instead, Joe was always out playing some sandlot sport – baseball, football, basketball, ice hockey – or just hanging out at the Quinby Park shelter house.

There was a relatively large group of girls and guys there just about any evening after school. Collectively, they were referred to as the Quinby Boys. Even the girls.

Since Joe's family lived half their lives on food stamps, or handouts from the Carpenters Union, to Joe, passing college prep courses seemed like a colossal waste of effort. Besides, Bill and Joe had part-time jobs on the weekend busing tables and washing dishes at the Elks Club.

Somewhere along the line, Joe discovered that a C-minus, or even a D-plus grade average would get him through to the next grade. To him, homework was something to be copied from others or just never completed. What helped him survive was a natural talent for speed-reading and a high retention rate from whatever he had read. If he made it to homeroom early, he could read and regurgitate the highlights of the science, history or English homework that was needed.

Naturally, this confused and frustrated his teachers. Joe would eagerly participate in every class, even going as far to ask complex questions. He would easily score high on every exam but never turned in written homework. When asked about this flaw, he always shrugged his shoulders and replied that he did not have time.

No one could ever explain to him what the difference of graduating high school with a C average would make in his life.

When asked, he just answered that all he wanted after graduating, was to join the Navy, and become a member of an Underwater Demolition Team.

CHAPTER SIX
April 1965

Ten weeks before graduating from high school, he and his father drove downtown, stopping near the Navy recruiter's office on East Market Street. After they parked, they both sat there in his Dad's rusted, 1955 Ford panel truck. While he was eager to go in and enlist, his father rested both hands on the steering wheel, sat silently staring at nothing, lost in his memories. He sat there quietly, not knowing what to do. Occasionally, he would glance at his father, who had remained stoic in the driver's seat.

At that moment, T. William Tyler, Sr. wanted to tell his boyish, seventeen-year-old son how life really was; how going to war was nothing like the movies portrayed it to be. How, on the morning of November 20, 1943, his father was a 19-year-old Marine aboard an Assault Landing Craft and, as a member of the 2nd Marine Division, his Company was just minutes away from beginning America's first significant assault of the western Pacific: The Battle of Tarawa.

The father wanted to explain to his son what it was like watching the huge landing ramp fall open into the chest-deep ocean and getting his first glimpse Betio Island. He wanted to say he witnessed several friends, standing not more than an arms-length in front of him, get killed before taking their first step off the transport.

Joe's father, for the first time in his life, wanted to say out loud how the sudden reality of war caused him to vomit and soil his fatigues. He wanted to add that over the next three days, 5,000 fellow marines would join them; 1,000 would die before the week ended, and another 1,500 would be severely wounded.

His father knew the war in Vietnam was heating up, that going into combat was hell. But more importantly, his father knew that coming home from war could be even worse. He knew that his son's combat memories could never be erased, that his son's friends and family would never, could never, understand what Joe's combat life was like.

More important (and later that day, more regrettably), his father desperately wanted to find the courage to tell his son that, although he never said it, he loved h more than he would ever know and that his father did not want his son to go to war.

Instead, his father looked to his right into his son's boyish face and asked, "Are you sure this is what you want to do?" Joe nodded, and with that, they both got out of the truck.

In May of 1961, President Kennedy made several announcements directing the future of the United States. That speech was carried live on all three TV networks. One of the initiatives from that address, that one most remembered by the newscasters, newspapers, and most American citizens, was his challenge to put a man on the moon before the end of the '60s decade. Within that same speech, Mr. Kennedy presented a military challenge that would have a lasting effect on the American armed forces: The President asked Congress to apportion over 100 million 1960s-era dollars to expand and strengthen the Special Forces. The President asked this to counter the Soviet Union, who was sending weapons, vehicles, and anti-aircraft to North Vietnam, to Laos and Cambodia.

What the public did not know was a few weeks before the President's address, he met with the Chief of Naval Operations, who detailed his idea to develop select members of the Navy's famed Underwater Demolition Teams (UDT) into counter-guerrilla units. These would be the Navy's Special Forces teams that would operate from sea, air, and land.

Joe was 13 when Mr. Kennedy made that nation-wide speech. Same as 99% of the rest of the American public, all he remembered was the President saying they would put people on the moon by the end of the current decade. He had either forgotten or was not paying attention when President Kennedy talked about his request to expand America's Special Forces into the Navy, Marines, Air Force, and Coast Guard. In fact, when his father co-signed for him to enlist in March of 1965, the American public was unaware, and very few military people even knew that there had been Top-Secret changes to the Navy's famed Underwater Demolition Team Frogmen; they had morphed into the now famous SEALs. Ten months after enlisting, he had an opportunity to learn everything there was to know about them.

◆ ◆ ◆

Nine weeks later, and just two days after his graduation ceremony held at original Mollenkoff Stadium from Warren G. Harding High School, his parents dropped him off at the military recruitment office where seven teenagers, all Trumbull County residents, were sworn in as members of the United States military. Four were headed to the Marines, one to the Army, himself, and another guy to the Navy. After being congratulated by both parents, he hugged his mother tightly, and she whispered how proud she was of him. When he stepped back, she was crying. His Dad clasped a steady left hand on his shoulder, shook his right hand, looked him in the eye, and mumbled something like, "you're on your own now."

With that, both parents turned and left.

The seven new recruits from Trumbull County Ohio boarded a grey military van and settled in for the two-hour trip to the Cleveland Military Indoctrination Center. After finishing their physicals, they signed documents giving body and soul to their respective military branches. They raised their right hands and swore the same oath as they had in Warren, vowing to serve and defend their country against all enemies, both foreign and domestic, as directed by Lyndon Baines Johnson, President of the United States of America.

All his life, he was taught that when you give your word that you were going to do something, you always followed through. Always. Therefore, when he raised his hand and promised both God and the President that he would faithfully defend the weak, and fight their enemies, to his death if necessary, he meant it with all his heart and soul.

At the end of the physicals in Cleveland, he was pulled out of the line and, to his surprise, instead of heading to Naval Great Lakes Recruit Training Center in Chicago, he received orders to report to the Recruit Training Center in San Diego.

The moment he boarded that plane at Cleveland Hopkins, somehow, he knew his life in small-town America was over. It was like winning the grand prize in the enlistment competition. Here he was; a 17-year-old kid who had never been away from home. Now, wholly unexpected, he had been assigned a seat, on a jet airplane no less, to southern California.

Joe anticipated recruit training to be like something out of the 1950s era war movies he had seen. The scenes from WWII flicks where the volunteers from Bo-Dunk, Tennessee, would arrive at boot camp entirely unaware of the horrors they were about to go through. After seeing those movies, he expected some large, nasty men to be hovering over him, yelling in his face, and shouting insults about his family; most of their language questioning his mother's and sister's sexual preferences.

There would be massive amounts of marching, drilling, fitness, obstacle courses, weapons training, and three-square meals a day. He looked forward to being challenged by these career military men; he had a deep need to see how he measured up when being with real fighting men. It never happened.

To Joe, Navy boot camp was boring. They had morning physical training, but it was not what he would call rigorous. No obstacle courses. They marched a lot -- to meals, to classes, to clinics -- but they never left the asphalt of the camp. Their 16 weeks of marching drills were designed to prepare them for one thing: 10 minutes of getting to, then formally leaving, the parade grounds for Recruit Training graduation.

On the plus side, no more daily lunches of butter and sugar, folded inside one slice of Wonder Bread for lunch, and occasionally, again for dinner, like back at home. Each day was monotonous. Most of their time sitting at desks in a classroom, or if they were lucky, classes out in the fresh air, sitting on wooden bleachers. At least when the classes were outside, they could watch the seagulls and enjoy the San Diego weather.

If he had to sum it up, he would say their primary training in San Diego was learning to "hurry-up and wait." They would double-time it to the mess hall, only to wait for 30 minutes once they got there. Likewise, they would march as a company to the medical clinics, then wait forever for yet another physical check-up.

The day they went to the firing range was the only time he felt energized to be at boot camp. They spent the first part of the day learning how to disassemble and then reassemble a Korean War-era M-1 carbine. After lunch, they headed over to the firing range. First, they spent an entire hour learning how to aim, adjust their breathing, then squeeze and not pull, the trigger.

Finally, it was his Company's turn to shoot live ammunition. Talk about pumped up! Joe finally had the opportunity to fire the same rifle his father had used in the Marines -- the same weapon his war-movie heroes used to beat the Japs and the Germans. The entire Company of 82 recruits went to the range about 1:30, waited two hours, got handed a rifle, sans any bullets, reviewed for the fifth time, the safety instructions they had learned that morning.

When told to do so, ten men would walk down the firing line and stand behind their assigned shooting mat. Once the instructor was positive each man was laid out in the proper prone sniper position, they were handed five rounds of live ammunition. When ordered, each man aimed their M1 at their assigned target that appeared 100 yards down range.

Once every man in the Company had completed their training, they marched back to the barracks. Total time on the actual gun range: Six minutes.

He was the only recruit with previous experience firing a rifle. As a teenager, he learned to shoot both a single-shot, 4-10 shotgun, and a .22 rifle. With all the thousands of rounds of .22-shorts that he had put through that gun, he became proficient in placing a small projectile through the center of small targets such as bottle caps.

Hitting a large target, with a large rifle on the Navy's firing range was a piece of cake, with every round in the bullseye.

Later that evening, while downing a few beers at the Chief's Lounge, their Drill Master was congratulated by his fellow DM's on his ability to train recruits at the firing range. Apparently, of the nearly 240 recruits on the firing line that day, Joe Tyler was the only person to place all five rounds in the center of the target.

After downing several more beers and, after being escorted out of the bar, their company's Drill Master headed to their company's barracks and entered their sleeping quarters at 2:30 AM.

After turning on every light in their barracks, the DM proceeded to throw two bright metal, empty garbage cans down the center aisle. As if the clanging metal noise, lights, and subsequent commotion were not enough to get everyone's attention, the inebriated DM began yelling through a battery-powered bullhorn. At 1:30 in the morning, he ordered all his recruits to get out of their racks and to stand for inspection.

Groggy, yet well trained, each man quickly threw their covers back and proceeded to line-up at full attention at the end of the bunks. With the men standing with their boxer shorts and t-shirts in various stages of disarray, the Chief began strutting down the middle of the barracks.

Looking straight ahead, they maintained tabs on their obviously drunken DM utilizing their peripheral vision. The Chief continued strutting for several minutes, ala, General Patton addressing his soldiers before D-Day. Once he reached the end of the aisle, he performed a very clumsy, military 'about face,' and nearly fell over. Regaining his balance, yelling loudly, ordered the entire Company to proclaim, in precision unison, that he was "The best damn Drill Instructor in the United States Navy."

Satisfied that his men were paying attention, he again utilized his loud Drill Instructor voice and proceeded to tell the entire Company that Recruit Joseph E. Tyler was the only recruit, ever, in the whole history of the United States Navy, going back "well over 200 years ago" from 1776 to 1965, to place all five rounds in the bulls-eye.

He slowly walked down the row of recruits and stood towering over him, patted him on the shoulder, and gave him a drunken wink. The Chief turned to address the remainder of the Company, but as he did, he forgot what he was going to say. After a few moments of scratching himself, he started talking, hoping that his original thought would return.

"As of this moment, Recruit Tyler Joseph no longer has sentry duty."

"In fact, he will no longer have any sentry duty. Ever!"

In his drunken state, he felt he made a historic proclamation, but his men failed to appreciate the significances of the moment.

"Further, due to his astute abilities and expert marksmanship, to wit, I was THE Drill Master that trained Recruit Joseph, and he soon became a legend in his expert marksmanship and recruit abilities!"

"Further, let it be known to all in this Company, that from this day hence, Tyler-the-Expert Marksman shall proclaim to behold Bunk One, which is now residing to be in the dominion to Recruit Double AA!"

Remaining within his drunken stupor, the DM ordered Aaron Anderson to step forward. Aaron did as he was told, glaring at Joe the entire time.

When the recruitment company was formed, Aaron, because of his initials, had first dibs on his choice of bunk. What made his bunk so special was its position within the barracks. AA enjoyed the top bunk in the corner, adjacent to two screened windows - one at the head of his bunk and the other on his left.

Fifty percent of the bunks in their barracks had no windows at all. Obviously, only bunks with windows got any air at all; and then only if they faced into the breeze. Because the window screens were only on the upper half of the windows, the bunks below them seldom felt anything.

During the late summer months in southern California of 1965, being guaranteed a soft, cool breeze at night was a luxury.

COPPERSUN 265

In Vietnam, he was a member of an elite, clandestine Navy SEAL extraction team...

. . . 50 years later, the nightmares continue.

Like 200,000 other Vietnam veterans, I've lived with PTSD for the past fifty years. Four years ago, someone suggested writing as a way to purge my subconscious. With the support of several friends, my meanderings developed into a 300-page novel: The storyline is constructed around how the tragedies of combat change a warriors life.

As a fellow South Dakotan, I would like to hear your views on PTSD, whether derived from the military, first-responder, or as the victim of an accident or an assault.

JOE WALKER
coppersun265@yahoo.com
# # #

Based on personal accounts and documented facts, *CopperSun 265* is the fictitious account of a 70-year-old Navy Special Operations veteran. Petty Officer Tyler's attitude about life was indelibly marked by the missions he carried out in North Vietnam in 1967 & '68. While Joe Tyler survived two combat tours on an elite, covert "Snatch and Grab" team, the brutality and secrecy of his missions combined to present an even more relentless enemy than he faced in combat: Post Traumatic Stress.

Amazon Keywords Search: Paperback Books Operation Footboy

"Aaron!" The Chief's bark was loud and sharp; everyone in the barracks snapped to attention. "You are to change the bedding and lockers with Tyler, forthwith. The Company shall remain at attention until both pass full, four-point-oh inspection!"

Once Aaron completed the move, the DM, being too tired to inspect them, headed toward his room and, talking out of the side of his mouth, told everyone to turn in.

After the lights had been out for five minutes, and the Chief's loud snoring gained momentum, Aaron yelled out, "Screw-you, Tyler." The rest of the Company laughed and began taken verbal shots at them both.

Joe learned a valuable lesson that day: To succeed in the Navy, making his boss look good can go a long way to making his life better.

CHAPTER SEVEN
June 1965

Four months earlier, Joe Tyler entered the Navy barely making the height and weight minimum requirements: Officially he was five-feet, five-inches tall and weighed 124 pounds. Teenage male growth spurts being sporadic and on their own genetic schedule, Joe grew an additional five inches in height and added 35 pounds to his now five-foot, ten-inch frame, all the gain reflected by hard muscle.

To accommodate his new body, the Navy had to twice reissue complete sets of uniforms -- once after the first eight weeks, and again the day before graduation.

◆ ◆ ◆

Forty-five minutes after graduation ended, each recruit got called to the Chief's office. Upon entering, the Chief handed each man their new orders and their flight tickets home. As each man turned to leave his office, a broad smile covered their face. Without saying a word, they went to their bunks, picked up their sea bags, and headed to one of the buses waiting to take them to the airport.

Oddly, Joe Tyler's name had not been called.

Tyler sat there, feeling stupid, wondering if he was oblivious to something that he was supposed to have known. Worse, Joe started thinking that he had somehow failed Recruit Training and was going to be told to do it again.

Joe was the last man standing, or sitting, as it were, on bare bedding springs in the middle of the barracks. Eventually, the Chief came out of his room and stopped in place when he saw Joe sitting there. The Chief stared at him, thought about it for a moment, then returned to his office.

After a few minutes, the DM came over, sat beside him, and began going through the Recruit Assignment Schedule. Sure enough, Recruit Joseph Tyler's name was not listed. After thinking about it for a minute or two, the Chief concluded that Joe needed to go to the Personnel Office and find someone who could solve the problem.

Everyone Joe spoke too at the Personnel Office seemed equally confused. Eventually, one of the clerks suggested he take a seat until they found someone who could solve his predicament.

Fortunately, he had just completed 16 weeks of training, where Hurry-Up-and-Wait was the primary lesson each day.

Three-and-a-half hours later, a gigantic human form stepped into the threshold of the office and stood motionless. The Creature's massive body filled the entire doorway – side to side and top to bottom. Standing rigidly erect, only his eyes moved as he sought-out his intended victim.

Like falling dominoes, the two dozen administrative people who, only moments ago, had been hustling and bustling about, became exceptionally quiet. Each person stopped what he or she was doing and stared in awe of the Creature before them, too intimidated to make the slightest sound.

In Joe Tyler's memory, even the telephones were afraid to ring.

Master Chief Petty Officer Barry Glenn was 45 years old, stood six-foot-five and, on a bad day, maxed out at 5% body fat. The Chief wore a dress-white, short-sleeved summer uniform with razor-sharp creases. His bicep/triceps arm combination threatened to tear the material straining to get around them.

On the left side of his chest was a magnificent display of combat ribbons, several rows high. Above the decorations, rested an Underwater Demolition Badge.

Chief Glenn's size 16 shoes had been polished to a mirror-like finish. Not seeing his target immediately, he took one step into the office. When he did, several office personnel subconsciously took one step back.

The Master Chief's piercing dark brown eyes locked onto Joe.

"Who are you?"

"Joe Tyler."

"I know that Butt-head."

Joe's butt cheeks spontaneously tightened.

"How old are you?"

"Sir?"

"Stop with the 'sir' crap. From this moment forward, you will refer to me as Master Chief. And?"

"And?" Joe repeated.

"Are you deaf?"

"Oh! My age? Uh, 17, Chief. Err, Master Chief."

"SEVENTEEN?" Barry Glenn bellowed and, when he did, several office people literally took cover behind their desks.

"You look 14. I'll be damned if my Navy is going to start sending me day-school brats to babysit."

"It's been a curse all my life, Master Chief."

"Do you shave?"

"Yep; two times a week. A third time if there's an inspection."

"Do you know why I'm here?"

"Not a clue." With that, Barry Glenn stepped closer to him, stood over him, and stared through him.

A disgusted look filled Master Chief Glenn's face. He shook his head and growled something menacingly that Joe did not understand. The Master Chief turned sharply, headed out the door, not bothering to look back.

Joe remained sitting there, hoping his pants were not soiled, and not sure of what to do next. He looked around the office for support, guidance, help. All he saw was pity. Remarkably few people even returned his look. Those that took a chance at making eye contact had only a glimpse of fear. The entire office staff stayed frozen in place, staring at the doorway, afraid to speak. Those that dared to make eye contact with Joe had a look of pity written across their faces.

Finally, someone in the office spoke up, suggesting that Joe had better follow the Master Chief. Coming out of his stupor, he grabbed his sea bag and hurried to the parking lot.

On the drive to Coronado, Master Chief Barry Glenn became only slightly more human. From the Chief's monologue, he learned that the military Joint Chiefs of Staff had declared that before entering BUD/S school, each perspective had to first go through intense psycho-testing.

Because coming directly from Recruit Training to UDT Basic Conditioning was a relatively new procedure, recruits had to qualify mentally before being accepted. If they failed, they were required to experience two years of active sea-duty before they could reapply.

Instead of living in barracks with 120 people like at boot camp, Joe had a dorm room to himself while staying at the Coronado base. Over the weekend, he roamed the Base. Because he was no longer a recruit, he could have left the Base that Friday afternoon and not returned until 6:00 AM the following Monday.

But, no one told him. In fact, other than someone asking him what he wanted to eat at the cafeteria, not one person said a word to him the entire weekend.

Thinking back, with his youthful looks and walking around in brand new dungarees while wearing a sparkling white, brand new enlisted man's hat, he must have appeared like some officer's kid trying to act grown-up.

Beginning the following Monday morning and continuing for the next two weeks, he checked with the Master Chief twice each day; at 7 AM sharp at the Chief's office and then again around 4 o'clock each afternoon.

In between seeing the Chief and some doctors or their assistant, he sat against a corridor wall at the medical clinic, both feeling like and be treated the same as a lab-rat waiting for a treat. The only other "patients" sitting near him, were the guys who had been to Vietnam. They were easy to identify as the all looked 15 years older than their age, and their faces tended to contain blank stares at something.

After the veterans were called for testing, Joe would sometimes go over, sit in the same chair they had vacated, and stare into the blank wall five feet across the aisle, just as they had. Whatever they were seeing escaped him. The walls were the same in every hallway and boringly unremarkable.

When it was his turn to tested, he sat in a room covered with white walls, a white ceiling, and white floors. The four examination rooms were identical in size, shape, and furnishings.

A four-by-eight-foot metal table sat atop the battleship gray linoleum floor. Three cushioned, metal chairs sat adjacent to and were lined-up neatly on one side of the table. A fourth chair, the rat's chair, sat on the opposite side. Behind the three chairs an elongated two-way mirror, about six feet in length, undoubtedly hiding additional lab technicians.

At random times each day, he would be invited into the room to visit with one or more of the doctors. Once seated and, after short introductions, exchanges of pleasantries, and conversations about his life, the testing would begin.

Sometimes he would be asked to describe what various ink splats represented. Other fun choices were being asked to rate a variety of geometric drawings or to arrange colored geometric blocks. Sometimes, because he was bored or just wanted to mess with the doctors, Joe would separate the colored blocks into "teams," get up from his chair and set each team at either end of the table.

If Chief Glenn was not in his office in the morning, Joe was told to just head straight for the clinic. In the afternoon, Joe was tasked with finding him. Because everybody knew the Chief, tracking him down was usually a matter of asking a variety of people at different locations all around the Base until he found him.

Intentional or not, searching the Base for the Chief introduced him to the intense training that he hoped he would one day have to endure. Observing what the BUD/S trainees had to go through each day, made his boot-camp calisthenics look like cub scout training. No matter the physical exercise, there were always several instructors shouting profanities as each trainee struggled through the various obstacles.

Once located, the Chief would ask him what he did all day. On average, their "conversations" lasted four minutes. After the first week had ended, the Master Chief came up behind Joe as he watched yet another group attempt to complete the obstacles in front of them.

"Dream on, douche bag!" he yelled in Joe's ear, causing him, literally, to jump an inch or so off the ground.

"If I have my way, you ain't never gonna make it that far. In fact, if it were up to me, I would pick you up by the belt loops and throw your candy-ass face off his Base, forthwith."

The Chief neither waited for nor expected a reply. He did a one-eighty, then headed back to wherever he had been going before he decided to harass him.

"Thanks," Joe yelled after him, "hope you had a good day, too." With that, Joe headed off to the mess hall for his third wholesome meal of the day.

The end of the following week, as he sat with a few of the other lab rats, someone said Master Chief Glenn wanted him to make an appearance in his office, forthwith. When he knocked on the wall adjacent to his open office door, the Chief was sitting, sorting through a variety of muted, colored papers on his desk, and looked up.

"Looks like you didn't make it, ass-wipe," the Chief said with a smirk on his face, not bothering even to ask him to come in and sit down. "It took a handful of white coats two weeks to figure out what I knew when I first looked at your sorry ass. I would say I feel bad, but I couldn't be happier."

The Chief looked at a manila envelope on the corner of his desk nearest the doorway. "You leave here first thing tomorrow morning, baby-cakes. Those are your orders. Oh, and since you wanted to be a mechanic when you grew up, I volunteered you to be a boiler tech."

Master Chief Glenn smiled to himself and then, to emphasize he was through, swiveled his chair toward the windows behind him, lifting his hand in the air as a signal for him to leave. Joe picked up the big envelope then headed back to his room.

A smaller white envelope containing his airline tickets had been taped to the outside of the more extensive vanilla-brown package. Inside were his airline tickets. The first card said Atlanta, Georgia with a departure time early the next morning. The second said Providence, Rhode Island.

Joe changed directions to where he was headed and instead, went at the personnel office to see about transportation to LAX. While he waited, he unwound the string that held the big manila envelope closed and took out his orders.

The Chief was right – nothing in there said that Underwater Demolition Training would be in his future. Instead, he had been assigned to the Engineering Division aboard an anti-submarine aircraft carrier, the USS Essex, CVS-9. He was to report no later than midnight the next day.

While sitting there, he thought about a few additional Navy life-lessons that he could add to his repertoire.

First: People above you could, and would, crap on you for the sheer joy of doing so. To wit: Master Chief Barry Glenn.

Second: Senior Petty Officers either lied a lot or just had no clue what was going on. For that life lessons, he had only to remember most every Chief he had met the past four months.

The first Petty Officer he met was the person who handled his enlistment. He told Joe that his recruit training would be at Great Lakes in Chicago. Yet, here he sat in San Diego.

At Boot Camp, their drunken Drill Master said each recruit would get a one week leave immediately after graduation. Instead, when he finished Recruit Training and, thanks again to Master Chief Barry Glenn, he did not go home like the other recruits but was driven directly to Coronado.

Another promise: After their one-week leave, each man would have orders to attend the school they chose when recruited, before heading to their permanent duty station.

Because of not making the mental cut to become a Navy Frogman, he was flying to his first duty station at oh-dark-thirty the next morning.

Apparently, no one remembered the promised one-week leave. Instead, Joe was now headed to the USS Essex CVS-9.

CHAPTER EIGHT
Fall 1965

In the 1960s, the enlistment slogan was "Join the Navy and See the World." Joe had not seen the world, but in 20 weeks he will have seen more of America than he would have ever dreamt. Not to mention he has been able to fly on jet airplanes. Now, within 24 hours, he would be a "fleet sailor," learning what a boiler technician does aboard an aircraft carrier. At least, that is what was what he thought was supposed to happen.

Joe arrived in Providence late the next evening and took a cab to the coastal town of Quonset Point. When they got to the Naval base, the driver asked if he should take him to the administration building or to a ship. When told that he had orders to go to the USS Essex CVS-9, the driver replied by informing he the ship was setting sail in the morning for Boston; meaning he had gotten to the base just in time.

The cab driver knew the base quite well. he looked for a ship but saw nothing that looked like a warship. "See that big, tall, building at the end of the road? That's it. That's your ship."

All he could see was a big gray building, about a half-mile ahead of them, with what looked like a string of white Christmas lights strung from the top. They went down the pier, past a couple of seagoing tugs and then pulled alongside the fantail gangway. he got out of the cab and threw his sea bag over his shoulder and looked in awe at the mighty warship.

The USS Essex was huge. His jaw physically dropped and, with his mouth open, looked back at the cab driver. The driver, who had been watching Joe, replied with a wide grin and a wave; his identity as being a small-town hick was apparently confirmed.

Within his small, naive brain, he knew he was going to love being in the Navy. In his first four months, he had been to Southern California, an airport in Atlanta, and would soon board one of the most massive ships in the Navy, that, by the way, was docked in the smallest state in the Union.

How cool was that?

Joe walked-up the long gangway to the hangar deck and handed his orders to the Duty Yeoman. The Yeoman in turn, took them to the Officer-on-Duty who was sitting in a small office area, drinking coffee. The two of them discussed something for a moment, and then the Yeoman came back and asked Joe to follow him.

Soon they arrived at a four-by-four-foot hatchway near the back of the hangar bay. Because the deck was relatively dark; the light was coming up through the hatchway was welcoming.

Joe scurried down the ladder with his sea bag over his shoulder. He was not sure what to expect, but whatever it was, it was not there. Everywhere he looked were bunks stacked four high, held by chains from the overhead. Beneath the bottom bunk, were flat metal lockers, six inches tall. Most had keyed metal locks securing them. The only sound in the sleeping quarters was men snoring.

One of his new shipmates came over and quietly introduced himself, adding that he had just gotten off watch. he found he an empty bunk, saying he would help him get settled the next morning. For the first night, he would have to be without sheets and a pillow, but the sailor did manage to find he a spare blanket. The sailor pointed to a narrow passageway, saying that the head (toilets and showers) was off in that direction. Before leaving he, he mentioned that the ship was departing for Boston in the morning.

When he awoke the next morning, the lights were on, and most everyone was gone. he slid out of his bunk and landed on a linoleum floor in his bare feet. he must have been more exhausted from a long day of travel as he never heard reveille called, nor the people surrounding him who were talking and laughing. he got dressed in his dungarees, deck boots, and chambray shirt, went to the head and returned to his bunk and attempted to figure out what his next move would be.

Once again, his new friend came to his rescue. Together, they began a circuitous journey through a maze of passageways to the mess hall. After going through the cafeteria line, they found a table and sat down to get better acquainted. Justin McDonald was a second-class petty officer, equivalent to a sergeant in the Army. Justin was in his fourth, and final year of service and would soon be heading back home to Minno, South Dakota. His father had just purchased a new fast-food franchise, something called Burger King, and Justin would help him get the restaurant up and running.

Joe admitted the obvious; he was fresh out of boot camp and gave Justin the cliff notes of how he happened to be assigned to the Essex. he then peppered him with questions about the ship, what to expect, etc.

Justin answered by saying the ship's regular crew is about 2,600 including officers and enlisted. Depending on which flight wing is onboard, it can get up as high as 5,000. he finished by adding that currently, there were only about 900 on board. The reason is that the ship was headed to dry-dock in Boston, principally, to fix a broken flight elevator.

When Joe asked him what time they would be leaving Quonset Point, Justin started laughing then added the ship had left port at dawn. he looked at him surprised and admitted that he did not feel the ship moving.

After breakfast, they walked to the open fantail area just below the flight deck. he was amazed to see the east coast of Massachusetts on the not-to-distant horizon. Later that evening, the big boat pulled into the Boston dry-dock area.

The next morning, Monday, October 25, he awoke to the 6 AM reveille call, showered, put on his dungarees, and headed up to the hanger deck for their divisional roll call, mentally prepared to take on his first day as an actual crew member of an American warship. The enthusiasm of getting ready for his first roll call was about as exciting as it ever got aboard the USS Essex.

Even though he was designated a Boiler Technician, the boiler and engine rooms were off limits to him and any other lowly ranked sailor while the ship was in dry-dock. Only senior petty officers, Naval officers, riggers, and mechanical engineers and were permitted to enter the boiler room area.

By noon, all but 12 of men from the entire engineering department had received orders transferring them off the ship and to their new assignments. Of the 12 military personnel still assigned as the Engineering Crew, two were officers, four were petty officers, and six were E-3s; rookie firemen, like him.

In dry dock, the giant ship was a beehive of civilian workers, both day and night. Each day, two firemen, one petty officer, an engineering officer was to remain on board for Watch detail. Each day an E-3 was positioned at the central hatchway leading down to the boiler room area. Why they had to be there is remains a mystery. Other than observing the workmen climb up and down the ladder, they never did anything.

Each Duty Watch lasted four hours. The eight hours they were not on watch were spent resting in their quarters, going to the mess hall for a meal, or for he, exploring various areas of the ship.

On his days-off, Joe toured Boston; its history, landmarks, and universities and colleges. he had grabbed one of the many free tourist maps on his first day in Boston and just started walking. To prevent getting lost, he always focused on the Boston Common area as his daily starting point.

At dusk on Tuesday, November 9, 1965, a strange thing happened on the northeastern part of the United States: Human error caused the electricity to go out throughout New England and the eastern metro areas of Canada. The Great Northeast Blackout, as it came to be called, left tens of millions of people stranded in the dark.

The ordinary problematic streets of Boston soon hosted world-class traffic jams. People were stranded in elevators. Hospitals went on emergency generators. As it got darker, people figured-out that neither the streetlights nor any other lights were coming back on. Tension flooded the streets as people, avoiding eye contact with one another, scurried about.

When the blackout occurred, he was standing on a corner of Beacon Street after spending the day exploring the stores and shops adjacent to Boston Common. Joe watched as a nice-looking young blonde lady struggled with three large paper bags of groceries. After a minute or two, he approached her and offered to help. Being fearful, she did not acknowledge his presence. Wanting to get away from him, she took a couple of steps toward the curb. When she did, bag number three began to slip from her grip. Joe, moving quickly, caught the bag and prevented the contents from spilling to the ground.

The blonde lady was both startled that someone had approached her and yet relieved that the stranger had saved her groceries. Once she recognized he was wearing Navy dress blues, she decided Joe was safe.

That being settled, she thanked him, mentioned that she lived a few blocks away and appreciated his coming to her rescue. She introduced herself as Patricia Krause and talked nonstop all the way to her apartment. Patricia lived on nearby Marlborough Street, a few blocks from the Public Gardens.

She told him about her job at John Hancock Insurance, how she lived with two other girls, and that her landlady only rented to females. She added that her elderly landlady discouraged visits from male friends, so, although she appreciated his assistance, he would not be allowed to enter their building.

Joe had yet to say a word, even to introduce himself, and was somewhat amused that she thought he had other intentions. He did not. In fact, he had first assumed she was married, hence all the groceries. Besides, he wanted to get back to the USS Essex, which was about a three-mile walk from where they first met.

Because his instinct was to always help someone in need, assisting her with the grocery bags and making sure she got home safely was all that had entered his 17-year-old, small-town-mind. Arriving at her building, they had to walk up several concrete steps to get to the front door. Joe offered to hold two of the grocery bags while she fumbled for her keys and unlocked the door.

She thanked him, handed him the third bag and, using her shoulder opened the doors.

"When we go in, be very quiet." After having laid down all the rules and regulations about how he was not to come in, her statement took him off guard. Three steps inside the building and the landlady opened her door. She stared at them both for a second and then gave him the once-over.

"I was worried about you," she said looking back at Patricia. "I'm glad you found a nice gentleman to escort you home."

"Yes ma'am," he immediately chimed in with his best boyish, awe-shucks grin. Joe even managed to pull off his white hat even as both arms wrestled with the grocery bags. His effort was received as a sign of southern hospitality and manners by the landlady.

"When I saw her struggling with her groceries and all, and with a bunch of strange people hollering and swearing at one another, and them cars going every which way, well, I thought I'd better help her get safely home to her family."

After a short pause, he added, "Leastwise, that's what my folks taught me to do."

With that, the landlady smiled, closed her door, and went back inside. Patricia glanced over at him with a look of total surprise. Joe shrugged his shoulders, returned her quizzical look, and mouthed: 'What?'

Still stunned, Patricia turned and began walking down the hall.

Joe followed her to her first-floor apartment, held the three bags in his arms and his hat in arms as she fumbled for the keys to the apartment door.

The roommates, Barb, and Nicole, were sitting across from each other in the living room, drinking scotch on the rocks. Candles were flickering from a variety of positions, which gave the room, with its high ceilings and elongated windows, to be what Joe thought of as turn-of-the-century Bostonian style.

When Joe entered the main sitting area, Nicole, who was sitting by a lantern paging through an old magazine, glanced up, more as a reflex, and went back to her magazine. After a second, it hit her: there was a strange male in their apartment. Nicole snapped her head up and nearly spilled her drink.

"He followed me home," Patricia chimed in. "Do you think we can keep him?"

"If it's okay with prune face out front,"

Barb chimed in, "then it's okay with me."

Barb paused for a moment, looked at Nicole, then added, "But you have to share him."

Nicole got up and poured two fresh glasses of Scotch and sat them on a table near where he was standing. Patricia asked Joe to hand her the groceries as she was opening the refrigerator door.

Because the electricity was out, she hurriedly pushed the groceries inside and quickly closed the door.

After she stood-up, he gave her one of the glasses. Raising their glasses with a toasting gesture, they touched rims as an acknowledgement to their newfound friendship.

Pat, as she preferred to be called, took a long, full practiced swig from her glass. Joe put the glass to his lips and, for the first time in his life, tasted 12-year-old Scotch Whiskey.

"By the way, that was some Southern charm you laid on her."

"It even surprised me when I heard the words coming out of my mouth."

With that, they toasted one another again and went into the living room to join Barb and Nicole. Patricia was about to introduce him when she suddenly remembered she never asked his name.

At 10:30, Joe excused himself, saying it was a four-mile walk back to the dock area and his morning duties began at 6 AM. Fortunately, the walk back made his head a little clearer. On the way back, Joe could not believe how much his life changed in the past several months. Today being the best example. Here was, on the east coast, 17 years-old, two weeks away from his 18th birthday, fresh out of boot camp, and four months out of a Podunk Steel Town, USA.

That day, he found himself among three attractive young ladies, all in their mid-20s, college-educated and working at white-collar jobs (and not some factory) in one of the most sophisticated cities on the East Coast.

A few weeks later, Joe received approval for 10 days' leave, beginning December 20th.

CHAPTER NINE
Christmas 1965

The Tyler family had grown over the years with the addition of two brothers: Hal, who was 9, and Kennedy, age 4. Just before he left for the Navy, his older sister, Karen, had gotten a decent job and moved into a loft with one of her high-school girlfriends.

After he departed in June, older brother Bill had remodeled the attic, which provided him a private sanctuary within his parent's house. When he was not sequestered in his attic hideaway, Bill could be found either working at Kunkel Florist or, at Kent State University attending classes.

Joe's first few days at home were spent visiting relatives with his parents. Although he preferred wearing civilian clothes, his parents insisted that he was always in uniform when they visited family or close friends. Everyone was amazed by his change in appearance. He left as a too skinny, too short statured boy and returned six months later almost unrecognizable.

While his mother was relieved to hear about his UDT school rejection, his father was disappointed.

On Christmas Eve, he offered to help his mother wrap presents for Hal and Kennedy. She told him there were none. T. William Sr. had found what little money she had tried to save for the boy's Christmas, and either drank or gambled away every penny.

Fortunately, his dad was not home when he heard the news, as he probably would have confronted him. Wanting to provide something for them, he went two houses over to the Santone family and borrowed one of their cars.

Because it was late on Christmas Eve, the only place he could find open was the Rexall Drug Store on West Market Street. He bought what little he could find from the toy aisle.

Having to live with the memory of the two youngest boys not having at least one present under the Christmas tree, was not something he wanted to think about the rest of his life.

Joe refused to talk to his dad all Christmas Day.

On December 26th at 8 AM, he was sitting at the table eating breakfast, teasing, and laughing with his younger siblings when his mother answered a knock at the front door. While not paying too much attention, he was aware she was talking with two male adults. She called to him, saying there were two people from the Navy wanting to see him.

As he approached the door, he could see that all the color had drained from his mother's face. Her knuckles were white from twisting the apron over and over in her hands. Tears had formed in the corner of her dark brown eyes. Inside the doorway stood two Navy Shore Patrol Petty Officers. Both wore full dress-blue uniforms; both looked very somber.

"What can I do for you two?"

"Fireman Tyler," the taller of the two addressed he as the other handed him some official documents. "We're here to take escort you to the Cleveland Airport."

"Whoa. Stop right there. I'm on leave until the 30th." His eyes narrowed, and his body language clearly demonstrated that he was not about to go anywhere.

"These orders supersede all other orders. You need to get your gear and come with us."

His manner was military serious. "Now."

Joe glanced at the paperwork and knew he had to go. He turned and looked at his mother. The tears in the corner of her eyes let loose and began to run down her face. The two younger brothers had come over to see what was going on. He gave her a long hug, told her he had to do what the two Shore Patrol Petty Officers wanted.

Joe headed up the narrow wooden staircase to dress in his military uniform and pack what little gear he had with him. All his other military clothing was still aboard the Essex. As he was packing, Hal came into the room, crying.

"Can't you stay? Why can't you stay?" Hal was sobbing and could barely get the words out. "Tell them to go away. This isn't fair!"

Joe sat down on the bed beside him, put his hand around his brother's small, skinny shoulders, and gave him a firm, brotherly hug.

"Listen, big man. I am in the Navy and, when you are in the military, you must always obey orders from your superior officers. What may not seem fair to either you or I isn't in question here."

Joe gave him another big hug, then gently raised Hal's face toward him. Throughout the rest of his life, he distinctly remembered the look on his younger brother's face. Hal's eyes stared deep into Joe's eyes, pleading, not understanding, yet not saying a word.

"Hal, always remember this: When you give someone your word when you promise to do something, then you have to do it. I promised the Navy, gave them my word that whatever they needed me to do, I would do it."

Joe paused, searching for something else he could say to ease his younger brother's pain.

"You'll be okay, little man. You got to be strong for little Kenny. Hal, you gotta remember that your word is your word. If you agree to something, you gotta follow through."

With that, he stood up, again put his arm around Hal's shoulders and together, Hal in front of him, they walked down the stairway.

Next came little four-year-old Kenny. If Hal had not wholly broken his heart, Kenny finished the job.

Once he and Hal had come down the stairs, Kennedy looked up and stared at the travel bag in Joe's hand. When Joe's feet reached the main level, he got down on both knees and reached out for Kennedy.

Kennedy stayed where he was standing, out of his grasp, his feet frozen in position, staring into Joe's eyes. Tears began flowing down his little-boy rosy cheeks.

"You said we would go sled riding!" he protested. "You said we would go this afternoon. You just got home. We haven't played yet!"

"You've been with everybody but me. When do I get my big brother?"

With that, the tears ran even harder. Joe remained kneeling. Slowly, he reached toward Kennedy, wanting to hold those tiny hands, wanting to hug his baby brother. Before he could reach him, Kennedy jerked his hands out of reach and slowly, began stepping away from him. "

Go. Go away. Just go. Go!" With that, Kennedy turned and ran out of sight.

Joe stood up and let out a deep sigh. He looked down at Hal and then his mother, who was not all that much taller than Hal. "I'll let you know where I end up."

With that, the two Petty Officers turned and went out the door. Joe followed them across the porch and down the steps. He got in the back seat of the official government dove gray Ford. He took one last glance at his mother and Hal as they stood out in the cold, on the snow-covered porch.

The Navy trio drove west out of town, connected to the Ohio Turnpike, and then headed northwest to the Cleveland airport. The smaller of the two petty officers were seated in the front passenger seat. He turned to look at him as he spoke.

"Just so you know. This is hard for us, too. Our orders said to pick you up on Christmas Day, but we told our boss you weren't at home."

They all sat in silence for 10 minutes before he asked to see his orders. Within the large, official manila envelope were plane tickets to Los Angeles. His orders only stated that a member or members of the United States Navy Shore Patrol, Los Angeles, would meet him at LAX and escort him to his new duty station.

Joe's only thought: Now what?

CHAPTER TEN
December 26, 1965

No Shore Patrol awaited him at the deplaning gate in Los Angeles. Joe hesitated for a few moments as he debated whether to continue waiting at the gate or to head to the baggage claim area. In the end, he stayed within the general terminal area, strolling through the nearby stores on the concourse.

An hour later, two somewhat hefty petty officers, white armbands covering their left biceps, NAVY SP embroidered in bold blue and gold lettering. He remembered thinking how sharp they looked against the men's, dress winter blues. As they approached, Joe introduced himself and shook hands with them both.

Now that Joe appeared to be a 'seasoned fleet sailor,' he was treated as a human being and appreciated the easy exchange of camaraderie they had shown. After introducing themselves, they asked about his sea bag. Since he had none, the three of them went out to the Navy sedan.

Shortly after they departed the airport, he noticed they were going east instead of Joe's preferred direction, south. That was the direction to the Coronado Naval Base. When Joe asked where they were headed, the guy in the passenger seat mumbled something about heading to downtown LA, where their offices were located.

They turned off the freeway toward downtown. As they were heading east, the driver asked if anyone was hungry. Simultaneously, and not caring what the answer might be, he began maneuvering the car to the far-right lane.

Joe kept quiet and took in the scenery. The Shore Patrol driver soon made a quick right into a small strip plaza and parked their "official government vehicle" in the No Parking Zone in front of a little, family-style restaurant.

Joe followed them through the front door and was overwhelmed by the magnificent aromas of authentic Mexican cooking. The fact that Joe had never tasted Mexican food before was about to change. He stood back and read the menu, which was written on a giant, wall-sized blackboard behind the register.

His escorts were apparently well known to the people behind the counter. They were greeted in Spanish by the father, who was standing behind the cash register. Both Petty Officers answered in Spanish, then proceeded to hold a three-way conversation. The only word Joe understood was gringo, which, when spoken, caused everyone to look at him and smile. Feeling like the village idiot who was standing at the edge of a cliff and wondering what to do next, he smiled back.

Being hungry and willing to try new foods, he ordered one hard shell beef taco, a ranchero chicken enchilada, and another burrito with "Camarones Diablo."

Everyone smiled and laughed, and a rapid exchange began between the entire family, even from the uncle in back at the dishwashing machine. The two veteran sailors guffawed and slapped each other on the back.

Apparently, he was the target of their jesting.

When their food came, one of the SPs paid the bill, and they each grabbed a Coke from the cooler. Together, they went outside to enjoy their meal in the warm, December 26th Southern California sun. Before Joe began eating, the SP passenger guy touched his right arm and provided a warning.

"The key to eating hot, spicy food, is never to allow the food to touch your lips. When you finish the burrito, then eat the enchilada and the taco."

The SP's face registered genuine concern as he spoke to Joe.

As an 18-year-old from small-town Ohio, Joe never forgot eating his first authentic Mexican food, primarily because it was hot enough to bring tears to his eyes and produce a fair amount of sweat on his forehead. Wisely, Joe took the SP at his word and did as he was told. The Camarones Diablo burrito was extremely hot, but, wonderfully delicious.

Joe, being an experienced person from a decade of physical altercations under his belt, the same Joe who never allowed anyone to know if he was in pain, outwardly, showed no regret about the food eaten.

While they ate Joe asked if they knew anything about where he might be headed. Each replied in the negative. In fact, the SPs had hoped that he might shed light on why they had to retrieve him from the airport the day after Christmas. Joe proceeded to fill them in on his short career, from enlistment to Mexican food consumption. The two SPs shrugged their shoulders; none of what they had heard struck them as unusual.

However, they were eager to hear about his relationship with the three ladies in Boston. Joe answered all their inquiries truthfully. They, of course, did not believe him. After an hour of start/stop traffic, the trio arrived at the combined Military downtown offices. They suggested Joe bunk down in one of their holding cells. After all, because this was a Sunday and the day after Christmas, the SP's were not expecting any calls from the LAPD and county sheriff asking them to give some drunken sailor a cell for the night.

At 6 PM, two new SP's arrived for the overnight watch. The two new guys were even more massive than the original two. While they did ask if Joe liked pizza, they did not bother to wait for his reply. About 25 minutes later, someone showed up with two large pizzas. One of the new guys handed Joe a paper plate with two large pizza slices and told him to help himself to some Coke in the un-locked vending machine in the hall.

They all settled in to watch Bonanza and The Ed Sullivan Show on a color TV while eating the two large pizza. While Joe had never watched TV in color before, he thought it better to keep that fact to himself.

The next morning at 6 AM, the two original guys returned to take command of the 12-hour day shift. They handed Joe two meal chits -- one for breakfast and the other for lunch -- valid at the diner around the corner. They added that Joe was free to roam downtown LA but should return before 5:00 that evening.

This routine continued daily, with the second crew ordering either pizza or chicken to be delivered for dinner each night around seven.

On Thursday, December 30th, 1965, Joe's new orders arrived from NavBuPers (Navy Bureau of Personnel). Accordingly, he was "to report to Master Chief Barrymore Glenn, Senior Instructor BUD/S, forthwith, at the Naval Amphibious Base in Coronado, not too far from San Diego."

Joe was elated. His new friends were impressed.

"How'd you get into that?" One of them yelled as Joe went in to pack his ditty bag. "How old are you, anyway?"

The other chimed in with his own questions as they both followed him to the back. "I thought you had to have at least two years' fleet even to be considered for UDT?"

"Hey, Tyler, who slept with your mother to get your butt in so quick?"

"It wasn't his mother they slept with, butt-wipe, it was his sister."

"Better yet, I bet it was Tyler himself. Hey, Tyler, who'd you have to have sex with to get them orders?"

"That's why he didn't sleep with them Boston broads. He's queer!"

"That it, Tyler? You gay? You find some commander who was sweet on your little child self?"

Joe ignored them as he gathered his meager belongings. Walking past his agitators, Joe stopped, turned, and asked, "Who's driving?"

Riding in the back seat of the gray Navy sedan, Joe thought about what he had gone through since enlisting in March. His initial enlistment was to become a member of the Navy's Underwater Demolition Team. Last Fall he had eagerly taken all the UDT/SEALs mental tests only to be told that he did not make the cut.

While his hopes and dreams had been crushed, Joe had come to terms with the fact he would spend the next five years as a fleet sailor. Instead, "sea-duty" had lasted one full day and being part of the Sixth Fleet lasted all-of-a few weeks. As they drove south in the Navy Ford sedan, Joe found himself feeling like he missed southern California.

The two Shore Patrol guys were escorting him to an amphibious base that had been reconfigured for BUD/S training, whatever that meant. Three hours later, Joe found out.

HAPTER ELEVEN
January 1966

Checking-in at the personnel office on the base, Joe discovered Joe was three weeks early -- well ahead of the other trainees. Joe headed over to his temporary living quarters and, within an hour of getting his gear stored, Master Chief Glenn stopped by.

"Hey, Tyler, heading to chow?" He asked this in such a friendly manner it caught Joe off guard.

"Master Chief Glenn," Joe replied, walking toward him with his hand extended. The Chief held out his big meat paw and, as they shook hands, the Chief patted him on the right shoulder with his big left hand like they were old friends who had not seen each other in years. Although somewhat puzzled, Joe went with it.

While they walked together toward the mess hall, the Chief asked about his time on the Essex, what Joe had thought of Boston, and whether Joe had caused the infamous blackout. Joe told him about his one day out to sea and how Joe had not been aware that the big ship had left port. This got a hearty chuckle from the Big Man.

Joe followed by saying that he never got to see the boiler rooms, the engine rooms nor propeller shafts. A huge grin covered the Chief's face, and he replied saying he never thought Joe would. While Joe tried to relax and just go with it, he began feeling like he had been set up;

precisely why, he was not sure. Joe left a few months ago thinking the Master Chief was Satan's gift to the US Navy. Yet, at that moment, he was more like some kind old teddy bear.

After they went through the chow line and sat down to eat, the Chief got down to the reason he wanted to get together with Joe.

"Okay, I knew when you left here in October that you would be back for the January BUD/S," he said matter-of-factly. Sensing the Chief wanted to talk about a lot of things, things that were important, Joe sat there quietly, listening intently.

"I didn't want to tell you at the time, but the various people who made you jump through the mental trials say everything points to your being an excellent candidate for advanced warfare training, which is the step beyond BUD/S."

The Chief paused for a second to think about how he should continue.

"I gotta tell you, though you bring, no, make that "you present, a few difficulties which we, meaning you and me, gotta overcome. I contacted a friend in Washington, and she was able to get you on the base ahead of the other trainees. I would not have done it except, for you, this is imperative.

"As always, I will be your training group's Senior Instructor for Phase One, Basic Conditioning. Do not let the words "basic conditioning" fool you. The training will be a real ball buster, specifically designed to weed out the mental and physical weaklings. Every day there will be guys ringing the bell, meaning they drop out.

"Then it really gets tough.

"Week Five is Hell Week. If you are lucky, you will get a total of four hours of sleep during the entire seven days of training. Hell Week is the hardest training you will ever face in your life. It is designed to take you past the edge of your mental and physical capabilities.

"Hell-Week is where we cull the herd; where we separate the top two-percent America has to offer. By the end of the fifth week, 90 percent of the original trainees -- guys like you who were all gung-ho to become a frogman and somehow survived the first four weeks of basic conditioning -- will be gone."

The Chief paused to eat, not looking at Joe. Slowly, he raised his head toward him, trying to read how Joe was digesting, if you will, what the Chief was trying to tell him.

"To be honest, I'm not sure you can handle it. And I cannot interfere with your instructors to help get you through. You are entering the game with three strikes against you. First, that baby face of yours is going to be a magnet for punishment. It's going to attract the wrong attention."

After pausing for effect, Barry Glenn continued.

"Second, you just turned 18. In their eyes, that makes you unworthy to wear the Frog.

"Your Third and final strike is that your instructors are seasoned warriors, guys who just returned from six to twelve months combat, are pissed they had to leave, and even more upset they were told to be here to train guys a bunch of draft-dodging head-shrinks say they should."

The Chief went back to eating. Without taking his eyes off his meal and anticipating that Joe was about to ask some questions, the Chief raised his left hand, palm facing Joe.

"Guaranteed they will come at you like maggots on road-kill."

Again, the Chief paused to let Joe think about it.

"Beginning tomorrow morning, you need to push your durance levels beyond anything you ever thought you could. You need to push yourself to take control of your brain."

With that, he put his utensils down and stared right through Joe. "If it were me, I would wake up every day at 0430 say to myself that, looking back, yesterday really was easy. So today it's going to be really tough."

At 2200 (10:00 PM) each night, your last conscious thought would be, today was easy; tomorrow Joe would really have to really push it.

"Exercise. Eat a lot of protein and carbs, drink lots of fluids. Run everywhere. Swim in the coldest water you can find and crawl through the thickest mud. Go non-stop for 16 hours. The next day, do it again. But do it better. Do it quicker. Push it. Push it. Push it.

"Train your brain to accept what you are doing. Every cell in your body will be screaming at you to stop. When your mind says no, tell yourself, go. Until you have been there, been through BUD/S Basic Conditioning, and especially Hell Week, you have no idea what pain can be; you'll be begging for the Devil's disciples to let you into Hell, if only to relieve the agony.

The Chief paused again and then added:

"I'm telling you now, Tyler, because you have the kind of brain that'll accept it."

Now the Chief's eyes narrowed, he sat as far forward as his size and the table would allow.

"If you do not do what I am telling you, you will hate yourself for the rest of your life. And THAT, you can take to the bank. Joe, I get letters all the time from dozens and dozens of bell-ringers, each wishing they had stuck it out. Each pleading with me to pull some strings and so they can retake the training. I cannot express this enough: This is a one-and-done training. You either do it now or never do it at all. There are no second chances."

The Chief sat military upright and stared at Joe.

No one had ever talked to Joe so seriously in his whole life. Not his family. Not his friends. Not his teachers. No one. Ever. Master Chief Barry Glenn was the first, and only, for that matter.

Joe looked down at his tray and slowly stood up from the table. As he picked up the tray, he heard these words come out of his mouth. "I will not let either of us down. Thank you, Chief."

The words came from somewhere deep in his soul. He spoke them softly. Forcefully. Reverently.

As Joe walked away, he began repeating, "yesterday was easy," over and over to himself.

Somehow, from somewhere deep inside, Joe knew there was nothing that he could not overcome.

Sitting on the edge of his bunk, he swore an oath to himself: Beginning now, that evening, he would run until he reached the peak of unholy exhaustion. He would push his aching muscles to go do more. Awakening each day, his first conscious thought always be to push through his pain threshold; no matter the physical consequences.

That evening he put on a t-shirt, gym shorts, and shoes and prepared to take on the world. As he opened the door to the dormitory, Joe was greeted with his first obstacle: the wind blew hard enough to pull the door out of his hands and cold rain whipped in his face.

After hesitating a moment, he took a deep breath, joined the elements, and stayed out well after 11:00 that night. At 5:30 the next morning, he went out again. In fact, Joe spent the next 21 days training his body and fighting his mind as it continuously told him to stop, rest and find a different occupation.

Basic Underwater Demolition/SEAL Class 35 was officially formed later in January of 1966, and just as the Chief predicted, the instructors came at him relentlessly. Sure, they harassed all the frogman wannabes, but it was apparent that not one of the instructors felt Joe was old enough or qualified enough or qualified enough, to be there.

From the moment the trainees awoke until they returned to their barracks, the instructors would verbally abuse, taunt, and practically insist they drop out so that the real men could proceed unhindered, with their training.

And every morning Joe said out loud, "Yesterday was easy. Today I will push through whatever they throw at me. I will not fail. I cannot fail. I made it through yesterday. And yesterday was easy."

UDT Basic Conditioning routine consisted of fast-paced calisthenics, running on a sandy beach wearing combat boots, then swimming in the ocean. After breakfast, they pushed through the obstacle course, including crawling through twenty yards of muddy water. They finished their morning workout by running several hundred yards over rocky terrain. While he may have always been the last swimmer to get out of the water, Joe was generally listed as having the fastest times on the various terrain and obstacle courses.

The only week they did not stick to the basic routine was Hell Week. Hell-Week is unfathomable to anyone who has never been through it: Five-and-a-half days of continuous, tortuous mental and physical endurance. As the chief had predicted, the fatigue, coupled with sleep deprivation - a grand total of four hours over the entire training week - caused everyone to question their personal motivation for wanting to endure the physical and mental torture they were putting themselves through.

One starless, moonless, rainy night, the men were separated into eight-man teams. As part of a team-building exercise, each group held a massive rubber raiding craft above their heads as they portaged over slippery rocks and various sized boulders. Wearing only leather combat boots with their usual t-shirt and gym shorts. High tide was coming in, causing the cold waves to crash against their bare legs and the rocks even more slippery, making it even more challenging to maintain their balance while trying to hold the immense, heavy boat.

The man behind Joe slipped and fell onto the rocks, his ankle severely twisted. Without anything being said, a man from the opposite side of the rubber craft left his position and assisted the injured frogman. The remaining six men bore the additional weight and continued moving toward their assigned destination. In the end, they finished as an eight-man team, and within their targeted time.

That lesson epitomized what becoming a US Navy SEAL was about: no man was ever to be left behind.

The lack of sleep caused disorientation, intense physical pain, and a few trainees nearly drowned. Add to that the dismal wet and cold that took many men to the brink of hypothermia. By the end of Hell Week fifty percent of the remaining trainees found it too much to overcome and "rang the bell," signaling their decision to quit.

Per the chief's prediction, of the 116 men who had initially begun Basic Conditioning four weeks earlier, 36 remained to attempt Hell Week. By the end of the week, only 18 men advanced to Second Phase. Getting through Hell Week - in fact going through UDT, SEAL Qual School, Escape and Resistance, and for one or two, Advanced Warfare Training - left each man with a tremendous sense of pride, achievement, brotherhood, and self-confidence. Becoming a Navy Frogman produced a new sense of who they had always been as a person. Deep with each man's soul was a conviction that as an individual, they had the courage and intuition to accomplish most anything they attempted. But when they joined forces with one another, they became infinitely stronger.

And almost unbeatable.

In June, after finishing their last day of Dive School, Joe stopped by the Master Chief's office. When he entered Barry Glenn's office, the big man looked up, smiled from ear to ear, came around his desk, shook his hand, patted him on the back.

Returning to his chair, Barry said, "Sit down. Take a load off. Give me a sec to finish this paperwork." He got busy scanning and signing several documents. Without looking up, he added, "Twenty-four years in this man's Navy, and I end being a glorified yeoman to a group of guys, most of whom won't be here in two months. By the way, congratulations on surviving First Phase."

"Chief, I wanted to stop and thank you for getting me here early and pushing me to prepare. If it were not for you, I would not be sitting here. Now, I owe you, big man!"

With that, he stood up, reached across the desk to again shake the hand of the man who he now admired.

For his part, Barry Glenn kept seated with his head buried in the documents before him and shrugged his shoulders as if to say it was nothing. Once Barry finished his paperwork, Joe asked if they could get together for dinner that weekend.

"I got a better idea," the Chief replied. "How 'bout joining my wife and I for some ribs tomorrow afternoon?"

Although he answered the Chief in the affirmative, Joe did so to hide the amazement on his face. Nine months ago, the Chief treated Joe like his very presence at Coronado was a personal insult to him, and a major insult to his Navy.

Until 60 days ago, Joe just assumed the big man was without a soul. And now he finds out the Chief has a human heart, was married, and had a family. The fact that Master Chief Barry Glenn was a normal human being had never entered his mind.

CHAPTER TWELVE
March 1966

Marsha Glenn was the kind of person everyone warmed up to, immediately. From the moment she opened the door and welcomed him to their small ranch home, Joe felt at ease. Like the Chief, she was in her late 40s. While her hair was a darker brown, it was her gorgeous hazel-brown eyes that caught Joe's heart and undying admiration.

"Barry's outback babysitting his ribs. Just go out the door in the back of the kitchen, and you will find him. I'll be out to join you in a few minutes."

As Joe entered the back-patio area, the Master Chief looked up and smiled.

"Man, glad you're on time. Grab yourself a cold one. These ribs need another 15 minutes; then they'll be ready."

Marsha came outside 10 minutes later with a large bowl of homemade potato salad. They made small talk as the chief continued his final preparations for serving the ribs.

After everything Joe had been through the past three months, relaxing with them on a warm San Diego Saturday afternoon in June, could not have gotten any better. Sitting with them, listening about all the different places they had lived, the duty stations the chief had served, and their life together, was the first time Joe felt utterly comfortable since Joe had entered boot camp the past June.

The Chief had enlisted in the Navy after World War II, spending all his time in the Pacific theater. He first attended UDT school right after the Korean Conflict; afterward, he transferred to Pearl Harbor. He graduated from the very first SEAL class in 1962 and had been one of the top enlisted men to develop SEAL training ever since.

After a few hours, Joe needed to head back to the base to begin studying for the second phase, Dive Physics. The chief offered to drive him back, which Joe readily accepted. On the way to the base, Barry presented his thoughts as to where Joe might be headed after he completed the last four months of BUD/S.

By now, Joe knew Barry had reviewed the results of his initial two months and assumed that Barry was among the group that made recommendations for the various post-school assignments.

"My gut feeling is that you're going to end up assigned to a recon or demo squad somewhere, maybe even in Nam. I realize your heart has been set on working underwater, but I don't see that happening."

"Like I said, Master Chief, I wouldn't have made it this far without your guidance; not sure how I can thank you enough. Just know that whatever I end up doing, I'll make you proud of me."

The Chief, the new, human Barry Glenn, smiled slightly and nodded his head. They both remained quiet for a while when something popped into Barry's head.

"I almost forgot to tell you something. There will be a test sheet for a third-class petty officer on your bunk sometime tomorrow morning. Answer 'C' to every question. That will give you a high enough score to pass."

"Really? What's the test?"

"Boiler room operations." The words no sooner came out of Barry Glenn's mouth as he began laughing out loud to himself. Joe was going to ask him if he was sure he should answer every question with the same letter but decided to let it slide. If the chief told him to respond "C" to all the questions, that was good enough for him.

When Joe returned from the mess hall the next morning, the test answer sheet was lying on his bunk. It took less than three minutes to answer all 100 questions.

The short version of his Dive Training is this: Joe almost flunked out. His problem? Without fins, he could barely swim on the surface of the water. Even with swim fins, he had trouble finishing the 300-yard requirement within the minimum time limit. Fortunately, he excelled at every other area of dive training, finishing near the top of all the academic issues.

On the last day of Dive School, the lead instructor told him to consider spending his career on land, adding that if Joe flunked the UDT portion of the training, the Marines would possibly take him as a part of their long-range reconnaissance group.

The instructor's remark took Joe by surprise. He did not know then, and still does know now if the instructor was serious or not. As it happened, Joe passed Dive training, although he ranked 30th out of 32 in the class.

The Third Phase was six weeks of land warfare, focusing on SEAL Qualification Training (SQT). It was very intense. The first week was spent on classwork; the other five weeks focused on mission planning, operations, tactics, techniques, and procedures utilizing the core tools of their trade. The course concluded by testing their competency in core tasks and how they would react in high stress "gut check" environments.

The SQT classes were divided into four-man squads, each of whom were to qualify in specific areas of field combat, such as explosives, marksmanship, rappelling, etc. Joe's designated qualification was mission-specific in two areas: search and rescue (referred to as SAR) and extractions. Extractions meant getting to their target (bad guy or good guy) and getting out of a geographical area without being detected with enemy soldiers hunting for him.

Joe remembered thinking of the game he invented as a kid: The one where he threw a rubber ball somewhere out in the woods then tried to find it. The object was to get out of the woods without the "enemy soldiers" capturing him.

After SQT, they moved on to Phase Four, Jump School: a three-week course in parachute jumping. They expected to go to Fort Benning, Georgia, and train with the Army Airborne guys. Instead, they flew in a Chinook Helicopter to an area north of Yuma, Arizona.

At first, jumping out of the plane and gliding to the ground was exciting. When it came right down to it, the idea of floating gently to the ground, completely exposed, while hoping not to get killed by an unseen enemy sniper watching him was not on his Top Ten list of favorite things in life.

When he returned from Yuma, Joe had a note on his bunk that said to meet with Master Chief Glenn, forthwith. In Navy language, forthwith meant now, as in - do not even stop to pee. When Joe arrived at his office, he stood up, reached out his big paw, and they shook hands.

"Gunners Mate Third Class Tyler, let he be the first to recognize you as an elite member of the United States Navy Underwater Demolition Team and welcome you as a frogman and as a member of SEAL Team One."

"Thank you, Master Chief." After they shook hands, both grinning from ear-to-ear, the Chief presented Joe a small, rectangular box. Inside this box were two brass petty officer pins displaying one chevron with an eagle above it. More importantly, there were two UDT Frogman metal badges; badges that forever designated him as an official member of a unique brotherhood.

After all the ups, downs, twists, and turns since joining the Navy, Joe's lifetime dream had officially come true.

"Sit down. I have a few things to discuss with you."

Joe did as he was instructed, but deep down, all he really wanted to do was admire his UDT/Frogman insignias.

"Listen up, Tyler; I only have a few moments before I've got to leave and meet with the Base Commander. You're being sent to advanced warfare training in the Philippines."

The Chief paused to observe Joe's physical and emotional responses to the news he had just delivered. As per his training, Joe showed no emotion nor change his physical attitude. He continued to sit erect and stare at the Chief as he awaits whatever else Barry Glenn had to say.

"Everything that happened to you from the time you set foot in Yuma for Jump School, up to and including 100% of anything that is about to ever happen to you in this man's Navy is highly classified. By that I mean you cannot tell anyone, and by anyone, I mean no living soul. You will hold this secret for the rest of your life or until it becomes apparent that this information is no longer classified as Top Secret."

The Chief again paused and stared at Joe.

"Roger?"

"Roger that!"

Joe was about to ask a question when the Chief barked out, "Attention on deck!" and snapped out of his seat and stood erect.

Without looking around, Joe followed Chief Glenn's movements and stood upright, staring at the wall in front of him.

"At ease, gentlemen." It was the Base Commander, Lt. David Del Giudice.

"Sit down, Chief." The Lieutenant's voice was civil, but, as Commander of SEAL Team One, even an ordinary, polite gesture came out as a command. Joe relaxed slightly, then turned to face him. To his surprise, the Base Commander was holding out his hand to shake his.

"I assume you're Petty Officer Tyler?"

"Yes, sir!"

"Sit down, Tyler. Relax." As he said this, he was studying Joe's face. He pulled up a chair next to Joe and they both sat across the desk from the Chief.

"I suppose the Master Chief was explaining about your next billet?"

While he was looking at Joe, Lt. Del Giudice directed his question to Chief Glenn.

"Yes sir, we were about to discuss the travel requirements."

"By the way, Chief, I stopped by to let you know we need to delay our meeting until tomorrow, 0700. Can you make that happen?"

"Yes, sir."

"Petty Officer Tyler." The Base Commander had turned in his chair and stared at Joe for a moment. As he did, Joe felt, rather than saw, the commander's eyes searching for something.

"The majority of your instructors were impressed with your efforts. A few said you are a natural born point man. Every instructor commented on your, uh, youthful appearance, but also said that it probably made you more determined to do whatever it took to finish near the top of each class.

"Now that we have met, I understand their concern about how old you really are. Seriously, you do not look old enough to be in recruit training, let alone moving on to AWT."

Joe glanced at the Master Chief for reassurance. In turn, the Chief looked down at his khakis, found something to pick at, but permitted the slightest of smiles to appear on his lips.

"I'm 18, sir. The Navy accepted my enlistment when I was 17."

"Eighteen." As the Base Commander softly repeated Joe's answer, his head moved slowly, back, and forth, from right to left.

"At 18, you're one of the youngest yet to get through Qual School. Your physical presentation, meaning uh, your baby face, almost brought you down."

"Sir, I started school a year younger than I should have and…."

"I read your jacket." The Base Commander cut him off with a combined bark and gentle bite, then continued. "The US Government has done an extensive check on your background. I know your father was a Marine, fought at Tarawa and later at Iwo Jima.

"I know your mother was born in South Bend. Your older sister is attending Kent State, studying accounting. Your older brother, Bill, took two languages in high school and is also enrolled at Kent State University in the Humanities department."

Lt. Del Giudice quickly added, "By the way, there are a lot of government agencies that would love to talk with him."

"You also have two younger brothers and, if your father had not forced you into taking auto-shop, you probably would not have graduated.

"I also know you scored exceptionally well on all the clinical psychological testing, a significant qualification by the Navy to getting you fast-tracked into UDT."

"Somehow got the attention of a Lt. Jeffrey Wheeler, whom you'll get to meet in a couple of days. In contrast to your high school curriculum, your written test scores here at Coronado placed you at the top of each of your classes. Add to that, every Qual School instructor insist you are a natural born point man."

The Base Commander paused before asking his final question: "Tell he this: How did you expect to become a frogman if you can barely swim?"

Joe would have preferred continuing with his silent routine but realized this was not a rhetorical question and the Base Commander, the sole person holding Joe's future in his hands, was waiting for an explanation. He looked to the Chief for support.

However, the Master Chief, upon hearing the Lieutenant's question, sat upright in his chair, and physically leaned forward. He too wanted to hear Joe's explanation.

"Sir, I thought Underwater Demolition was, uh, well...," Joe squirmed as he fought to find the right words.

"Well, I thought it meant all under the water," Joe said, looking back at the Commander. "Until I got my orders, I had never heard of BUD/S or the SEALs. Sir."

Joe stopped talking, as it was evident the Lieutenant was not looking for details. Lt. Del Giudice sat there for a few seconds, pondering, as he stared at Joe.

Finally, he got to the point.

"I have not signed off on your AWT. In fact, I came in here with full intentions of overriding their request to get you to Cavite in time for the beginning of their next training class. Part of me still believes that sending you to a fleet UDT to gain seasoning would be in the best interest of the United States Navy."

As he spoke, Joe felt his own attitude change. It was not anger, but it was confrontational. The Base Commander and the Master Chief recognized the change in his body language, and the room got tense. The Base Commander glared at Joe for a second or two, then slowly stood up, never taking his eyes off him. The Chief and Joe followed his movement, both slowly rising to their feet.

There was a long pause, and Joe felt his future, his dream, in danger.

After a few seconds, the Base Commander finally spoke. "

Don't screw up. Don't get killed."

With that, Joe began breathing again. As the Base Commander began his departure, he paused at the door, then turned and looked at the chief and Joe.

"Chief, get him to Cavite." After a brief pause, he added, "Petty Officer Tyler, when you see Lt. Wheeler, give him my regards. He wired a week ago, pushing me to get you there in time for the next training to begin. And you can thank him for getting you out of the last few days of Jump School, not to mention and entire Escape and Resistance class. But don't worry, Hell Week Two will cover that."

"Roger that, sir."

Once he left, the Chief and Joe sat down, Barry Glenn picked up the conversation as if nothing had happened. Only now, he sounded more like the Master Chief Joe first met nine months ago.

"You need to read and sign these documents, then hand them back to me forthwith. They state that you volunteered for advance jungle warfare training and, upon successfully completing your training in the Philippines, you will be assigned to the Military Assistance Command – Vietnam for further evaluation under combat-theater situations.

"You cannot reveal to anyone what you do, what you have done, nor the chain of command from which your orders are received. Further, you will execute various operations wearing non-military clothing, no markings, patches, dog tags, etc., that connect you directly to the U.S. Government. In the event you are captured or killed in line with the duties of which you are freely volunteering, the United States Navy, the Pentagon, and the American government will disavow any knowledge that you exist.

"This agreement will continue to stay in effect for the next years."

Master Chief Barry Glenn paused and stared into the eyes of his young protégé.

"Petty Officer Tyler, do you understand everything that I have just explained to you?"

"I understand."

"Do you have any questions?"

"No Master Chief. No questions."

Upon hearing that, Master Chief Glenn slid two documents in front of Joe. Without reading them, he signed both and pushed them back to the Chief.

The Master Chief collected them, signed his own name beneath Joe's, placed one copy in a dark-colored accordion file behind him, and the other with Joe's traveling documents, sealed the large envelope, and then handed it to Joe.

Joe noted that the dark-colored accordion file had his name on stenciled in the upper left corner. It read:

<u>TOP SECRET</u>
TYLER, Joseph Edward
USN-B-91148210
<u>TOP SECRET</u>

"Your training station is located outside Cavite City in the Philippines. Your flight departs LAX at 0630 tomorrow, the van leaves the base promptly at 0315. You are to wear civilian clothes beginning at 0300 tomorrow and continue dressed as a civilian until you have been formally received at the Cavite Naval Supply Depot.

"Upon arriving at the Cavite Training Base, you are to hand that envelope, intact, to Lieutenant Wheeler, by personally placing it in his hands."

The Master Chief stared at Joe Tyler. A better description would be to say he stared deep into Joe's brain. After a short pause and a deep breath, he handed Joe another large envelope.

"These are all your travel arrangements, tickets, transportation, chits. Keep them on your person always, even when you are asleep. Are we clear, Petty Officer Tyler?"

Joe stood up, and they shook hands.

"Roger that."

"Good luck, Joe," the Chief added, his voice back in friendship mode. "I'll try to keep tabs on you, but my clearances and authorizations only go so high."

He paused to open a small desk drawer on his left, pulled out a little, tan-colored envelope, and handed it to him. Joe looked inside, paused, then gave Barry Glenn a quizzical look, as the envelope contained five, $20 bills.

"That's from Marsha and me."

Barry Glenn took another deep breath, this time followed by a long, caring sigh.

"Joe, you've changed a lot, both physically and mentally, over the past year. I read in your personnel file that 80% of your pay gets sent home each month. Because you are required to wear civvies until you reach the Philippines, we thought this might help you to buy some new things."

The two friends stood staring at one another for a second or two, both wanting to say something, yet both knowing nothing need be said. Joe accepted the gift, thanked the Chief with a nod of his head, then turned and left.

CHAPTER THIRTEEN

August 1966

Joe's trip to the Philippines was yet another adventure in military travel.

First, he flew commercial airlines on a 5 AM shuttle from San Diego to Los Angeles. At 7 AM he departed LAX for Honolulu. After taking a taxi to Pearl Harbor, he and five fellow travelers went to Guam onboard a military transport.

For the most part, the vast plane contained equipment and supplies. Along either bulkhead, a row of four seats faced one another. It was hard for anyone to notice that Joe was the only person on board the aircraft not wearing a military uniform. This fact did not go unnoticed by either the flight crew or the other military travelers. Joe ignored the glances and stares from his fellow passengers by either sleeping or reading a book.

Once in Guam, he reported to the Regional Seventh Fleet headquarters and dutifully waited in line behind two of his Hawaiian travel mates, both mid-ranked naval officers. The receptionist, a female Second-Class Petty Officer, smiled at them, handed out new paperwork, and directed each to their next destination. While it is not a big deal today, back then, there were very few enlisted women. Joe had been in the service for about a year, and this was the first female Petty Officer he had ever seen.

Before he spoke, she looked at him with a questionable expression on her face. Joe introduced himself and handed her the 11 x 14 envelope containing his orders and his training history.

As she read through the documents, she would occasionally glance up at him, a quizzical look on her face. Finally, she told him to have a seat. And wait. She said it just that way.

Two short sentences:

"Have a seat."

"Wait."

There was a half-dozen empty chairs across from her military-issued light green desk, her small domain clustered in the corner of the room.

Three hours later, around 5 PM, she looked at him with a face that said, 'keep waiting, plebe.' She proceeded to make a big show of locking all the paperwork in the file cabinet behind her. After straightening the items that remained on her desk, she grabbed her purse and headed out the door. When she left the room, her pug nose was pointed high in the air.

She never said goodbye, good night, or good luck. Joe just assumed she was in a hurry and forgot.

Once her ample apple figure disappeared through the doorframe, he pulled several of the plastic chairs together and laid down for a quick nap. No sooner had he figured out a comfortable lying position when a male, third-class Petty Officer stepped through the door and asked him to go with him. Together, they walked about a half-mile to the air transport facility.

After a quick identity check and a review of his orders, someone pointed to another massive, military transport. Joe walked across an active tarmac, went aboard the plane, and introduced himself to the flight crew. Their snap reply was *sit down, strap in, shut up*.

After their military transport plane arrived in Subic Bay, he found his way to the flight line office. Still dressed in his civilian clothes, he told the officer on duty who he was and where he was headed. The flight line officer appeared nonplussed and told him to wait while he figured out the transportation needs.

Ten minutes later, the officer said to go over to the mess hall, grab dinner, and report back in an hour. When Joe arrived back at his office, two Marine MPs came to escort him to the helicopter staging area.

Unlike the guys who picked him up last Christmas in Warren or the even guys at the airport in Los Angeles, the two Marines had active sidearms and were all business. Together, they rode in an open jeep and, after passing through security to get on the tarmac, pulled up next to one of the helicopters.

The pilot was walking around his machine, inspecting every nut and bolt. As the jeep pulled next to the Huey, the MP in the passenger seat jumped out as the vehicle rolled to a stop. As the MP and pilot spoke, the pilot kept glancing over in his direction. Finally, the pilot glanced his way, shrugged his shoulders, and signaled for him to get onboard.

With that, Joe jumped out of the back of the jeep, thanked the driver, shook the pilot's hand, and, without saying another word, climbed into the passenger area of the Huey, and strapped in on the bench seat behind the pilot. While the pilot and his co-pilot had the bubbled glass and shoulder harnesses to hold them in, all that protected Joe from falling out was a worn-out, three-inch-wide seat belt.

Apparently, doors on military helicopters were an option.

There was another headset hanging beside him, so he put it on with the intent of listening to the military air-traffic chatter. As he adjusted the headset, he overheard the pilot say something to the extent it was his first time having to babysit some admiral's 15-year old grandson on a ride to a Naval base.

After the helicopter sat down at the Cavite US Naval Supply Base, the pilot waited for him to clear the wash of the blades then he revved the engines and took off again.

Lt. Jeffrey Wheeler, the friend of the Coronado Base Commander Lt. Del Giudice, pulled up next to him in his jeep. The Lieutenant was informal about his rank and most everything else. He was dressed in well-worn jungle tiger-stripe fatigues and, unlike most officer in his position, drove the vehicle himself.

Because he was expecting him, Jeff Wheeler introduced himself, shook hands and told him to jump in the front passenger seat.

The "L-T" as he was supposed to call him, was a graduate of Annapolis and had gone through BUD/S, and Advanced Land Warfare training. After his impressive training, Lt. Wheeler had served four years of active duty, including three years as an advisor to the South Vietnamese guerrillas.

Jeff Wheeler was a co-author of the military manual, "Covert Jungle Insurgency Through Non-Conventional Allocation of Multi-Divisional Military Deployments." At the Cavite Advanced Warfare Training Facility, Lt. Wheeler had the final word on every member of the armed forces, regardless of branch, military rank, or even what country.

Upon leaving the Cavite Naval Base, they drove through the darkened residential streets of Cavite City and proceeded to wind their way over dirt roads. The LT talked most of the way, filling him in on what to expect, what he would be learning, and why he was there.

Joe only recalls the LT asking one question, and he saved that until they reached the quartermaster's building at the training site.

"How old are you? I mean, really? I know what your jacket says. Before you answer, you have my guarantee that you will go through this entire training, regardless of what you tell me."

"Sir, I really am 18. I know I do not look it. Judging from what I've heard, you handpick everyone that comes here. But like I told Master Chief Glenn before I started

110

BUDS, I will not let the Navy down. I won't let him down, and more importantly, I promise never to let you down."

Many military historians consider Cavite to be the birthplace of America's Advanced Warfare Training. Back then, specialized teams, such as the now famed US Navy SEAL Team Six, had yet to exist. The men-with-green faces, as the North Vietnamese came to call them, laid the groundwork for future mission specialist by inventing new techniques in block training and ambush preparations, along with new designs in weaponry for specialty missions, along with a variety of communications procedures and equipment.

No matter what the military affiliation or even country of origin, at the Cavite base, the men bunked, ate, and cross-trained together. Throughout the entire process, the man who pioneered the original idea, Lt. Jeffrey Wheeler, personally chose and oversaw the development of each candidate.

Unlike today's elite training camps, in 1966, there were no failures: trainees repeated specialized training techniques until they got it right. Also, cross-training with other nationality's military units exposed them to a variety of tactical techniques. For example, while working with Green Berets, Joe learned a ton more about kill-zones, cross kill-zones, and flanking positions.

Working with the Air Force candidates, Joe became better at the triangulation of targets. The Aussie's knowledge of interpreting the landscape and understanding color variations of the vegetation was unique. Because of their experience, Joe's skill of anticipating an enemy ambush and predicting precisely where enemy soldiers would be positioned was off the charts compared to other SEAL point-men.

The Korean Tiger's approach to setting an ambush was different from anything he had ever trained or read about. For example, American SEALs who specialized in stealth, liquidation operations, focused on taking out the enemy personnel as quickly and quietly as possible. The Tiger's, on the other hand, approached their quarry like a hungry pride of lion's intent on getting a meal.

The Korean's began their assault by assigning one or two team members to identify and eliminate the weakest three or four members of the targeted group.

Another Korean Tiger Special Operations team member specialized in taking out one, and only one person: The opposition's leader. These men did this as either a sniper or, depending what the conditions warranted, by coming up behind them and slicing their throat. In either case, once their target was deceased, and the ambush concluded, they would cut-off their victim's ears and attach them to a thin leather strap that hung from their waste. However, if they wanted to make an impression on other country's warriors or, (especially) visiting dignitaries, they hung them around their neck.

Other Korean Tigers focused on communication personal, while the balance of their squad had narrow and precisely designated kill zones.

The Korea Tigers were in superb physical shape and highly skilled in a variety of martial arts. Often, after regular training ended for the day, he spent many an evening working with a couple the Tigers to improve his hand-to-hand combat techniques.

An integral part of Jeff Wheeler's Advanced Warfare Training idea included cross-training with other nationalities. The few who went through AWT had their military skills advanced several levels.

Therefore, the training groups were divided into individual squads that received advanced training in mission-specific clandestine operations.

Unlike Coronado, where teammates learned every members' function, there was no cross-training at Cavite. Why? Because of the secretive nature of the three primary, clandestine operations: Psych warfare, surveillance, and extractions. In the unlikely event, such as a team member would be captured the procedures of the other teams would not be compromised.

Joe trained as the point-man on a four-man fire team that specialized in extractions, aka, snatch, and grab missions. Snatch meant their focus was on clandestinely kidnapping a bad guy. Grab meant their target was an American or allied prisoner, squirreled away in some remote jail controlled by either the NVA (North Vietnamese Army) or Ho Chi Minh's Communist Party.

◆◆◆

Near the end of AWT training in Cavite, individual teams experienced what Lt. Wheeler called Hell Week Two, or "H2." Hell Week in Coronado was designed to identify an individual's combined mental and physical limits. H2 was a joint operation consisting of six-person teams: an officer and five enlisted personnel from a variety of military backgrounds. The focus was on cooperation and total acceptance of your individual brothers to do their job professionally.

The week-long training course started innocuously and without any prior notice. Four different teams departed at 30-minute intervals and targeted to a specified destination point in the Philippine jungle. The objective was to get to the objective without being caught by the enemy soldiers. What Jeff Wheeler failed to mention was that each group's destination point was, in fact, a makeshift enemy prison camp. He also neglected to say that the so-called, "enemy troops," were 75, superbly trained Philippine Special Warfare guerrillas.

Should an individual be unlucky enough to be "captured by the enemy," you were forced to take off your jungle boots and socks, then walk barefoot the remainder of the way to the targeted destination. To make things more realistic, their captors tied the prisoner's wrists in front of them, pulled his elbows behind them, then slid a 4-foot-long bamboo stick between their bent elbows and spinal cord that kept their elbows pinned behind them, thus the prisoner's wrists would be forced up and under their rib cage. The result made it both hard to breathe and consistently placed pressured against their liver and heart.

Fortunately, the Marine Lieutenant who headed Joe's squad assumed that anything as comfortable as an eight-mile hike in the jungle, mainly since it was part of hell Week Two training, should be regarded with a large amount of suspicion.

About 200 yards from the beginning of their trek, Joe's instincts began to fire-off and, as the squad point man, he stopped their advance. The Lieutenant came forward, and Joe told him he had nothing more than instinct to base his decision to prevent the squad from advancing forward.

That was a good enough reason for the Lieutenant and he, in turn, told the rest of the squad to become one with the jungle. After finding a relatively secluded spot, Joe sat elbow to elbow with a seasoned Marine Lieutenant and discussed several alternate routes to their destination, designed to avoid probable ambushes.

While Joe was proud to say that they got to the designated area undetected, their accomplishment was not well received by the enemy Camp Commander. Joe was uncertain whether the Camp Commander was more upset with the fact that a team had avoided his troopers or the way the American squad acted when they strutted into his camp. The team came into camp, acting like some cool, high school dudes. They acted like they had just won the top prize in a Stroll competition.

They smiled, congratulated one another, then let the whole camp know they were there. The Marine Lieutenant, full of bravado, walked up to the Commander's tent to find out what they were to do next.

(What every man learned that day was to stay hidden in the jungle for 24 hours, observe the camp activity and then, as a team, decide what they should do next.)

Instead, a dozen enemy soldiers secured the five of the enlisted men, then shoved them, forcefully, face first into the dirt. The Marine Lieutenant, hearing the scuffle, turned to look at what was going on. Before he had entirely turned around, he was slammed into the ground by four, powerful "enemy soldiers."

They half carried; half dragged the LT away.

The rest of the team were brought to the front of the main tent and commanded to get down on their knees, place their hands behind their heads, and interlock their fingers. The guards tied their wrists, and then their ankles. They finished by tying a third rope which secured their wrists to their ankles. The connection caused their bodies to arch backward and constricted their ability to breathe.

Joe's position was at the end of the line. To relax and focus outside the situation, he found a stain mark on the tent and stared at it intently. While doing so, he could sense his fellow prisoners fidgeting nervously and stealing glances at one another. Joe thought of the whole thing as a big game knowing full well that while he might get a little roughed up, he certainly was not going to die. After all, he had been roughed up a lot growing up in Warren and always managed to come out of it.

Not to mention surviving "Basic Conditioning" and "Hell Week."

Was he uncomfortable? Yes. But physically, not any worse than what he had recently been through the past several months just to get to this point.

After several minutes, individual guards came up behind the other guys in the squad, placing black canvas bags over their heads. Once each man was secured, three guards came over to Joe, untied all his restraints and told him their "general" wanted him to observe the other guy's punishments before he died. Deciding to play along, he tried to look concerned. Two guards stood to either side of him, each tightly holding an arm and wrist. Standing he in front of each prisoner, they went down the line questioning each man for details about the "mission" they were on.

Each man replied with answers from the Geneva Convention Manual: name, rank, and serial number. In turn, each got kicked hard, either in the back, the side or the stomach by a guard wearing jungle boots, rolled in the dirt, pissed on, buckets of dirty water thrown at them and made to lay in the resulting mess.

When Joe's turn came, an enemy officer came over to him and, very softly, but quite menacingly explained that what happened to his partners was nothing compared to what they had in store for him. To avoid the terrible things that were about to happen, all he had to do was answer some questions, truthfully and honestly. Joe stood there, controlling his breathing and heart rate, staring straight ahead.

"Where were you going on your mission?"

"Point B, which I assume, is right here," he answered without taking his eyes off his newly discovered tent stain.

"What was the point of your mission?"

"To the best of my knowledge, to avoid meeting you."

With his face inches from the right side of his head, the officer screamed at him.

"What was the point of your mission?" His spittle went into Joe's ear.

"Man, I'm the lowest ranked guy here," he said, turning his head to look at his advisory. Calmly, and quietly, Joe added, "You think they're going to tell me anything? Do you show your lowly ranked messengers what your General's orders are?

"You can do what you want to me, but I'm so low on the totem pole, I normally end up in the dog-house anyway."

He paused, turned his head forward, found his stain, then added in a very calm voice, "What else can I help you with?"

The officer demanded his name, rank, and serial number. Joe answered with nearly the right name and the proper rank. The serial number he gave out was 100% fictitious.

The officer walked over and discussed something with his General. The officer signaled to a couple of his guards, who in turn threw Joe to the ground and dragged him by his heels some thirty yards across the prison's rocky parade yard. Reaching their destination, the guards forced him into an awkward sitting position next to a five-inch diameter wooden pole, then made him sit with legs and arms wrapped around the pole.

First, they tied his ankles together. With another rope, they tied his wrists together. Joe looked at his captives and smirked, "I was treated worse than this playing dodgeball in my fourth-grade gym class."

Bad move. A guard came over and roughly pulled a black leather hood over his head. At first, Joe only shrugged his shoulders. But when he relaxed all he could smell was someone else's sweat and the putrid aroma of another person's vomit.

Joe heard their boots in the sand and gravel as they walked away and remembered thinking that if this is how he is going to spend his night, it was not so bad. All he had to do was sit and lean against the pole and fall asleep.

That bit of wishful thinking lasted, at best, about a half hour.

Not being able to straighten his arms or legs became extremely uncomfortable. Soon his calves, knees, thighs, hips, back, and shoulders became stiff and sore. Sitting in one spot even made his butthurt. By the next morning, he would have given them anything they wanted, all they had to do was let he stretch. Fortunately, a few hours later, a young guard came over, untied him, and whispered he was taking Joe to the latrine. The guard told him to be civil and not cause any undue attention. It felt terrific to straighten his body, so he did as he was told. When they got to the latrine area, the guard took the black hood off his head.

Even today, Joe can still recall how sweet the air smelled, even in the latrine; but mostly how good it felt to stretch again.

After he had done his business, the guard blindfolded him again, but this time with a just a black rag that covered his eyes. The rag blindfold was much better than having the hood over his head, plus he could now see out of the bottom of the blindfold. When they returned to the original post, the guard again had him sit with his legs and arms around the post. However, this time, Joe's back was to the officer's tents. The guard tied his wrists and ankles rather loosely. Once finished, the guard looked around to make sure that no one was paying attention, then squatted down in front of him.

"Keep quiet, and they'll forget you're here. Don't try to break free and run or we'll both be beaten with a stick. Joe thanked him, leaned against the post, and promptly fell asleep.

Guessing by the shadows on the ground, it was just before noon when his young friend finally reappeared with water. It tasted like rusted tin, but it was wet, so he gulped it down eagerly. The guard pretended to check all his ropes and blindfold, then told he would be back with more water. About an hour later, the guard returned with another tin-cup of rusty water and a carrot he snuck from their mess hall. Before he left, the guard told Joe that someone would soon take him to the Commander's tent.

"Soon," took another four hours. The young guard escorted the still blindfolded Tyler to the front of the Commander's tent. Joe had to shuffle barefooted across the prison camp's parade ground as an ankle rope secured his legs. His hands remained tied behind his back. Once they reached the General's tent, the guard told him to stand at ease and not make a sound. Joe did as he was told.

Ninety minutes later, strong hands suddenly grabbed him under both armpits, held him in the air as they climbed several wooden steps. When the guards dropped him to his feet, he almost lost his balance. His guards quickly untied his ankles and wrists before removing the blindfold from his eyes. Once his vision became accustomed to the light, the first thing he saw was the Commanding General standing behind an old-fashioned wooden desk.

"Welcome Petty Officer Joseph Tyler, please sit down." He was too congenial and way too friendly. His accent was thick, making it hard to understand what he wanted. Mentally, Joe prepared himself for whatever bad was apparently about to follow.

"I hope your night wasn't too unpleasant. I truly realize how sore your legs and arms can be when you can't stretch."

"Yes, sir. It felt good to be able to walk over here." His reply dripped of sarcasm; a point missed by the General.

"Many of your friends didn't have it as good as you. In fact, they got no rest at all." The General sat down in a wooden office chair, began slowly rocking back and forth as he stared at him. He stared back for a few seconds, found a spot on the wall behind him and glued in. Finally, the General swiveled in his chair, selected a handful of papers, swiveled back, and laid them in front of him on his desk. Looking through the many documents on his desk, the General made a point to check off the names above Joe's.

"There were several members of your group who decided this morning that a steak-dinner, a comfortable cot to sleep on, and healthy meals each day was a better way to spend their week here."

The General looked again at the paper in front of him and then added, "To be exact, seven of our current residents took advantage of our hospitality."

The General stood up, attempting to standing tall in his five-foot-eight frame. After a few seconds of staring at Joe, he came around to the front of his desk, sat on the corner and began talking to Joe in a guy-to-guy friendly manner.

"All your friends had to do was sign some unofficial paperwork saying they are employed as a member of the US Military, and fill in their name, rank, and serial number."

The General brought out a piece of paper with Joseph Tyler's name on it and two pages of something that looked like Chinese writings.

"Looks like more than my name, rank, and serial number," he offered.

"Legal Mumbo-jumbo. I give you my word on this."

Joe pondered the paperwork for a good two minutes, hoping it would cause his captor to begin squirming. It worked; the General started to get restless.

"Have you ever seen Bridge on The River Kwai?" Joe asked him, refusing his clipboard.

The General looked at him with a quizzical expression on his face.

"It was a British movie that came out about ten years ago. Basically, the story was about a company of Brit soldiers who were captured and forced to build a railroad bridge over a river. Along the way, the Japanese Commander locked the British officer in a tin box for a week and let him bake in the sun."

"Get to the point," the General commanded.

"After being treated like an animal for a week, the base commander offered the Brit a steak dinner and a glass of wine to sign paperwork he couldn't read. My point is this: Sir, with all due respect to your rank, sir, I can't sign anything, no matter what the offer. Sir."

The General was going to say something but stopped himself. Instead, he sighed, stood behind his desk, and then called for the guard. When the guard came in, Joe stood up and allowed him to take his arm. Without saying a word to one another, the guard escorted Joe back to his pole.

On the sixth morning, a gray military bus pulled up to the camp. Joe's new guard friend came over as the bus was arriving, pulled Joe's blindfold off, released his ropes, and brought over a cup of cold, non-rusty water in an actual glass.

As Joe looked around, he could see several other prisoners, all in a variety of apparel, and physical appearance, getting onboard the bus. His guard-buddy stood alongside him and told him it was time to go back to Cavite.

When they passed in front of the main tent, the General called out to him in perfect English.

"Hey, Tyler, how old are you?"

"Eighteen."

"You look fifteen," he shouted with a big smile on his face. They waved to each other, and Joe continued making his way over to the bus. Before he got on board, he turned one last time to say goodbye to his new friend and maybe find out his name. Joe finally spotted him, wearing camo jungle gear with a bayoneted rifle strapped to his back. He was among a squad of other guerrilla fighters ready to enter the jungle to capture more unsuspecting American and allied warriors.

When the bus returned to camp, it stopped in front of Lt. Wheeler's tent. When the men got off the bus, they loosely assembled in two lines.

"Tomorrow morning at 0500, we begin the final two weeks of training. The focus will be on hand-to-hand combat and new weapons training. By 'we,' I mean you."

The men all chuckled as the Lieutenant never joined their physical training.

"I'm transferring to Cam Ranh Bay tomorrow at 0700 where I hope to revisit with some of you in the next few weeks. Good luck and God's speed."

With that, they were dismissed. When Joe got back to his hooch, he showered, put on clean skivvies, dark blue workout shorts, a white T-shirt, and running shoes, and walked over to the mess hall. He had a small protein-packed brunch and then headed over to their makeshift outdoor gym.

Since Basic Conditioning in Coronado ended, pushing his body to perform had become, his way of reconnecting with himself. An hour after brunch, he put himself through a strenuous upper body workout, ran the hills that surrounded the training camp, then ended up at the firing range.

The relatively new Stoner 63A carbine and the light machine gun had recently been made available for the exclusive use of the SEALs. Beginning with the first round, Joe fired, he understood what a well-made machine he was holding. He put several hundred rounds through the latest carbine model, the XM22E1, shooting from a variety of positions, enjoying every trigger squeeze. After that, Joe fired nearly 2,000 rounds through the model XM207 light machine gun. Joe left the firing range that afternoon, hoping that both weapons would be available to him when he got to Vietnam.

First, he had to get there.

CHAPTER FOURTEEN
November 1, 1966

Upon completing 12 weeks of Advanced Warfare Training at Cavite, he was ordered to report aboard the USS Henderson DD-785, currently stationed in Honolulu. The orders concluded by saying his next duty station would be Cam Ranh Bay, South Vietnam. Once there, he was to report to Lieutenant Commander Jeffrey Wheeler, Military Assistance Command, Vietnam - Special Operations Group, Combat Central Command (MACV SOG)

Lieutenant Commander? That meant since leaving Cavite two weeks ago, Lieutenant Wheeler had been promoted. The fact that he would be reporting to someone who knew all about him was great news.

Because he would be living onboard a Navy destroyer for a week or two, he thought it better to wear the standard work uniform that enlisted folks wore while out at sea. After leaving the AWT personnel office, he went to the Quarter-Master's building and drew out two pairs of dungarees, two chambray shirts, along with three sets of white t-shirts and skivvies. That done, he headed to the laundry pool and had his Petty Officer Third Class crow pressed on his shirt sleeves and his name stenciled above his pocket.

Two days later, sea bag in hand, he arrived at the pier where the Henderson had docked, walked the short gangway onto the fantail, and reported onboard. he handed the Officer-

On-Deck his paperwork and, per the OOD's instructions, he found an empty bunk in the engineering department. After claiming an empty top-level bunk, he settled-in to spend the next few weeks aboard his new home.

Three days out to sea, as he sat a table on the mess-deck, alone as usual, eating his lunch. Lost in thought, he heard someone say his name and looked up.

Petty Officer First Class Skylar Mertes came up and asked if he could sit down. While he welcomed him, he did so with suspicion. Mertes was the first person to not look upon he as an alien from another planet.

"Officer Wodianka said we were cut from the same cloth and I should get to know you."

Mertes paused to let that information set-in.

"I've been assigned to this tug for five months and, for the most part, haven't gotten to know a single soul which, by the way, is fine by me."

Joe stared at him for maybe four or five seconds, then pointed to the seat across from him. Mertes set his metal tray on the four-person table, then sat in the plastic chair across from him. Because the warship was traveling at a relatively high rate of speed, it pitched and yawed over the ocean on its way to the war zone. They both balanced their trays with their left hands, as the ship rolled left, right and front to back, seemingly at the same time.

The two men swapped the traditional get-to-know-you banter, both semi-lying as they were trained to do. Mertes was the sole proprietor, co-inventor, onboard genius, repairman and all-around whiz kid for a 1/10th scale version of an unmanned helicopter being tested for anti-submarine duties. While most people think of military drones as being a modern invention. The Navy was testing drones back in 1966.

"I'm not sure what you mean by us being 'cut from the same cloth.'"

This was truer than the college-educated, super-smart, Mertes could even conceive. Mertes began to count off facts, using his fingers to emphasize each point.

"Number One: I'm not an Electronic Technician, and you're not a gunner's mate."

Joe paused for effect.

"You're wearing new dungarees, and that chambray shirt has a third-class gunny's crow, yet you bunk with the engineering black gang instead of the gunners-mates. When you came aboard, you had a quarter-filled sea-bag."

"And, number four, your orders went directly to ship's Captain instead of the ship's office. Obviously, you are a), not planning on staying onboard for any great length of time and b), have no concept of what a gunner's mate does aboard a Navy destroyer."

Mertes smirked, gave he a look of 'the prosecution rests,' and returned to consuming his lunch.

Joe sat there, not moving, staring at him wondering what he should do next. What he did was place his elbows on the table, fold his hands under his chin, and stared at the top of Mertes' head for several seconds.

"What's your point?" Mertes sat upright, pushed his tray away, and looked at he. "My point is this: I'm stuck here for a while. Until I figure out who and what you are, and if nothing else, I found someone to share a few meals and talk with. That is, at least until you disappear. We can talk about sports, music, family, current events, or how the Navy is completely screwed up."

Mertes paused, took another couple of bites off his tray, then looked at Joe.

"If you want to talk about your life and what you really do for the US Navy, that's up to you. I will not ask. For the most part, he, I really don't care."

Both men sat there, stared at their trays and, occasionally, took another forkful of food.

"Joe, if that's your real name, whenever you want to come up and see my toy, that's up to you. I am always available, and I have gotten you clearance through Chief Warrant Officer Presley, who, by the way, said he knows you. Not to mention that he added you were in some kinda training with him, one-time during his career. Since he looks thirty and you look sixteen, I cannot, for the life of me figure out when that could possibly have been."

Joe stared at Mertes for a minute, sat upright, and picked up his fork. he was hungry, and the food appeared to look appetizing. Besides, Chief Warrant Officer Presley sounded familiar to he, and he did not want Mertes to read that from his face.

Joe lifted his head, said, "Fine by me," and then proceeded to focus on his meal.

From that moment forward, they became arms-length friends and shared an occasional meal or two together each day.

Apparently, everyone aboard the ship knew Mertes was a spook.

They also knew that Tyler was supposed to be a Gunner's Mate Petty Officer Third Class yet did not know anything about the ship's weaponry. Joe never told him about his actual training and continued to speak in generalities about his past. Their conversations eventually settled into a routine of sports, music, family, current events, or the number one fallback conversation, how the Navy is screwed up.

Joe went to look over the drone and was eager to learn about what it did and how it worked. Mertes was always tinkering with the machine, most of the time trying to get the large cameras to operate within some big, clunky, remote-control box and, at the same time, not interfere with the drone's guidance system.

Looking back, he enjoyed his time with Mertes and often wished he had had a chance to know him post-military.

November 27, 1966 is a day Joe remembers for several reasons.

First, it was his 19th birthday and, other than himself and his mother, no one cared.

Second, it was the day he got his first glimpse of South Vietnam.

Third, in the early afternoon, so he was hanging out with a couple of the men from the engineering gang taking a break from their boiler-room duties. Most everyone stood near the rail on the port side of the ship's fantail, himself, and a couple of other sailors, catching their first real glimpse of the east coast of a gorgeous country.

At that moment, he did not realize his view of the countryside would change before the day ended.

"So that's Vietnam," one of the guys stated to no one as they looked toward the jewel-like, dark green hillside along the coast a few miles away.

"Doesn't look like much fighting going on from here."

Their spectating was interrupted as the chief boatswain's mate, whistling the designated notes over the ship's loudspeakers to get the attention of the crew.

"Now hear this. Now hear this. Petty Officer Tyler report to the bridge. Petty Officer Tyler to Commander Elfelt's stateroom. That is all."

This was his third week aboard the warship, and he was aware there was a lot of scuttlebutt going around about who he was, as it was quite apparent to everyone that as a third-class gunners-mate, he knew nothing about the ship's armory nor ever took a duty watch in any of the ship's operations.

Add to that, instead of bunking with boatswains and other gunners-mates, he bunked in the engineering quarters, i.e., men that controlled the machinery that pushed the big ship across the ocean.

After the announcement over the ship's loudspeakers, the dozen people standing near him on the fantail went silent and stared at him; a few even stepped back a little so as not to be accused of guilt by association.

Joe gave everyone a surprised look, which in this case was genuine, shrugged his shoulders and asked out loud to no one in particular, "Wonder what that's all about?"

As he began to head forward along the starboard passageway, one of his engineering shipmates yelled from the fantail, "Hey Tyler, maybe they finally figured out you ain't got a clue about being in the Navy."

Joe turned, smiled, and put his hands up in a "got me" manner.

Another man added, "He heard you turned the wrong valve and sent black oil to the Commander's crapper. heard his crapper exploded and shit flew everywhere when he hit the flush valve."

This elicited a lot of laughter, and, as a group, they continued to joke and speculate about his soon-to-be-handed-out punishment.

Meanwhile, as he headed forward along the outboard starboard passageway, everyone near the rails or along the bulkhead would step aside and give him room to pass. Their looks were a mixture of unease and compassion; it was if Joe was the proverbial a "dead man walking" to the gas chamber, and they did not know what to say.

Because he had never been in this portion of the ship, upon stepping onto the bridge, he had to ask the Officer on

Deck where to go. As he turned to walk in the direction the OOD had designated, the officer, an Annapolis newbie Ensign, began to rebuke him in front of the other enlisted people on Bridge.

"Petty Officer Tyler, the next time you enter this bridge, you will do so with your lid on, you will salute, and you will address the OOD as Sir! Am I making himself clear?"

If that was meant to intimidate Joe, it did not. He mumbled a "Yes, Sir" and then began to salute. His right arm froze in midair and stopped the saluting progress. By Navy rule, he could not salute with his head uncovered, and his enlisted man's white hat was hanging from his back pocket.

In the end, Joe's intent to comply with the OOD commands turned into a half-ass wave, which angered the young Ensign even more. However, before the OOD could sputter his indignation, Joe had moved off in the direction of the ship's Captain's office.

Come to think of it, there were a lot of things in the Navy Joe could never get the hang of: Like, why did they always call the stairway ladders? Same with the walls; they were called bulkheads. Toilets were called heads. Who came up with that?

And the food was always served on the mess deck instead of the dining hall.

Okay, that last one made sense. As he stood outside Commander Elfelt's stateroom, Joe hesitated before knocking while he attempted to remember the regulation concerning putting on his white hat before entering a senior officer's quarters. If he left it off, should he still salute him? After all, the Captain was the Lord and Master of the ship.

In the end, he held his hat in his left hand and rapped his knuckles three times on the outer bulkhead, just under the Captain's nameplate. The Commander called him in, and when Joe slid the curtain back, it occurred to him that in the past few weeks, he had never seen him.

Commander Elfelt sat at his desk, scanning the pages of Petty Officer Tyler's service jacket. His physical appearance was tired, mean, and grumpy.

Naturally, Joe assumed the Commander's irritation was somehow caused by himself. Immediately, his brain began racing, searching for something he had done wrong; something recent, that is. Naturally, he thought, there could have been a few things from the hell Week Two training, but, as hard as he tried, his little pea-brain could not regurgitate anything that would upset such a high-ranking officer.

"Who are you?" he asked without bothering to look up.

"Sir! Petty Officer Joseph Tyler reporting as ordered, sir!" Joe practically shouted, just as he had seen them do in movies at the Robins Theater back in Warren. After being dressed down from the OOD, he figured by throwing in a lot of military-sharp "sirs" would be a good opening defensive position.

The Commander lifted his head wearily as he swiveled his chair to face him. When their eyes met, his Commander's body language turned from wonderment to incredulous. He looked Joe up and down, then stared into his eyes.

A burning sensation began percolating in the back of Joe's head. Simultaneously, his stomach began regurgitating whatever that greasy stuff was that he had at lunch. Joe started to shift his weight from side-to-side; wanting to excuse himself and go pee. Thinking about it, he felt more at ease when he was an "enemy prisoner" at Hell Week Two. As that thought floated through his brain, it made him begin to smile.

"How old are you?"

"Sir?"

"How. Old. Are. You?"

"Eighteen, sir. No, check that. Today's my birthday. Make that, 19!" he paused, let his smile about Cavite come through, then caught his enormous mistake. His brain screamed to him: SHUT UP AND WIPE THE STUPID SMILE OFF YOUR FACE!

Why did he just tell the ship's Captain about this being his birthday? Did he somehow think the Captain called him to his stateroom for them to sing Happy Birthday together?

A new thought quickly appeared in his brain: Do they still make stupid sailors walk the plank?

Joe closed his eyes, let out a long, slow breath, and stood ready for the verbal smackdown about to come his way. Based upon a lifetime of mental conditioning, Joe's whole being quickly shifted from confusion to defiance. His muscles hardened as he braced himself for the Commander's assault.

Commander Elfelt paused, then sat back in his chair. His demeanor slowly changed from that of a senior officer to that of a curious elementary school counselor. A long, slow sigh escaped his lips.

"Relax, Tyler. Stand at ease. Seriously, you do not look 19, 18 or even 17 to me."

"I understand sir. It has been a curse my whole life, sir. It made BUD/S especially tough, sir."

"If I hadn't read your jacket and reviewed your training, I would have guessed that you were a junior in high school."

Joe stood as erect as possible and tried to look older.

"Do you shave?"

"Sir?"

"Tyler, I'm not in the mood, nor in the habit of repeating myself. Let's try this again: Do you, Petty Officer Third Class Joseph Tyler, shave or not?"

"Not very often, sir, maybe twice a week if I remember to do so. Or, if there's going to be an inspection." For good measure, he added another, "Sir."

"Okay, let's start again: Who are you?"

"Sir?"

"Tyler! Work with me here!" Joe wondered to himself if the Commander was rubbing the pain in his head or trying to make Joe disappear.

"Sorry, sir. I was confused by the question."

In truth, he was stalling for time, trying to figure out if he was testing to see if he would tell him more than he already knew about him. Commander Elfelt sat there and stared through him.

"Joseph E. Tyler. Petty Officer Third Class. Bravo 914-82-50-54." He tried is best to sound all military and stuff.

At his newest reply, the Commander stared hard at him. The ship's Captain was trying to figure out how the person in front of him had graduated from Advanced Warfare Training, or better, how he got in the Navy in the first place.

Joe avoided the glaring look on his face and instead told himself to stare intently at a mark on the Captain's office wall, err bulkhead.

"Can't say any more than that, sir."

"I know all about your training, Petty Officer Tyler, but too many redactions cut up the important parts."

Several seconds had passed without him saying anything. Commander Elfelt broke the silence, "Tyler?"

"Sorry sir, I heard you but, uh, I don't know what you mean by redactions."

"Blacked out."

The Captain's voice dropped off wearily, and he thought for sure he saw him age another year. Think man, think! Since he had never considered reading his own service jacket, he was even more clueless than usual.

"Sir, I'm not supposed to talk to anyone about my training, where I've been, nor where I'm going." Joe took a chance and looked directly at the Commander.

More forehead rubbing, however, this time, he added the heavy sigh.

"Okay, Tyler, here is what I do know: When this ship left Hawaii, I had orders to go to Midway. We're out less than four hours and new orders arrive saying to head to the Tonkin Gulf, forthwith."

The Captain looked through him, at which time Joe knew he had guessed right - he was the cause of Commander Elfelt's grumpiness.

"Just before we depart Pearl you show up with a partial sea bag and wearing starched and pressed new dungarees. The Officer-On-Duty becomes confused. While he sees the gunny crow, the orders specifically direct the OOD to assign you a bunk in engineering quarters.

"The word from my staff is that you had to ask what size the cannons were. If you truly are a gunners-mate, you would have known without asking."

As the Commander spoke, his voice began increasing in volume. A vein bulged-out at the exact spot where he had been rubbing his forehead.

"Instead of your jacket going to the Personnel Office, your orders are addressed For My Eyes Only, sealed, and stamped Top Secret. Inside it says to sail to international waters off Cam Ranh Bay and await further orders."

Commodore Elfelt's grumpy mood was reaching a new high point.

"So, what happens next? Here we are on station and do nothing more than sail around in figure eights for two hours. A few minutes ago, I got a message that PCF-116 will be here at 1530 hours (3:30), to pick up Chief Warrant Officer Presley and Petty Office Third Class Tyler."

The Commander paused.

"I asked Presley what he and you have in common. He said you were in Coronado together."

So that is why Presley's name sounded familiar to Joe. They had gone through BUD/S together. Joe never got to know Presley as he thought that was a regular officer, and not someone who came up through the enlisted ranks.

The Commodore paused, then added, "And by the way, I'm well aware that Cavite is a Special Forces training base."

The smartass in Joe wanted to correct His Highness and tell him it was designated as an Advanced Warfare Training facility and was not just for Green Berets, or, as they were commonly referred to, as Special Forces. In fact, Cavite trained multiple military branches from several countries, including the elite Philippine commandos.

"I'm no Green Beret nor Army Ranger if that's what you're thinking, sir. I'm true blue, United States Navy."

Joe straightened to his full five-foot-nine and three-quarters inches and resumed staring straight ahead. Somewhere deep inside, he felt the bad attitude within him begin to stir again. He earnestly wanted to tell the Commander that he was done here and was leaving.

The Commander either got the hint or simply decided he was not going to get anything more from Joe. He turned toward his desk, wrote something in Joe's personnel jacket, signed it, put it in a large sealed envelope, then handed the whole package to him.

"You are dismissed."

As Joe left the Command Deck, he heard the boatswain mate notify the deck crew to prepare to take the Swift boat alongside. Everything was moving so fast Joe did not have time to say goodbye to his new friends. He packed skivvies, a hand-towel, toothbrush, comb, and hurried to the fantail.

The Swift pulled along the leeward side, and both crews made ready for the two departing men to jump onto the gunboat's rear deck. Before he got into a good position to leave the Henderson, CWO Presley threw a small bag onto the gunboat's fantail and jumped on-board. Joe followed and had no sooner put his second foot down when the Swift's crew let go of the ropes and gunboat began maneuvering away from the big warship.

In less than a minute, the coxswain opened the throttles, and they headed in the general direction of Cam Ranh Bay.

The person that helped him catch his balance when he jumped aboard was a veteran First Class Boatswain's Mate. An "old salt" in Navy vernacular.

"I'm Ty. . ."

"I don't give a crap if you're the bastard child of Saint Lucifer himself. You will be dead in three days, three weeks, or three months, so no one, 'specially me, gives a crap who you are or how you got here."

"Exceptin' maybe your whore mother," he added. "Then again, I doubt the Navy could ever figure out what Panamanian brothel the bitch is working, so she ain't never going to get to be asked, neither."

Without skipping a beat, the First-Class continued his unsolicited, crude, yet seasoned, combat military advice.

"Look, Polly-frog, stay the hell out of my way and don't touch none of them weapons. In fact, squat down on the deck like you are taking a crap, keep your hands in your pockets, and don't even look at me until we secure."

With that, the Boatswain turned, grumbling, and swearing as he walked away.

Joe, smiled, and watched him leave. For the fleetest of moments, the bravado in him thought of tossing the old guy overboard. Instead, he took a deep breath, walked to back of the gunboat, and purposely leaned against the 50-caliber machine gun, instead of squatting, as the Boatswain had ordered.

Looking back toward the Henderson, he waved goodbye to his shipmates. A few returned the wave. The majority ignored him and went back to work preparing the warship for an upcoming shore bombardment.

Joe scanned the helo-deck until he spotted Mertes standing with his hands on his hips; his feet spread wide apart to keep him balanced. When their eyes connected, Joe gave a big overhead wave.

In return, Mertes flipped him off.

In less than a week, and in the hardest, cruelest way possible, Joe learned what the Boatswain had said about not getting to know who anyone, was a lesson that endured his entire military career.

CHAPTER FIFTEEN
November 28, 1966

Having been promoted to Lieutenant Commander (LCDR) Jeff Wheeler oversaw Seal Team One and Two Special Ops platoons operating in I Corps, also known as Eye Corps.

As the most northern military tactical zone of the Vietnam War, I Corps encompassed the five South Vietnam provinces that shared their borders with North Vietnam, Cambodia, and the Gulf of Tonkin. Because of this, I Corps saw the heaviest fighting throughout the entire Vietnam war. Unfortunately, their location also meant a disproportionately higher percentage of combat deaths and wounded.

Over the past two days, five greenies – graduates of AWT without actual combat experience – had been assigned to Cam Ranh for further evaluation. Among them were two Australians from the SASR, two South Koreans from the famed Tiger Brigade, and Joe Tyler.

Because Jeff Wheeler hand-picked each man chosen to be at Cavite and designated their mission-specific training, he was acutely aware of the strengths and weaknesses of the five men he chose to become members of Operation Footboy.

In addition to their outstanding performances in the Philippines, each brought with him a specialized trait that could not be taught: An innate predisposition that would first sense danger, accompanied by an accounting of where enemy soldiers would be positioned.

Wheeler's final evaluation of each candidate was to place them in positions where interaction with the enemy was almost a given. From personal experience, Wheeler knew it was one thing to be trained to combat the enemy. Nevertheless, coming face-to-face with another human being and then, without hesitation or second thought having to kill them – well, that took a completely different mentality.

Joe awoke Monday morning, November 28, 1966, at 5:30 AM in a two-man hooch at the combined Navy/Marine base in Cam Ranh Bay, South Vietnam. At 9 AM on the 28th, he and the other four new men met with LCDR Wheeler in his temporary office at the MACV Compound.

Their meeting was atypical Jeffrey Wheeler: no one sat, no welcoming speech, no Q & A when he finished.

"Good morning, guys. I assume introductions are not required. You have been chosen as prospective members of a Special Operations Group that will operate out of Eye Corps. First, there are two or three additional assignments that you will need to successfully complete. You will not be working together; instead, your missions have been chosen to reflect your future assignments. There is a high probability that you will contact the enemy."

Upon hearing this, the five new men twitched with anticipation. Wheeler concluded the meeting by instructing each man where, when and with whom they were to report to, the next morning.

Once finished, everyone was dismissed.

Per Wheeler's instructions, Joe joined the crew aboard one of the 50-foot Swift boats. As a function of US Military's Operation Market Time, their primary assignment was to intercept sampans and other boat traffic within three miles off the coast in the northeastern portion of II Corps area. If called upon, they also provided support for Army units operating in the region.

Each Swift patrol boat had a regular crew of six or seven, with either a junior grade lieutenant or master chief petty officer as the Officer in Charge. Each enlisted man had volunteered for this unique duty; most had extended their enlistment obligations to get their jobs. A Vietnamese Navy liaison had been temporarily assigned to various gunboats designated to inspect sampans and other Vietnamese vessels traveling along the coast.

Their first two patrols were routine. Joe used the time to get in sync with the crew on a variety of boarding and defensive positioning assignments. His primary duty was to operate the single mount 50-caliber machine gun whenever they pulled alongside a foreign boat.

Most fishing boats held two to four fishermen out for their days' catch. Often, they would pull alongside larger Junks that had entire, multi-generational families living on-board. A twin-barreled 50-caliber machine gun tub sat atop and to the rear of the pilothouse. Because it could swivel in a 360-degree arc, the gunner had a clear field of fire in every direction.

Behind the cabin area, on the port side was the aft steering station, basically a replica of the pilothouse. The boat's skipper would usually position himself there when going alongside the various vessels to be searched.

While every search has the potential for danger, searching a dozen watercrafts every patrol and finding nothing tends to make things relaxed, almost tedious. he had to remind himself that many of the Vietnamese vessels they came upon would be manned by non-combatants.

However, his third day patrolling the coastline turned out to be a day that would live with he the rest of his life. That morning they joined another PCF in search of a large Oriental junk off the coast of Thein Biehn, north of Cam Ranh Bay. While the other crew boarded the Junk from the leeward side, they stood guard, maybe 30 feet off the windward side.

All their weapons were aimed at the junk, safeties off, belts loaded. Because the shipping lane where they were operating was busy with boats heading in several directions, they always had one member of the crew watching the opposite direction to protect their flanks.

That morning the crew member was he. Suddenly, a grenade exploded in the direction of the original PCF. Almost immediately, several weapons opened fire - some from their Swift, others from the first PCF, and a couple from onboard the junk.

For a split-second, everything went quiet. Then their radios came alive with several people shouting at once.

Then the commander of a nearby Coast Guard cutter reported Joe was coming in from zero six zero and he could see the black smoke roll from her stack as she turned in their direction. Joe could also hear the ship's boatswain calling General Quarters even though she was a half a mile away.

The gunboat's firefight lasted maybe eight or ten seconds, which he learned was normal. The grenade landed short of the other patrol boat and other than spraying shrapnel into the bow, it did no damage. The junk was riddled with holes. Two of its crew lay dead, one was missing, and two others were gravely wounded.

The PCF crew member and interpreter who had boarded the junk had immediately flattened themselves on the deck within the first nanosecond of trouble and came away with a few scratches from flying debris.

Their crew boarded and found North Vietnamese propaganda leaflets, a couple of boxes of grenades, and primers for explosives. Men from their boat secured the prisoners and transferred them to the Coast Guard cutter.

Afterward, Joe discovered the safety on the M16 he had shouldered when the action began, was still in the Lock position.

Not good.

An hour after they departed the area, they received another call, this time for shore support, eight miles northwest of their position. The Chief aligned their Swift to the northwest and pushed the dual throttles all the way forward.

Joe sat atop the cabin in the bucket, behind twin 50-caliber machine guns. As the boat raced forward to join the fight, he double, and triple checked the weapons to ensure the tracer belts were correctly loaded. he also checked and rechecked that the safeties were in the off position.

As the gunboat drew within a mile or so away, they began hearing sporadic rapports from the soldiers M16s. The Chief backed the throttles back by fifty percent. A minute of quiet then thump, thump, thump as the Army platoon launched three mortar rounds. The rounds exploded followed by a minute or so of intense firing.

Then silence again. Soon, the Chief eased the boat slowly along a nearby shoreline. Every man aboard the gunboat became hyper-alert. The crew's veterans were experienced to this type of combat. Each man gripped or held a variety of weapons, their fingers resting lightly on the triggers.

Within the angles of their respective kill zones, each man searched the jungle foliage for any sight of the enemy. While everything appeared to be tranquil, the tension on the gunboat rose.

A voice broke over the radio with a command to stand down. It was from a Captain on one of the helicopter gunships.

"Hold your fire. Hold your fire. Friendly cattle in the area. Repeat. Friendly cattle in the area. Stand down."

Joe let an audible "say what?" escape from his lips, then looked at the other guys to see if he was awake or dreaming. The Chief looked up at him, smiled and simply said, "Later."

They continued their close coastal patrol for another hour or so, and then slowly swung out to sea. After the Chief ordered them to stand down, he secured and covered the guns, jumped down the side of the cabin, and asked the front gunner to explain exactly what had happened to make them break-off the attack.

"Sometimes it is cows, sometimes it's water buffaloes. You'll get used to it. One time, we had to stop firing at Charlie on account of some rubber trees were getting damaged."

Again, something else they had failed to tell him in Cavite. Amazing.

Later, the crew heard that two American soldiers were wounded. The VC KIA (Killed in Action) body count was six. Several VC got away by mixing in with the cattle. Joe was ending his first week of combat patrols and, because adrenaline had rushed through and subsiding in his system twice, he felt a bit drained.

It was only 11:30 in the morning and his day was about to go wrong and then later, turn much worse.

CHAPTER SIXTEEN
December 1966

During coastal patrols, the sampan traffic slowed down in the heat of the afternoon, presenting an opportunity to break out the "sea rats" - canned rations of pretend foods the military thoughtfully provided for them. The gunboat's crew would take turns either being on watch or sitting on the side of the boat opening the cans of, well, of whatever someone had put into dark green tins a decade earlier.

Seriously; a decade earlier.

Occasionally, the crew would try to guess what was in the can by judging the shape. The best guess was usually SPAM as, 80% of the time, that is what it was. The hard part was guessing the year it was canned.

Joe recalled opening cans that were dated 1955 -- two years after the Korean War had ended. Eleven-year-old "food." Life was good. Yum. On their third day of patrol, a newbie came aboard. Because of his new guy's greenie designation, he was instantly promoted to veteran status and, being the good guy, he was, decided to share his vast combat experience -- three patrols -- with him.

Jerimiah Julius ("JJ") Smith was from Dewey, Oklahoma. Quick to smile, easy to talk to, eager to learn, JJ was an all-around good guy to be around. Because of the first two confrontations that morning, JJ was earning his combat sea-legs rather quickly.

As they sat there, the chief announced they were going to do a raiding party on an American Destroyer Escort (DE) that had been shadowing them since early that morning.

A raiding party meant that they would go out to the DE, pick up a couple of junior officers, take them on dry land, or at least awfully close to shore, and have them hold an M16 as they draped a belt of machine gun shells over their shoulder. They would take a few Polaroid pictures of them, thereby proving to their family and friends what great warriors they were in the Vietnam War.

In exchange, one of the Swift crewmen would go on-board to get a tour of the ship. Their target was the food freezer. Once down by the mess area, they would mention that they had not had ice cream for several months. The cooks, feeling sorry for them, would always offer a dish. They would negotiate to get their hands on a five-gallon container -claiming that they personally should not have ice cream without their buddies joining in.

Once the ice cream container was secured, they would make their way to the main deck and signal the PCF. When the gunboat arrived, the gunboat's designated hunter/gatherer would throw the ice cream to one of the crew and jump onboard.

The chief would pretend to get an emergency call necessitating that they must leave immediately. Once the gunboat got a couple of miles away, they would all strip to their skivvies, and, using their hands, would dig in and slurp the ice cream. Because the temperature was usually 90+ degrees, the ice cream would soon melt in their hands, slide down their arms and legs, then drip into the water below them.

Soon sharks began circling by the dozens. Once the ice cream had been depleted, the chief would start the engines and drive off a mile or so. With the area clear of sharks, the senior crew members would jump in the ocean, splashing and horsing around like teenagers, while the greenies - JJ and he - stood shark-watch, each with an M16, locked and loaded.

The real fun began with two of the regular crew offered to stand guard so that JJ and he could join the others. JJ stripped down quickly and was in the water before he knew it.

For some reason, he felt suspicious of their generosity and hesitated. The two crew members grabbed him, threw him overboard, and laughed when he came up for air. Soon, the rest of the crew would scramble back aboard. Naturally, all the commotion in the water along with the fresh scent of ice cream, quickly brought sharks to the area, providing extra fun for the seasoned crew members.

Ha-ha, NOT!

Especially since JJ and Joe were splashing in the water and smelling like the shark's favorite dessert. Their attempts to get back on board were met with the crew pushing them back in again, laughing harder and harder. Finally tiring of the game, the crew allowed them to scramble aboard.

While they were using their T-shirts to dry off, a couple of the regular crew prepared for the closing act of the afternoon.

The sharks had now gathered in higher numbers than before. Someone leaned over the side and filled the currently empty cardboard ice cream container with saltwater. As the chief started the engines and put the gears in neutral, another crew member would pull the pin on a long-fused grenade, then and put it in the cardboard bucket full of saltwater.

The additional weight of the explosive caused the bucket to drift toward the ocean floor slowly.

The sharks were now in a frenzy as they followed the container downward. One of the more giant sharks' bit at the container just as the grenade detonated. There was a muffled concussion, accompanied by a massive mound of the ocean, spraying water along with shark body parts, everywhere.

Later that afternoon, maybe around 1600 (4:00), they got a call from a P-5 Marlin pilot that a fishing boats, a sampan followed by a single person vessel, traveling south a few hundred yards off the coast, a mile to our south. What had initially gotten the pilot's attention was the fact that the winds were increasing, and the small boats were too far from the shoreline.

The crew quickly transformed themselves from vacationing teenagers to the Navy-trained, military combat patrol unit. The chief repositioned our approach to provide the gunship time to observe the target's activities. The primary fishing vessel was a narrow, 14-foot sampan. A lady, casually attired under a wide-brimmed hat, sat toward the front, holding an infant on her lap while her husband sat in the back, controlling their small, outboard engine. Between them, a tattered, tan colored tarp covered their worldly belongings.

Joe quickly noticed that there was not any fishing gear onboard.

The other members of the crew noticed, too, and prepared for trouble by slowly checking and rechecking their weapons.

Because he was positioned behind the aft 50-caliber machine gun, his "kill zone" would be the occupant of the Vietnamese traditional small, saucer-shaped fishing boat that drifted 10 feet behind the sampan, attached by an old anchor rope.

Inside the six-foot, round, wooden vessel sat a little old man, probably the child's grandfather. He had a thin build with long, wispy white hair that was complemented by an equally white goatee. He sat alone in the small craft, which rose and fell with the swells of the ocean.

Most people would look at him and see a grandfather, an old man who had spent his entire life fishing to supply the food required to keep his family alive. Joe's intuition began firing warning signals as everything about the old guy felt wrong.

Joe's eyes locked onto the old guy's chest area, trusting his peripheral vision to catch sudden movements. His right hand pressed lightly against the firing mechanism on the weapon.

The old guy grew noticeably tense as the chief and the gunny began boarding the sampan. Our interpreter ordered the husband off the sampan and onto the gunboat. One of the crew helped him onboard the Swift and then had him sit crossed legged on the deck in the center of the gunwale.

Next, the interpreter ordered the lady off the sampan. This caused the old guy to become noticeably more agitated. Joe intentionally, and quite loudly, chambered a round in the 50 Cal and aimed it at the old man's chest, more for effect than to fire the weapon. Hopefully, the noise and the powerful gun pointed at his chest would cause the grandfather to remain stationary.

To the contrary, the old guy became significantly more agitated.

Meanwhile, the sound of him cocking the mighty weapon got the attention of the crew, causing everyone on board the swift to become more intense, also. The interpreter began speaking to the woman in a soft voice, reassuring her that no harm would come to the baby.

Hesitating, the mother handed her infant to the chief so that she could climb onboard. Like her husband, she sat cross-legged on the deck. When she was in position, the Chief, a loving smile across his lips and a slight twinkle in his eyes, handed her the child.

Once the baby was securely cradled in her arms, she smiled at the Chief and thanked him.

What happened next, happened in slow-motion. It began when the old man produced a Chinese-made grenade from between his legs, screamed an epitaph, and brought his right arm back to throw the grenade into the sampan. His initial movement caused adrenaline to rush furiously throughout his veins and, at within the same micro-moment, several months of intense combat training took control of his reflexes.

"Grenade!"

At the same moment Joe heard himself shout, he squeezed and released the trigger on the massive weapon in front of him. Every member of the crew impulsively dropped where they stood. In the next half second, two rounds from the uber-powerful 50-caliber machine gun penetrated the old guy's frail mid-section, causing his torso to literally explode. A third round, flying on the same trajectory, passed through nothing but air.

The way Joe remembers it, the old man's head remained stationary, momentarily levitating above the exploding torso. Their eyes locked together, and, as his head slowly fell into the ocean, he swears the old guy is laughing.

A second later, the now stronger ocean breeze carried a shower of organ parts, bone fragments and massive amounts of fluid in Joe's direction. Blood and organ tissues painted his body from head to toe, as his mouth filled with a rusty, coppery taste.

A muffled concussion occurred under water, somewhere below and toward the port side of their swift boat, shocking him back into real time. An enormous surge in the ocean lifted and shook their craft, and then everything went quiet.

Joe remained standing behind the weapon in a frozen mental state, as the smoke drifted past him from the machine gun's muzzle. Soon he felt everyone's eyes on him. Not wanting to return their stares, he instead looked at the Vietnamese the lady who sat there, clutching the infant tight to her chest and rocking back and forth.

Her husband, his hands still tied behind his back, was frantically using his legs to push his body back toward the bulkhead.

Suddenly, Joe's digestive system went into spasms, and he began vomiting SPAM and chocolate mint ice cream. His lower digestive system also exploded, causing him to foul his dungarees. Finally, the enormity of what he had done caused his knees to weaken, and he collapsed into a cross-legged sitting position atop his own filth.

After a short debate, the chief decided not to secure the woman's arms; instead, he had her sit cross-legged near the cabin's bulkhead. She sat away from her husband, her ankles now securely tied, still holding tightly to the child who was whimpering softly into her breasts.

Attempting to clear his head, Joe made a wobbling effort to stand and take a deep breath. Fully clothed, he jumped into the ocean. Once in the water, he took off his deck boots and threw them onboard. Likewise, he removed all his clothes and threw them on deck.

One of the crew picked up the clothing and laid them out for the sun and the warm breeze to dry. The interpreter began to yell orders at the husband as another crew member untied his hands and removed his blindfold. The crew member handed him several rags, and the interpreter told him to clean up the mess Joe had made.

Because he was in the water and unencumbered by any clothing, the Chief threw Joe a diving mask and told him to inspect the boat's hull for possible damage from the grenade. Finding nothing serious, he swam the rest of the way underwater toward the stern, keeping tabs on several sharks that had begun to gather below him.

Using the propulsion ducts and transom cleats, Joe pulled himself on board. Though his clothes were still damp, he put them back on and prepared to assume his duties. The chief had he climb to the twin machine gun tub above the cabin, where the wind and the sun would finish drying his clothing.

Because his boots were still wet, he used the shoestrings to hang them from the gun tub rail where they could dry faster. Once he had everything in its place, he leaned back against the gun tub, took a deep breath, and let out a long sigh, to calm himself.

After a few steady breathes, Joe forced his mind back to the war and his new responsibilities. He loaded and locked the tub's twin machine guns, sat upright, and began scanning the horizon.

Sitting atop the gun mount provided him the bonus of not having to look into the faces of his fellow shipmates. When he was underwater and examining the hull, the chief and translator re-boarded the sampan to complete the inspection. Hidden under various household items were multiple North Vietnamese Army live mortar rounds and several Chinese-made grenades.

Two hours after transferring their prisoners to a Coast Guard cutter, they received another call for immediate help. While heading north to new coordinates, the Chief called he down to the front helm.

"How're you doing'?"

"Everything is copasetic," Joe heard himself answer, not sure that even he believed in what he had just said.

The Chief allowed the conversation to hang there a few seconds, then added, "The first is the worst, especially because that crazy old bastard was so close. If the old guy had tossed that grenade on the sampan, ain't none of us be here talking right now. Roger that?"

"Yeah, I copy that," Joe said solemnly. "Everything happened so quickly that I didn't think; it was all reflex."

Joe stood there as the Chief rechecked their course headings.

"You reacted quickly. Decisively. Your training kicked in, and you knew what had to be done without thinking about it. You took out the old bastard."

The Chief paused to recheck the Swift's alignment.

"Look, everyone has doubts when they are in combat. Those that hesitate before firing, well, they ain't here no more. Those that don't, like what you did, survive."

The Chief went back to his duties, glancing port and starboard, checking his headings before he continued.

"Mostly, that shit happens at a distance. Grunts in the bush usually just keep lighting it up until Charlie stops shooting back. Unless they are KIA detail, the grunts rarely see squat. You -- hell, that happened 15-20 feet away from you. Everything is wide open out here on the water, 'cause there ain't nothing to hide behind. Your guy was sitting there, pretending, and acting old, innocent and all. What you did was righteous!"

As he paused to scan the horizon in front of them, he stood there beside him, wishing the Chief would shut-up.

He did not.

"You warned your crew brothers before you cut his ass in half. You saw it, no one else did, but you saw the grenade, and you neutralized his ass. Ka-blam! You saved that baby's life, and his mama, too. Better yet, you saved MY life. Did what you had to do without hesitation or nothing. That's pretty heavy shit."

Another pause, then he added, "That's going to earn you some kind of star." "I don't need a star, Chief. I did what I was trained to do."

"Whatever. But I still gotta write it up." It was as if the chief had lost the will to shut-up.

"So, what else is bothering you?" The Chief paused for a second, gave him a quick glance, and then turned back to his job.

"Is it what happened afterward? The vomiting and all? That ain't going in no report. Ain't anyone on this boat ever talk going to talk about it, either. They do, and they are talking in a higher voice the rest of their miserable life."

"Thanks, Chief." With that, he started to walk away, tired of hearing the Chief's voice.

"You and JJ grab them 16s. Extra clips, too."

Upon hearing this, Joe's intuition went-up a notch. About the only thing the Chief had not said was to prepare for more combat. Inwardly, Joe suddenly had a bad feeling about the near future.

As the Swift pulled into a small bay, the sound of rifle reports began coming toward them from two different land-areas of the bay. Recognizing the lighter, sharp cracking from the American M16s interspersed with the heavier sound from Russian-built AK47s, it made it easy to ascertain which Army was which.

As the Swift became visible to the Viet Cong, the whole bay erupted, and the crew found themselves in the middle of a full-blown battle between two, good sized opposing military forces.

Bullets began flying over their heads or splashing the water short of their gunboat. Occasionally, a wayward round would hit the Swift with a plinking sound. It reminded Joe of the sound hail makes on a car during a thunderstorm.

Up front, the Chief was talking over the radio, maneuvering the boat, and yelling orders to the crew, all at the same time. The plinking noise from incoming rounds increased as their boat took a few more shots on the side of the hull.

The front gunner opened fire in the direction of the enemy muzzle flashes just as the Chief pushed the throttles wide open. The boat began zigzagging left and right as they charged toward the beach. Without warning, the gunboat made a hard turn to starboard and sped along the curved shoreline where the enemy was entrenched. The front and back gunners joined the top gunner, resulting in four heavy machine guns firing simultaneously toward the enemy positions.

In the meantime, JJ and Joe had put their M16s on fully automatic. Once the swift completed the turn, they both leaned tight against the outside of the rear bulkhead in preparation to spray the enemy positions. It was at this point that JJ did something dumb: he stood up with his shoulders and head exposed over the deck and sprayed an entire clip into the jungle.

"Are you frigging nuts?" Joe yelled at him as he grabbed JJ's belt and pulled him down beside him. They both leaned their backs tightly against the bulkhead. As JJ inserted a new clip, he was smiling from ear to ear, grinning like a teenage boy seeing his first boob.

"What? I wanted to get some, too."

"Yeah, right!" Joe screamed at him. "This ain't playtime at Mare Island. You will get killed jumping up like that. Watch how I do it"

With that, he slid up the bulkhead with his back still tight against the wall. Facing away from the target, he positioned the rifle over his head, holding it upside down and pointing the barrel toward the enemy's entrenchment near the shoreline. As he squeezed the trigger on the M16, he slowly swung the weapon from right to left until the clip was empty. When the clip emptied, Joe slid back down next to JJ.

"See. Effective and a helluva lot less dangerous." JJ looked at him and smiled, and then imitating all his actions, slid up the wall, sprayed a full clip from his weapon and then slipped down next to him. JJ winked at Joe as he inserted another clip into the rifle. In the meantime, an American Army platoon had outflanked the Viet Cong to their right, forcing Charlie to retreat and put their backs to the shoreline and the bay.

Sensing their dilemma, several Viet Cong turned away from the American platoon, threw themselves onto the sandy beach and began directing their fire power at their gunboat. The Chief responded by swinging their gunboat in such a way as to present a smaller target.

In doing so, the Chief had turned the boat so quickly that JJ and Joe did not have a chance to get to the other bulkhead for protection. Both men heard the bullets zipping above them. Additional plunks could be both heard and felt on the side of the boat, inches below where they were sitting.

As the gunboat continued to maneuver, Joe got the Chief's attention to make him aware that he and JJ were changing positions. The Chief acknowledged by nodding his head. Without looking back, he reached behind him and tapped JJ on the shoulder, signaling a "follow me" gesture. Looking to where he wanted to end-up, he bolted for the other side for protection.

Just as he had done before, Joe slid up the bulkhead and emptied his clip into the beach area where the enemy soldiers were beginning to take cover in the sand. When he slid down, he looked over to watch JJ take his turn.

Except JJ was not there.

CHAPTER SEVENTEEN
December 1966

The Chief suddenly repositioned the gunboat so that the Swift was facing toward the shore, with only the topside twin '50s exposed to the enemy positions. As Joe began to scurry around to the other side of the cabin, he noticed the chief had been leaning against a side rail, bleeding from a leg wound. While the Chief claimed to okay, Joe ripped apart the trouser material where his leg was bleeding and found a deep tear through the back quad.

Nothing life-threatening, but it would need stitches.

Joe grabbed the first aid kit and pulled out a fist full of gauze. Within a minute, he had stuffed the cheesecloth into the wound, wrapped the tape tightly around the Chief' thigh and then applied a tourniquet above the injury for good measure.

As Joe turned to resume his search for JJ, several rounds hit the front cabin of the boat, just below the top gun mount, causing him to hesitate for a moment before deciding to keep moving.

The incoming rounds suddenly trickled to a stop. The Swift's twin machine guns stopped firing, too. What few VC remained apparently decided to give up. The US Army infantry advance quickly and secured the prisoners.

Once all the firing stopped, Joe stopped, too. Not because the guns went quiet but because he had found JJ. He was still sitting where Joe had left him, his chin resting on his chest. Four inches lower, Joe saw a three-inch wide, wet, red hole. Behind JJ, blood, and shattered bone covered part of the bulkhead. Streams of blood were running down the Navy grey paint and pooling where JJ's body slumped against the outer bulkhead.

Joe was about to step toward him when the Chief reached out, stopped him, and pointed to the area to JJ's left. Four bullet holes formed an irregular pattern where Joe had been sitting. Had he not moved when he did, parts of his internal organs would have been beside JJ's on the bulkhead.

Joe turned and walked to the back of the boat and sat on the fantail, his legs dangling over the stern. The day's events raced through his mind:

. . . swimming with the sharks after eating ice cream.

. . . a family comprised of a grandfather, husband and the wife holding an infant, trying to sneak mortars to enemy forces.

. . . the old man trying to blow them out of the South China Sea

. . . a gun battle between a US Army Company and a Viet Cong Company that had taken place in dense jungle adjacent to a beautiful, picture postcard, white sandy beach.

. . . teaching JJ how to fire his M16 without getting killed.

. . . his leaving JJ.

. . . JJ dead.

After seeing bullet holes in the exact spot he had just vacated, Joe realized he should be dead, also.

If only he had stayed and pushed JJ to go, it would have been him lying there and not JJ.

Because of his split-second decision, JJ was dead.

JJ and not him.

JJ - the kind of guy that had "it" all. Someone who obviously had a great life in front of him. Someone who should have finished the day, hell, finished the war, without a scratch.

If only: Two words that permanently changed Joe's outlook on life.

The sound of several helicopters approaching brought Joe back to reality. The Medevac teams had begun landing, the medics leaping to the ground and rushing to service the wounded. The helicopters landed and kept their blades turning, albeit slower than when they arrived. Soon, Army infantry soldiers arrived carrying the torn and mangled bodies of their wounded brothers.

Another helicopter began lifting off after receiving their allotted load of black body bags. The new occupants' red blood stained the clothing of the men that had transported them.

Two other Medevac birds were also being filled. A few times, their pallbearer's combat boots would slip in the deep sand, causing them to fall to their knees and, occasionally, dropping their precious cargo.

The Chief eased the PCF onto the sandy beach, one engine idling in a low forward gear, keeping them positioned against the shore. Joe and another member of the Swift's crew carried JJ Smith's body to the forward bow and slowly, reverently handed the body to two medics who had waded out to the knee-deep ocean.

A third medic came onboard the gunboat to check over the Chief, gave him a shot to ward off viruses and offered him a flight back to Cam Ranh Bay. The Chief declined, telling the "Doc" to sew him up where he stood.

Once the stitching had been completed, the Chief chased the medic off the boat, bitching about needing to get his beloved Swift back to the shipyards for repairs.

On the return trip, Joe, lost in his thoughts, remembered what the old First-Class Boatswain Mate had said when he and CWO Presley had jumped aboard: "You'll be dead in three days, so no one gives a shit who you were or how you got here."

While not getting it at the time, he got it now. From that day forward, Joe swore he would avoid getting to know anyone other than his Frogman brothers.

With JJ's death, any self-doubt or self-pity about killing the old man, dissolved. Now, he was glad he killed the old bastard. What he should have done was kill them all.

And why not? The VC could care less about him, his family, or how he grew up.

From that moment on, Joe had some major bad news for Charlie: The Vietnamese could keep their country, but he'd be damned if he would ever let Charlie, Charlie's comrades, the whores they were married to, or any other human piece of crap like them to ever harm his warrior brothers.

Joe recommitted himself to doing what he had been trained to do, and to do it better than any of his instructors had ever dreamed possible. If the military thought they had developed him into a highly skilled fighting machine, well, just wait: They had not seen anything yet.

"Congratulations, Charlie," he said out loud, "you succeeded in creating your worst nightmare."

When he got back to Cam Ranh Bay, he would find LCDR Wheeler and tell him he passed his baptism by fire.

As it turned out, LCDR Wheeler had other plans for testing his unique abilities.

In fact, harsh new lessons would present themselves to Joe within the next 72 hours.

Christmas of 1966 was a major, psychological turning point for Joe Tyler. Unfortunately, it would take him the next 50-years of his life to figure it out.

CHAPTER EIGHTEEN

December 25, 1966

"There are a couple more, uh, tests I've placed on your agenda to convince myself that you are ready to join the operations team. Early tomorrow, you will be heading out on your own. Without providing specific details, I need you to evaluate the three forward listening posts located on the hillside perimeter, north, and west of the base."

"Roger that!" Joe said, trying to hide his excitement.

"Get with Stevenson and deep six those dungarees and boat boots. He will help you requisition whatever weaponry you think you may need. Tyler, you are on your own; this is your mission. Copy?"

"Roger that, sir." All the mental conflicts that he had earlier that morning evaporated. By 'his' mission, the LCDR meant that he would be operating solo and was to plan the evaluation then execute in a four-oh manner. It was up to him to initiate and review the topography, get the coordinates on the look-out locations, and check the weather reports.

Stevenson, LCDR Wheeler's yeoman, would not only assist him in getting new clothing, weapons, and gear but also provide the credentials required to talk to pilots, Marine, and Army personnel who were familiar with the territory. It even meant he was permitted to go into the highly secretive "war room" to get the latest intel, the positions, and most recent verbal challenges for approaching the listening posts and become aware of all other "friendlies" operating in the area.

Joe grabbed his food tray and happily dumped the contents in the garbage. With inspired purpose, he walked briskly to find Petty Officer Stevenson. For the first time since joining the Navy, he could be on his own, in the field, doing what he had been trained to do over the past 19 months.

Stevenson had all his credentials prepared. Together, they walked over to the quartermaster's supply building. On the way, Stevenson briefed him on the new jungle camo gear, called tiger stripes. Because of the horizontal camouflage design.

Joe secured three shirts, one long sleeve shirt, two pairs of and pants, and a dark green bandana. He also snagged a floppy hat designed to keep both the sun and the rain out of his face. The hat's wrinkled construction and camo material would blend better with the bush. Joe also got three new pairs of skivvies, all greenish brown in color. They are allotted three new pairs of socks but, with Stevenson's help, he got six pairs. Keeping your feet dry while out in the bush was huge, not to mention that their socks seemed to rot away after one or two uses.

Instead of jungle boots, the QM brought him two pairs of Converse tennis shoes. Recently, all SEALs began wearing these dark tennies because the platoons in the RSS (Rung Sat Special zone) leaving boot prints in the dusty trails. Joe was familiar with the Stoner 63, having practiced with it on the ranges in Cavite.

For his sidearm, he chose the traditional Colt 45 Model 1911, several extra seven-shot clips. At the supply armory, the Army Master Sergeant that oversaw the distribution of weapons and various accessories, suggested he go with one of the new chest/shoulder holsters versus the traditional hip placement. He explained that recently, many of the Army's Special Forces Green Berets had made the switch to holstering their sidearm higher for a variety of reasons.

Joe gave Stevenson a questioned look and asked him what Wheeler would think of he not following protocol on holstering his weapon. Stevenson said he agreed that having the gun off his hip would make working in the bush more natural and that the LCDR would probably support his "creativity."

The sergeant found a harness to fit him and again, Stevenson helped him "saddle-up." Stevenson helped him carry everything back to the hooch. He changed into the camo, strapped on the two K-bars, and put on a pair of new tennis shoes.

Next, he stripped and cleaned both the carbine and pistol, then oiled the chest holster and calf K-bar's sheath.

Later, as he finished going through the afternoon chow line and began looking for a place to sit, LCDR Wheeler walked-in and almost did not recognize him. He stood there, tray in hands, wearing tiger-stripe camos, armed with the chest-holstered Colt 45, sprouting the new K-bar on the back of his right hip.

Joe looked at him for a few seconds before he came up to talk.

"Are you going out early tomorrow?"

"No, sir. If it was all right with you, I wanted to slide out this evening. Stevenson pulled some K-Rats and was tracking down a PRC-25 for my communications. And I took all the new clothing to the river as soon as I got it."

Together, Joe and the LCDR sat down. Wheeler looked over his Colt chest harness, nodded approvingly, but never said a word.

The LCDR went through the mission objectives, brought him up to date other units he could encounter. Together the reviewed the terrain, moon status (none), weather (rain), escape routes/extraction points (none) and the bush code-words: both the challenge and reply were two random numbers that equaled thirteen.

After a short pause, "Stevenson has your call-signs and checkpoints. Tyler, I know you are pumped-up to finally be out in the bush. Nothing heroic. Report to my tent in three days. Copy that?"

"Roger that, sir."

"If you come across anything unusual that I should be made aware of, tell Stevenson 'PLUS-2' after the challenge code."

"Plus-Two. Roger that."

The LCDR was right: Joe was eager to get started.

One of the items on his observation list was an assessment of the main base at night. That meant he had

174

to find a secure position at the highest point possible on the northwestern hillside, allowing him to observe the base yet remain hidden in case any unfriendlies happened to wander out his way.

On his way back to the hooch, Joe met with Stevenson, got a radio, terrain map and his call sign: CopperSun.

His verification code would be 2-6-5.

Any response other than 2-6-5 meant there was some type of unusual situation. A higher number meant he needed to talk to his next in command – a lower number meant he was in trouble. After an early dinner, and armed with the Stoner 63 carbine, the 45 caliber Colt handgun, four grenades, two K-bars, and several clips for each weapon, he began to cross the base and head toward the northeast gate area.

A hundred yards before he got to the gate, he came across several Marines teaching a dozen Vietnamese teenagers how to play softball. Everyone was laughing and having a great evening. As Joe slowed to watch, a fouled ball came to rest near him.

Before he could get the ball, a teenage Vietnamese boy grabbed it, stood, and practiced his newly developed throwing technique. When practicing before throwing the ball, the ball looked awkward. It did not take a genius to figure out the kid was a natural lefty. Joe placed the ball in his left hand and, standing next to him, Joe's right hand holding the boys left, he slowly demonstrated the proper stance and throwing motion.

Finally, Joe gestured for him to throw the ball to one of his buddies out on the playing field. He threw an amazingly accurate ball to the other player and turned to his new American friend with a big grin.

While he appreciated the boy's friendship, Joe had an errand to complete. For some reason, Joe took off the gold Saint Christopher medallion and chain he always wore and placed it around the boy's neck. Again, the Vietnamese kid's face lit up like a three-year-old at Christmas. Joe patted him on the shoulder, turned and continued his journey.

Originally, Joe had planned to start his surveillance on the northern hillside and spend the next couple of days climbing the nearby hills on the west of the camp while making his way south toward the river.

It was dark and cloudy when he finally made his 50-yard perimeter check from where he would hunker down for the evening. Once he assured himself that he was alone near the top of the hillside, he found a hallowed area with naturally broken and fallen trees. Finding a tree trunk laying against other trees and tangled with the natural brush, he covered himself with mosquito netting and, hoping his Navy-issued insect repellent would continue working through the night, propped himself into a semi-sitting position to take a three-hour nap.

While sitting there, his hearing tuned to the cacophony of insect, jungle and military sounds that surrounded his position. Once comfortable, both physically and mentally, he fell asleep. Over the past 18 months, he had developed into a light sleeper; he trusted himself to awaken should any of the noises around him change, or worse, suddenly stop. The last thing he remembered before he slept, was smiling broadly to himself, recalling in his youth all the times he had wished he could, one-day, sleep in his private jungle, just as he was about to do that night.

At midnight, he awoke, slowly sat upright, and studied the sounds around him. After remaining motionless for a full 10 minutes, he threw a large rock down the hill and listened intently for another 10 minutes. Other than the insects becoming quiet for a few seconds, nothing changed.

Joe crawled away from his sleeping area and slowly stood tall within a collection of high jungle foliage, his carbine's safety in the off position. Another 10 minutes of committed listening and peering into the darkness, the jungle continued its natural symphony of Insect Concerto Number One.

Quietly, he moved fifty yards out, and over the next hour, checked the perimeter of his first night's lodging while observing how the base looked under the lights. He arrived back at his original position around 2 AM and, after deciding that everything was copasetic, took another nap.

When he awoke at 4:30, he repeated his half-hour listening routine. Everything appeared quiet, natural, and safe. He ate protein, drank unsweetened cherry Kool-Aid, then prepared to move out. Making a fire for coffee would have been stupid. Not to mention that carrying utensils was not something he ever remembered doing as a member of SEAL Team One.

Joe climbed to the highest point of the hillside and studied the various ingress and egress routes linking the northern side of the base to the surrounding villages, small towns, and transport lanes. Everything seemed well secure. From his current vantage point and, with the sun rising over the inlet of the bay, the defensive bunkers and mortar positions looked like they could hold their own.

Besides, they had artillery positions within three miles of the base, not to mention Navy warships and the Coast Guard always hanging around the bay.

At precisely 6 AM, his PRC-25 radio crackled softly, and he heard Stephenson's voice, "CopperSun. (Pause.) CopperSun."

Joe answered, "Two. Six. Five."

Their morning communication completed, he turned the radio off and hung it on his back. Before he moved out, he added a layer of green camo paint to his face, neck, and hands, policed the area where he had spent the night, then saddled up.

The journey over the top of the hill took him through dense foliage and fallen trees. Purposely, and slowly, he negotiated his way through the thickets, testing his navigational senses while practicing "reading" the jungle.

Within an hour, he spotted an Army forward listening post about 150 yards to his left. The bad news for them was that he got within 20 feet of the Duty Sergeant and sat there for two hours without their noticing.

Joe listened to their jokes, comments reflecting their dislike of their officers and theories about what they would do in a real combat situation.

As they broke out their lunch rations, he decided to join them. But first, he decided to have a little fun. Joe set the channel position to the brown-water Navy boys, turned up the volume and balanced the radio on the branches of a tree. Then he silently crawled around behind them. He no sooner got in position when the radio crackled with a Skunk call (a water surface vessel).

Joe almost laughed out loud as four Army infantrymen practically jumped out of their skin, spinning to turn toward the origin of the sound, their M-16s at the ready as they took defensive stances.

"Relax guys; it is only me." All four men jumped upon hearing an unexpected voice. When they turned in his general direction, it was apparent they were relieved and yet visibly pissed. To make things worse, he walked a couple of steps toward them before they even figured out exactly where he was.

With their mouths a gap and their brains still trying to make sense of the last few seconds, he calmly walked through their defensive positions and retrieved his radio. As he had his back to them, they could not stop staring at him, not sure what they should do.

"I'm starving. Any of you guys got an extra sandwich?"

Assuming a leadership stance, the Sergeant growled, "Who the hell are you?" He took a couple of menacing steps toward him, but Joe held up his hand in a "you don't want to do that" gesture.

"Base Special Ops. We're checking perimeter security," he said this in a manner suggesting that he was not alone. Then over his shoulder, he spoke louder and said something like, "Johnson, take their 6, and Murph, move west at two-seven about a hundred yards and check out the valley."

The grunts bought his bluff, anxiously looking around to see where the others were hiding.

Joe thought, "man, the Skipper is going to get a kick out of this part of his report."

"Don't worry guys. I've been sitting here for a few hours and, other than the fact you didn't know I was nearby you've done nothing wrong that I could see." They looked at him, not sure whether to believe him. Sensing this, he followed with a few choices quotes from the conversations he had overheard.

Joe thought their jaws were going to drop off, smirking at his success. After mentioning he had yet to eat that day, someone offered a roast beef sandwich. Joe thanked him and then visited with the squad's Sergeant. Meanwhile, the other grunts went about their assigned duties, albeit more astute then they had been previously.

Producing a topography map, the Sergeant updated the latest Intel and suggested a more accessible route to his next destination. Afterward, he thanked the guys and promised not to mention how he had surprised them in his official report. They shook hands, and he headed down the western slope of the hill, soon melting into the foliage, smiling all the way.

The remainder of the day was quiet and, as "normal" as one could expect in a war zone. Several miles away, to the south, west, and north of him, separate firefights could be heard as the war continued in all its glory.

Occasionally, the serenity of his private jungle -- nearby insects and birds, mixed with the distant sounds machine gun fire, mortars, artillery, and bombings -- was broken by the roar of Phantom jets overhead, along with a variety of different types of helicopters.

The rest of his day was spent working up and down the hillsides, observing and then bypassing two other Army positions, while he continued south toward the river. Around 4:00 that afternoon, as he sat, unobserved just outside the last lookout post, the skies opened with a torrent of rain. Nonplussed, Joe put on his poncho and continued his journey south.

Later that evening, with the river only a few miles away and the rain still coming down hard, he felt motivated to push on, quietly, efficiently, allowing the storm to obscure any unwanted noises he might commit. Even during heavy rain, the bush gave off its own distinctive rhythm. It did not take too long to familiarize himself with the vibration and the cadence of the rain falling on, and through the dense foliage.

An hour had gone by when Joe's instinct stopped his momentum and put him on high alert: something was wrong.

He froze, motionless, then slowly knelt to the ground. He slowed his breathing and got his heart rate down to 45 beats per minutes, which allowed him to better focus on the current state of the jungle environment.

Nothing stood out that could be identified as out of the ordinary. But darn-it, something was not kosher.

Joe kneeled in the mud and dampness, staying perfectly motionless for at least 30 minutes. As he was about to begin moving, something got his attention, and his instinct held him still. Early in life, he learned to pay attention to that inner voice in the back of his head. Qual School reinforced what he felt he already knew; AWT taught him to trust that mindset, unequivocally.

Joe pushed himself to listen harder with more focus. Still nothing.

Then it hit him; the problem was there was nothing when there should have been something. The natural rhythmic and diverse jungle sounds, even with the rain, were absent. Upon consciously recognizing the problem, he felt the tension the air as if his senses had rewarded had he. Now that he identified the problem, he needed positive identification as to what caused it.

When someone is trying to find you, and you do not want to be seen, one of the many keys to survival is to get small, become one with the surroundings and move as delicately as possible. In other words, get low and go slow. He did precisely that, continuing forward in his original direction, but now on his belly through the mud and slime, each movement with patience and measured quietness.

Every 10 yards, Joe stopped to listen, paying attention to any human-created sounds; especially those in front or behind him. After several dozen 10-yard movements, he could make out human voices, very faint, 30 yards in front of him. Assuring himself that no one was behind him, he continued crawling forward, now stopping every 5 yards to gain a precise bearing on the direction of the voices.

Though the sounds remained weak, they spoke Vietnamese, with several different people involved in the conversation. One voice was noticeably more commanding, while others agreed in short retorts. Occasionally, someone would ask a quick question which sounded more like verification or something of that nature.

Joe moved in another 20 feet and decided to pinpoint their exact location on his map, which he had laid on the ground, inches from his face. Utilizing a red, night-light, he triangulated his position, then searched for a likely place these people were meeting.

Because there were neither commercial nor residential reasons for them to meet out here, they had to be military. Joe chose the area where they were meeting, slowly turned and headed to higher ground. One hundred yards up the hill, he found a tall tree, then stripped his gear except for the radio, binoculars, and weapons.

Joe tried his best to keep what little trunk there was between himself and the enemy company while climbing as high as possible and not attracting someone's attention. Once he felt secure in his elevated position, he sat on a branch and locked his legs around the tree's trunk. Using his fingers to shield the optics from the rain, he put the binoculars to his eyes. Within seconds he spotted a company of enemy soldiers, most in Viet Cong black pajamas, a couple in North Vietnamese Regular Army uniforms, still others in a variety of different guerrilla warfare attire.

Back on the ground, Joe gathered his gear and made his way to the crest of the hill, about a half-mile winding trek, to the top. Reaching the summit, he gained a clearer view of the Cam Ranh Bay base camp. Judging by the activity at the base, it was apparent that no one knew about the enemy positioning for an attack.

Knowing that Stevenson would soon make contact, he committed the enemy position to memory. Unexpectedly, the rain stopped, and everything became eerily quiet. Too quiet.

Joe decided to head back down the hill toward the enemy position, but far enough away to stay out of hearing range of their camp.

"CopperSun. CopperSun." Stevenson made his contact call, but this time Joe's reply would be different. Facing away from the enemy position, he replied in a soft voice, "Two-six-five. Negative, plus two."

"Standby."

During the wait, he decided to split the difference between the enemy position and their own base camp, assumed that if it were to be a night assault, the VC would move around to the south end of the hillside, keeping the river on their right flank. As experienced fighters, they knew that trying to climb over the hill would expose them to possible American forward listening posts.

Even though the rain had stopped, because of the thick cloud coverage, it grew darker faster than usual.

"CopperSun, one-seven." Stevenson's voice, while remaining military professional, had a hint of anxiety running through it. What he was telling Joe was to change to radio channel eight, and that both the base commander and LCDR Wheeler would connect with him to evaluate the situation. He wanted to let Stevenson know that he was all right and in control, and he was switching to channel eight.

Therefore, his reply to him was, "Two-six-five, three-five." Two-six-five meant all was well; three-five was a challenge reply confirming he was switching to channel eight.

Both commanders got on the hook and, utilizing brief description points, Joe detailed what he had seen, including the coordinates as to where the Viet Cong were staging. He added that forty-five minutes had elapsed since he last visually confirmed the enemy's positions.

To summarize this situation, the commanders knew the location of the Viet Cong, but obviously did not know what the VC had planned, nor when they were going to execute their operation. While the base Command had to assume an attack would be imminent, they did not know whether their target would be the military base, the shipping docks, the bridge over the river or some combination of objectives.

Command probably either did not know, or least did not say whether additional enemy units were congregating elsewhere, as the base covered a rather long, narrow stretch of the peninsula which, theoretically, could be attacked at a variety of points along the northern and western perimeters.

What Joe did not know, was that an entire elite Marine Recon platoon had been deployed yesterday to circle the north end of the hillside and had reported that a second VC company had gathered and were preparing to attack the opposite flank.

Joe was ordered to get closer to the VC command, avoid contact, and to report enemy unit activity. His final communication would be to let Command know if the VC infantry approached the tree line across the road from the south-western entrance to the base. Joe took a deep breath and resumed moving toward the river where the ground would begin to flatten and where the VC would, in all probability, find it most accessible to traverse. Just as he started moving, the rain resumed and came down hard.

When possible, he moved the radio tight against his left ear but heard nothing. Two hours went by without hearing any military voice traffic, and he began to wonder what was happening. At 3:00 in the morning, Stevenson's voice called out in a loud whisper, "CopperSun, get small."

Before he could answer, the whomp-whomp of the American mortars sending flares high into the sky could be heard throughout the valley. He flattened out in the mud, trying to blend in with the foliage. He kept his head down and eyes closed as the flashes exploded high above, he and floated slowly toward the jungle treetops.

Just as they had been taught, without moving any other muscles, he opened his eyes. Less than 20 feet away, dozens of VC were moving slowly in the direction of the base camp. Several carried the Russian AK-47 assault rifle. Others carried small, but obviously heavy, bomb-laden satchels in knapsacks across their backs. Joe lowered his head the final five inches into the ground, as several Viet Cong soldiers began walking in single file, passed silently within 6 feet of where he was laying.

Because of their proximity, Joe slowly moved his left hand down and clicked off his PRC-25 radio. Once he was confident the last soldiers had gone by, he got to his feet and quickly moved up the hill another 100 feet. Once in position he began moving parallel to the VC column that had just passed by him.

Joe crept low for the short distance to his left and around the hillside to where the base was in full view. The camp had shut off most of the lights which meant they were staging defensive positions. Joe contacted Command, whispering, to make them aware of what he was seeing. Their reply was to move himself to higher ground to avoid being hit by friendly fire. He was to contact them once enemy soldiers got within 25 yards of the road that ran alongside the base.

Unfortunately, with the rain still coming down, he could no longer see where the enemy had gone.

Knowing it was critical to notify the base once the VC began settling into their positions, rather than staying in place or moving up the hill, Joe moved downhill to locate them.

Fifteen minutes later, through the rain and darkened sky, he found them. Their infantry was at the edge of the tree line and spreading out for their assault. Several mortar positions, each occupied by three-man crews, began setting up their mortar tubes. Behind them, the soldiers with the explosive satchels were receiving last minute instructions from their commander.

Joe needed to contact the Base Commanders and tell them what he knew. It was at this moment that Murphy's Law decided to present itself.

CHAPTER NINETEEN
December 27, 1966

Joe's radio battery had died, and he did not have a backup.

Realizing that he had to somehow let the base know the VC were preparing to initiate their assault, he slowly made his way downhill and about 60 yards above and behind the VC mortar positions. Joe pulled two grenades off his belt and set them in front of him. He would throw the long fuse first, then the short fuse, hoping for near simultaneous explosions.

While there was no way he could hope to throw these couple-pound, hand-sized bombs 180 feet, his intent was not to kill enemy soldiers but to cause a commotion and light up the enemy position from behind.

Karma should be on his side since he had recently shown some Vietnamese kid how to throw a softball. While that does not make sense to him when he said it out loud, it did at that moment. Besides, he figured the angle of the hillside and gravity would be to his advantage.

Joe pulled the pin on the 10-second grenade and threw it as far as he could straight down the hill. Next, he pulled the pin on the 6-second grenade and threw it as far as he could to his right, mostly in the general direction of the bridge that spanned the river. As soon as he let the short fuse fly, he got up and ran as fast as he could up the hill to escape the soon-to-be-rendered friendly fire, not at all worried about any noise he might make.

Within seconds, the first grenade exploded followed immediately by the second one. The flashes that came with the explosions achieved their desired effect of silhouetting the Viet Cong infantrymen right at the edge of the clearing and within clear sight of the American defensive positions at the base camp.

The grenades caused a panic within the VC ranks, as they had not expected to have any American forces on their six. A few of the VC turned and fired in the general direction of the explosions. This began a chain reaction, and other infantrymen started shooting toward the base camp.

In turn, their Army and Marine guys returned the VC fire and, well, all hell broke loose. All the while, he kept climbing high into the hillside, trying to keep as many trees as possible between him and any stray bullets.

Joe also wanted to be well above any friendly mortar rounds fired from inside their base that would come in his general direction. Having the words "Killed by Friendly Fire" on his tombstone was not an option. Once he felt relatively safe, he crouched behind a large tree trunk and watched the battle going on before him.

Fifteen months earlier, the scene before him would not have made sense. But he had learned so much over the past year-and-a-half, it was like watching a precision NCAA-D-1 basketball team manhandle a team of D-3 players. The VC were neither equal in training nor physical abilities.

Concurrently, the VC who had planned to attack the northern flank of the base, decided now would be an excellent time to join the fight. Big mistake: The Marine Recon Team were above them.

Having trained with Special Operations Marines in Cavite, he can tell you that these are some tough dudes who were among the best when it came to find and kill bad guys. When the VC on the north side launched their attack, they stepped into the middle of a Marine ambush.

When the VC began launching their sapper attack from behind the tree line, they were cut down by precision machine gun fire coming at them from two sides. Next, their mortar positions were wiped out by the Marines behind them. For the most part, the VC's planned dual assault was eradicated in less than 10 minutes.

Meanwhile, the VC on his end of the base camp were faring a little better since his radio had decided to quit. However, the few enemy soldiers that made it onto the base typically only penetrated a dozen yards before being permanently, and forever stopped. After a half-hour, everything went quiet.

With their attack thwarted, the retreating VC would be heading his way. He repositioned himself so that any enemy flanking to either side would be minimized and maintain the advantage of seeing someone approaching before they saw him.

Sitting on his butt, he leaned into a broken log and set his five remaining clips between his legs. The Stoner rested over his right knee with the butt of the stock pulled loosely into his right shoulder. The safety was off, the index finger of his right hand rested alongside the weapon's register, his middle finger resting lightly on the trigger.

Luckily, he never had to fire a single round throughout the night. He never slept, ate, or even took a piss. He steadfastly held his position, constantly focusing his attention on either the sounds of the jungle or the shapes of the leaves and other foliage.

Joe held his strategic, tactical position until the sun signaled a new day would be upon them within the hour.

Cautiously, Joe headed down hill, taking a more northernly route toward the base and near the road, cut to right while staying high in the tree-line. All his senses remained focused and on high alert for enemy soldiers.

A half-mile from the base, he met up with an Army squad conducting an enemy KIA count. After some light banter and an exchange of tactical information, their squad leader contacted the base to advise them that Joe would soon be coming in through the North Gate.

The clouds and rain from the night before had moved off, the remainder of the day promised to return to its typically hot and humid.

CHAPTER TWENTY
December 28, 1966

After Joe entered the camp through the Northern Gate, he worked his way over to his hooch. While a few buildings were damaged, for the most part, the defensive positions had been well-planned-out and extremely efficient. After a shower and a change of clothes, he climbed into his bunk. Sleep seemed like a great conclusion, his adventure, making lunch-call his great target time to begin enjoying life, as it were. Unfortunately, his morning nap was never going to happen. Twenty minutes after lying down, two Marines came into his hooch.

Joe awoke when he heard them walking toward their hooch. Since they did not seem to be in a hurry, he laid still, his eyes closed, hoping they would go away.

"Look at him. He probably didn't even know there was a war going on last night."

"In his next life, I'm going to join the Navy, see the world, get shore duty, and lie around all day." "Hey, Tyler," the first one shouted, "Wakey, wakey! Would hate for you to miss breakfast. C' mon man, get up. I've got something for you."

"I'm awake," Joe answered as he pulled the pillow over his head and rolled away from them.

"C' mon, man. Besides, I think I got something you might want," the first one continued. "Doesn't this belong to you?"

Joe rolled back over, sat up, scratched a few body parts, stretched, frowned at them both, and held his hand out with his eyes half-closed. The first Marine dropped his Saint Christopher medal and chain into his open palm.

"Isn't this yours? Didn't you give it to that kid when they were playing softball?"

Joe looked at the object in his hand, recognized the medallion, nodded his head, and followed with a quizzical look at his two agitators.

"They found it this morning on a dead gook kid about 30 yards from here. He was wearing explosives on his back. Guess he wanted to show his appreciation by blowing-up your hooch."

Joe thanked them as they turned away and left, proud of themselves to have completed their Boy Scout duties. He let out a sigh and stared at the Saint Christopher medallion for a moment, wondering aloud if Saint Christopher would work his protection system- better than it did for the kid.

He had a fleeting thought that if this were a John Wayne movie, Joe would have taught the kid to play baseball, and the youngster would have saved his life last night.

He made a note in his mental scorebook to never trust even the friendliest of Vietnamese. With that, he let out a deep sigh, rubbed both temples with the palms of his hands, and laid down to accomplish his goal of sleeping until dinner.

It was not meant to happen. Thirty minutes later, someone new entered the hooch. To Joe's relief, the stranger was wearing SEAL tiger-striped camos and carrying a sea bag.

"You Tyler?"

Without waiting for an answer, he continued, "I'm your new roomie, Kaffar. The Skipper wants to see you forthwith." With that, Kaffar dropped his sea bag on the wooden planked floor, laid down on the empty bunk, and fell asleep.

All the while, Joe sat there, trying to clear the cobwebs from his brain. Finally, he yawned, stood up, stretched, and got his gear. The Colt 45, extra clips, and both K-bars were always a vital part of his waking attire. In truth, Joe had developed the habit of always going to sleep with the diver's knife strapped to his right calf and the Colt under his crossed arms. This routine continued from the time he first got them, until the day after he arrived back in the States.

LCDR Wheeler had his back to Joe as he entered the MACV command tent. Jeff Wheeler was standing in front of the I-Corps military map, which was the northernmost theater of operations in Vietnam. I-Corps was adjacent to North Vietnam and was the first line of defense should the North Vietnamese Regular Army choose to invade South Vietnam.

"Stevenson said your radio died."

"Roger that, sir." "Next time, always replace the battery with a fresh one before you leave," this was stated more like a command than a suggestion. "Or didn't we cover that in Cavite?"

Uh oh. He was not summoned to be congratulated for a job well done.

The LCDR turned to look at Joe before he spoke again. While his face said in-control-professional-officer, a tad of anger found its way into each word.

"You threw the grenades that started the excitement?"

"Yes sir."

"Why?"

"Sir?" was what he said, but in his mind, he was thinking, this may be where the proverbial crap hits-the-fan.

"And don't sir me! What the hell, were you thinking, Joe? You screwed up a well-set ambush. You were trained better. I personally trained you better! The US Government, with my recommendation, has spent a fortune making you the perfect warrior. And this? This is what they produced? In case you have not figured it out yet, we are supposed to be the best of the best; the head of the food chain. You . . ."

Having made his point, he sat down, caught his emotions, took a minute or two to collect himself. After 30-seconds, LCDR Wheeler's eyes locked on Petty Officer Joe Tyler. shoulders slumped, and his tone softened.

"Relax. Sit down, Tyler. I am trying to understand what you were thinking."

Neither man said a word for at least 60-seconds.

"Skipper, from where I was at, from the last communication I got, I was directed to let you know when Charlie was 50 yards out. Having had a couple of the bad guy's platoons walk right on top of me, I thought it best to let someone know Charlie had reached the tree line. Lighting them up from behind seemed like the best move."

Joe paused before he finished.

"The way I saw it, making Charlie think they were being attacked from behind would cause confusion, disrupt their surprise and let you know how close they had gotten."

"Well, it was not a good idea! We knew your last position. We knew the VC's status. And we had good intel telling us where they were headed and what they were planning on doing when they got here. Granted, we did not know if you were dead or alive; but, by that time, your well-being was the very least of our concerns. Either way, it didn't matter."

The Lieutenant Commander studied Joe for a few seconds, then took a deep breath to calm himself.

"On the other hand, you had to know you were putting yourself in a dangerous situation by exposing your position." With that, neither of them said a word for several minutes. Wheeler sat looking disgusted, mulling over Joe's fate.

Joe sat there, wondering about his future. Not wanting to stare back at him, he found something else to occupy his eyes. Occasionally, he would glance toward Jeff Wheeler way, looking for a hint from his body language.

"So, tell me, in your purported concern for the safety of the base, did it even occur to you that we, as senior, veteran officers, that we might know more about counterattacks and ambushes than you?"

Once again, Jeff Wheeler's voice grew in force, and Joe noticed a vein starting to throb in his head, ala Commander Elfelt.

He began to squirm but did his best to hide it.

Wheeler took him from hero to idiot in one sentence. In truth, Joe had not given any thought to what the senior officers might be thinking. His mind began bouncing around, searching for an answer. Nothing came to mind before Wheeler spoke again.

"The facts of the situation included several combat-seasoned senior officers and a greenie in the bush. The officers had a job to do. They knew how to handle the situation. Tyler, you should have figured that out. You did not. You screwed up."

"I guess I needed to Confess and Correct, LT."

In basic SEAL training, everyone is taught that if you screw-up on an active mission, then CCC: Contact, Confess, and Correct.

"On the confession side, no sir, I did not give any thought to the fact that the situation was already under control by my superior officers."

His honesty seemed to touch Jeff Wheeler, albeit, ever so slightly.

"On the correcting side, I'm confused. What should I have done? Agreed. Not thinking that Command would have been planning something, okay, was wrong. I get that now. On the other hand, dealing with the facts as I knew them, I felt it was imperative to let the base know they were about to get attacked."

Joe paused for several seconds, then asked, "So, Skip, what would you have done in my place?"

Jeff Wheeler stared at his protégé for a few seconds as he considered his side of the argument.

"You should have positioned yourself behind their mortar emplacements, not their infantry, then waited until the next round of flares went up. As the flares fell, you should have thrown both grenades in such a manner as to take out a couple of their positions."

Joe let that sink in for a good 30 seconds, took a deep breath then let out a sigh.

"Relax Tyler. All things considered; you did a fair job. With experience, I'm convinced you would have acted differently."

That was not what Joe was expecting to hear.

"You apparently slept through close combat tactics during both SQT and AWT, as you missed the part where we stressed make yourself think of all, repeat, all the alternatives before you act. Yes, there were, and will be situations where you had to trust your instincts. However, in this situation, you had time to think things through. But you did not. And that is what bothers me the most! Whether or not you get killed is not, repeat, is not as critical as doing your job right and accomplishing your mission. Hooyah?"

"Hooyah!"

LCDR Wheeler began to pace slowly in front of his desk.

"Look, Tyler, all the training in the world is second to actual experience. On the plus side, I'm planning on including your recent situation as a training exercise in Cavite."

Joe began to relax.

"I want you back here at 1600. Chief Warrant Officer Presley will be leading an eight-man recon-team west of their operation area. You met Kaffar. Two others, Petty Officer's Tatge and Proctor, will make up the balance of the team."

"Where are we headed, sir?" Joe asked.

"We'll go through that at 1600." "Sorry Commander., I meant after Cam Ranh."

"Quang Tri. You and Kaffar along with Tatge and Proctor will be part of new Special Ops Group, Team 19. Your platoon officer will be LTJG Frank Sallie. Hooyah?"

"Roger that! Hooyah!"

In short, the LCDR had just told Joe that he had graduated from his in-country trials and was moving forward to do the job for which he had spent a year training: Joe had officially been promoted as a member of a Special Ops team.

Before they departed, Joe took another quick look at the wall map. Quang Tri was the northeastern most military forward operating base in I-Corps. It seemed close enough that you could throw a rock, and have it land in North Vietnam. Thinking about his assignment got Joe's adrenaline flowing.

He stopped by the mess hall, grabbed a sandwich, some fruit, and filled a canteen with cold water. He ate everything on the way back to his hooch. Finally, nap time.

At 3:30 that afternoon, Joe awoke ready and eager to go. About the same time, his new roomie, First Class Petty Officer Brenden Kaffar, also awoke. Upon sitting upright, Brenden asked if he had met with the LT, which was his way of saying good afternoon. Kaffar was in his late 20s, had 12 years in the Navy and was a 1964 graduate from BUD/S in Coronado.

Brenden began his first tour as an advisor in March of 1965, the same month he had enlisted. After spending four months with an ARVN guerrilla unit, he transferred to Brown Water Special Ops, working mostly 'snatches' (capturing bad guys) along the Tay Nihn River.

Brown Water refers to the Navy's efforts to patrol and secure the rivers and lagoons of South Vietnam. The sailors who operated these small gunboats called PBRs (patrol boat, river), went by many nicknames, including River Rats, Black Berets, and the Mekong Yacht Club. Although they were not BUD/S trained, they were elite riverine combat warriors and some of the bravest, non-special ops people in the military.

Kaffar liked his idea of his having two K-bars and carrying the Colt 45 across his chest. On their way to LCDR Wheeler's quarters, they stopped by the quartermaster's supply building, and he picked up an additional K-Bar knife, calf sheath, and a chest holster.

Kaffar suggested he take an Ithaca Model 37 riot action 12-gauge shotgun. The Ithaca had a short 18-inch barrel and a dull, unadorned stock with a plastic butt plate. In special warfare situations, it had distinguished itself as a significant "show-stopper" when operating in remarkably close proximity to the enemy. Besides the light weight of the Ithaca and the short barrel, the most notable feature was that it did not eject the shell casing out the right side, as was usual with most pump shotguns. Instead, it both loaded and ejected spent shells from the bottom. Designed as a close operation bush weapon, this design prevented a lot of mud and dust getting into the receiver.

After helping Joe get the Ithaca's harness adjusted high on his back, they made their way to the Skipper's tent. CWO Presley, Petty Officers Austin Tatge and Jimmy Proctor had arrived ahead of them and were sitting in wooden, folding chairs in a semi-circle around LCDR Wheeler's desk.

Wheeler started the meeting by giving a couple of historical facts on each member of the team. When he got to Joe, he referenced his short time in-country and highlighted his quick trigger action onboard the Swift boat. Wheeler gave him credit for alerting command of the approaching VC company that had attacked the base the previous night. The LCDR added, in a positive way, that his quick thinking of tossing grenades behind the enemy infantry alerted the entire base that the attack was about to happen. The LT did not mention that Joe almost screwed things up.

After LCDR Wheeler welcomed everyone, he began the meeting began by verbally outlining the Specific Mission Orders for Operation Footboy's Mission Elvis:

MO-1. Utilizing SOG's Insertion Gunboat, they were to pick-up an American CIA field operator and his South Vietnamese Army counterpart.

MO-2. The Spook-guy will designate both the snatch target's position and transfer coordinates.

MO-3. CWO Presley has overall mission command. Code name: Elvis. Each man assigned to this mission has an obligation to complete Mission Elvis successfully.

MO-4. Kaffar will be in the Two and command have overall the four-man fire team, Code name: Rat Catcher.

MO-5. Tyler is the One and will coordinate with CWO Presley and the Spook. Kaffar will be in the Two and command in the bush. Tatge the Five and Proctor the Six.

MO-6 follows SOG General Mission Order Number 6: Should you find enemy combatants; you will kill the enemy combatants and you will come back alive.

"Kaffar will stay in-line behind Tyler in the Two. He will have to keep tabs on where everyone is, especially which flank Tatge is on. Austin, as the five, you will scout both flanks. Proctor, you need to be extra vigilant on your Six.

Pausing, LCDR Wheeler made eye contact with each of man.

"The snatch will take place tomorrow night and will last into the next day. You shove off at 0430 tomorrow."

As each man rose from his chair, LCDR Wheeler held-up his hand to get their attention. Before he spoke, he looked at Stevenson and nodded his head.

Stevenson reached beside his chair and set one of the boxes on his lap. He opened the box slowly, then drew out a pistol, that was obviously smaller than the Military Colt 45 that they had been carrying. Next, he pulled out a long cylinder-like object and easily screwed it onto the snubbed barrel of the pistol. Once completed, he double-checked he chamber to make sure no bullets were in the register.

Stevenson sat back, admired the weapon, and passed it to the man on his left, Austin Tatge, who then passed it to the man on his left. As the men continued to receive their new weapons, LCDR Wheeler again began to speak.

"Men, before you, is the new Swedish made SK-22 pistol. Designed by a Frogman, and, for obvious reasons, it has been nick-named the Hush Puppy. The major advantages of the weapon are that it is foreign made, is lighter and better balanced than the Colt, is more accurate and is about two-thirds the weight of the Colt. In addition, the weapon uses the same ammunition as the Stoner."

As he spoke, the men continued to pass individual weapons to the man seated on their left. Eventually, a new SK-22 made its way to Joe. The first thing he did was to check the weapon's balance. Satisfied, he withdrew the Colt from its holster, discharged the clip and ejected the shell from the chamber. He double checked the older weapon and safely passed it to the man on his right until it made its way back to Stevenson.

Each man on the fireteam did likewise. Once they each had their new weapons, they holstered them across their chests, smiled to one another and returned their attention to LCDR Wheeler.

"When you get back, Presley will transfer to a new position in Saigon. The rest of the team, including myself, will catch a bird to Quang Tri. Kaffar, Tyler, Proctor, and Tatge will stay together as Rat Catcher.

Not knowing any better, Joe asked if he kept his CopperSun call sign.

"Roger that. Kaffar has always been Crossbow, same with Tatge as Raider. Proctor as Cowboy. So yes, Petty Officer Joseph Tyler, from now until the day you die, you will always be CopperSun."

Then, just for fun Jeff Wheeler paused, looked him squarely in the eyes and added, "Quite honestly, Tyler, I'm still not positive you're old enough to have a driver's license."

To Joe's chagrin, the other men on his team started chiming in with their own hoots, hollers, and questions about his birthright.

◆ ◆ ◆

On his way back to the hooch, Joe began to rethink the single-man, "listening-post check" that LCDR Wheeler had designed for him in the hills adjacent to Cam Ranh. Navy Frogmen/SEALs always worked in teams. However, there were many documented events where frogmen, rangers and Special Forces people have had to work alone.

If he had to guess, Joe now realized it was all part of his fast-track training qualifications. To date, he had passed every mental and physical exam the Navy presented, including responding immediately to the threat presented by the old guy in the 'fishing' boat.

Thinking about it further, for his final test, LCDR Wheeler wanted to know precisely how his 19-year-old protégé worked with guys senior to him in age, experience, and rank. More, how would he apply his training to future missions that would be, for all intent and purpose, learn-as-you-go under extremely high-stress-conditions?

The next morning, as the five of them made their way to the dock, a few of the younger grunts and jarheads stopped what they were doing and stared at them. Other than the fact that they all wore black Converse tennis shoes instead of combat boots, no two of them dressed alike.

CWO Presley wore all black: black jeans, black t-shirt and even a black, western cattle-rancher hat. While Kaffar, Proctor, Tatge and Walker camouflaged tops and bottoms, it appeared they had bought them at a second-hand clothing store. Of the eight pieces of clothing, no two went with any other piece.

While Tatge and Proctor wore camo-jungle floppy hats, better known as boonies, Kaffar favored the Australia bush hat. Joe preferred wearing camouflaged bandana hat tied in the back.

Each carried a K-bar on their hip, Kaffar and Joe also had a frogman's diver knife strapped to their right calf and hidden by their pant leg. Both carried their Hushpuppies in chest holsters, while the others still preferred them on their right hips.

Proctor and Tatge cradled their Stoner 63 light machine guns in the more traditional 'across the chest' position. Tyler preferred the semi-automatic Stoner 62 Carbine, which he carried across his shoulders. He transported the Ithaca riot gun strapped in a specially created harness, high on his back.

CWO Presley wore black jeans, a black T-shirt, and a dark brown jean jacket. He also fancied the Colt 45 to the SK-22 Hush Puppy as he would not be in a position where he needed to silence a barking guard dog.

CHAPTER TWENTY-ONE

January 2, 1967

The gunboat/insertion craft departed Cam Ranh Bay promptly at 4:30 and by 9:30 that morning, they arrived in the area to pick up their passengers. Presley slowly drove by the exact rendezvous spot while the rest of the team scanned both sides of the river for enemy activity, especially possible ambush positions. As they had discussed the night before, after they traveled past the site about a half-mile, they edged near the opposite shoreline, and Joe slid over the side of the PBR onto the muddy bank, armed with his two K-bars, the Colt pistol, and the riot gun. His face, neck, and hands were covered with green paint.

The boat proceeded another quarter mile, made a slow 180-degree turn, and headed back downriver. This time, the boat stayed near the same shoreline as the pickup point, and Jimmy Proctor went over the side with similar weapons and camo face paint. Proctor's job was to move into position behind the pair to ensure that they were not being followed or in any kind of danger.

In the meantime, Jimmy worked the jungle on the opposite side of the river to ensure there were no surprises. Should he see something, he was to neutralize the situation and get to his pickup point. If it was a situation he could not handle on his own, he was to do what he could, move away, then signal by firing three rounds with the Colt in semi-automatic mode.

Joe began his slow journey parallel with the riverbank. Only a quarter mile into his journey, Joe heard voices and stopped. Slowly, silently, he crawled forward to gain a better look. Joe came within 60 feet of four adult civilians - two men and two women - walking on a wide dirt path. Three or four children, all under the age of ten, followed along behind them. The youngsters were playing and joking like kids everywhere, seemingly unaware they were the middle of a war zone. They were non-combatant locals, so Joe stayed low, blended in the with brush around him, and let them pass.

Once the families had gone safely by, Joe completed his scouting detail for another a mile, and, after he was convinced all was clear, he moved closer to the riverbank and continued his search for anything unusual. Glancing back up the river, he noted that the two passengers were onboard. A few seconds later, Proctor appeared out of the clearing and jumped onboard.

Presley moved the gunboat away and, staying close to the bank, moved downriver, past Joe's location, and then made a slow U-turn toward him. When the boat was about 30 feet from his position, Joe stepped into the open, then jumped onboard as the PBR slowly moved past him.

With everyone onboard, they continued their northwest journey along the winding river. The CIA field officer and his Vietnamese counterpart discussed with Joe and Kaffar how the snatch would proceed. While the CIA guy handled most of the discussion, he asked Joe his ideas for getting to the village, establishing the perimeter and the optional exit routes.

The night looked to be perfect for the snatch. Dry weather, partly cloudy sky, and most importantly, no moon. They hid the boat under camo netting and tied-off next to the trunk of a tree that had fallen into the river. At 1:00 the next morning, Kaffar and Tyler went into the bush about 150 feet from the gunboat's location.

Kaffar positioned himself 30 feet behind Joe and to his right. They sat motionless, listening for any jungle noise that sounded or felt wrong. A half-hour later, the others joined them, with Presley alone on the gunboat.

Once gathered, the six of them moved forward, Kaffar positioning himself some 30 feet behind Joe. Another 40 feet behind Kaffar came the CIA operations guy with the ARVN officer close behind him. As planned, Tatge was in the Five slot, 50 feet behind them. Occasionally, Tatge would sweep right or left to make sure no one was flanking them.

Proctor was the Six and stayed back at whatever distance he felt was right. His primary function on the team was making sure no bad guys were lurking on their tail.

Whenever they were in the bush, Joe was never sure exactly where Jimmy was located. However, knowing he was back there brought comfort to him, and the entire team. Once they got to the targeted village, without any conversation, Joe circled to the left as Tatge went right. After a minute or two, Kaffar leading, the CIA guy and Vietnamese officer entered the village, moving in single file, quietly advancing to the target's hooch.

Kaffar took a quick look inside the one-room hooch, gave a thumbs-up to the others, then placed himself in a defensive position outside the entry. The two officers quickly went through the doorway and, within 90-seconds brought a middle-aged man outside, his hands tied behind his back, and a black hood over his head.

Brenden escorted them out of the village while the rest of the Rat Catcher team held their positions, double checking to ensure no one would try to rescue the American prisoner. As the four of them cleared their perimeter, a lady came out of the hooch screaming and crying; three pre-teens boys who looked very frightened followed her.

The Snatch Team gathered a hundred yards from the village and took the road most of the way back toward the boat. Once he had judged they had gone far enough, the CIA officer pulled the hood off the snatch-target so that he could better navigate through the bush. The Bad Guy had a gag over his mouth and had been threatened with the loss of his family's lives if he did not cooperate with them.

They reached the gunboat in good time. Presley started the engines and, with everyone onboard they moved up the river. After a quarter mile, Presley made a 180-degree turn and positioned the PBR perfectly in the center of the river. Once confident he had found the current that would move them forward, he cut the engines.

As the gunboat drifted downriver, Presley adjusted the rudder so they would slowly drift toward the left bank. Like a precision Swiss clock, Proctor came out of the tree line to their left. Proctor jumped on-board and, as his second foot touched the deck, Presley cranked-up the engines to ¾ power, and they continued their journey, unabated, downriver.

Soon the eastern sky began to glow. Overall, a well-planned snatch. However, for their newly formed Rat Catcher team, tomorrow morning would bring its own peculiar ending to their squad's first mission.

CHAPTER TWENTY-TWO
January 1967

Including the snatch-target, they now had eight people crowded onto their relatively small gunboat. Presley did his best to keep the PBR in the middle of the river for their three-hour ride to the transfer point.

Kaffar smiled as he watched his inexperienced Snatch & Grab Team settle-in for what they assumed was a well-deserved nap. After permitting them 10 minutes to get comfortable, Kaffar informed everyone onboard that it was standard practice for Charlie to take a few shots at them on their way home. The gunmen would typically be local farmer sympathizers who would fire one shot and then go back into hiding. The farmers would surmise (correctly), that every American boat that went upriver would usually make a return trip within the next 72 hours.

With that, everyone onboard kept their eyes peeled for snipers. Unless they knew precisely where the shots came from, Kaffar instructed them not to return fire. Their focus was to get their prisoner to the pick-up point, not to engage the enemy. As predicted, forty-five minutes later, they heard two loud reports from two different carbines located somewhere high in one of the thousand jungle trees surrounding them. About the same time as they heard the weapons, water splashed nearly simultaneously a good 60 feet from the boat.

.

This happened a couple more times before they got to the rendezvous coordinates.

While the others took the shooting in stride, it made Joe tense. Jimmy Proctor noticed his body language and began teasing him about how the snipers always aimed for the youngest guys.

Their transfer point was located at a natural 30-degree right bend, where there appeared to be a natural clearing on the inside of the apex. The potential landing site for the pick-up had a wide, white sandy area that had been carved out of the tree line. The opposite bank was at least one-hundred and twenty-five yards away, which prevented anyone from mounting a surprise attack opposite the landing.

Once Presley got the boat positioned against the white, sandy beach, the four-man fireteam got into position about fifty yards into the dense jungle, securing the pick-up site. Proctor, Tatge, and Joe were each assigned specific kill zones: Joe went toward the middle; Proctor was on Joe's left and Tatge to his right. Kaffar stayed nearby the gunboat, but well hidden in the jungle. After about 20 minutes, Joe reported in, "CopperSun. Four-by-four." Proctor followed a minute later, "Raider. Four-by-four."

They waited for Tatge to call.

Five minutes passed, yet they heard nothing. Finally, Kaffar announced "CopperSun Romeo Nine Zero. Bravo Romeo Four Five. Crossbow Six Zero." To translate,

Kaffar instructed the three of them to locate Tatge. Joe began by moving to his right at a 90-degree angle. Proctor would cross behind him and come up about 20 yards to his left. Kaffar would come up about 20 yards to his right.

Presley had stayed with the boat, along with three passengers. The CIA officer secured the prisoner, then handed the Vietnamese officer an M16 rifle while he took a position behind the 50-caliber. Presley started the engines and allowed the boat to drift slightly off the beach. This kept him available to captain the boat while the two officers provided cover fire.

With a few apparently simple commands, Kaffar had strategically set Proctor and he so that they formed three overlapping kill zones as they slowly made their way to Tatge's patrol position. Thinking about it today, just as he did later that day, he admits it was a stroke of professional, military tactical genius. Kaffar's training and experiences, combined with an ability to envision the physical circumstances, led him to position them to find Tatge, and, if needed, establish an ambush of their own.

After a few minutes, Joe spotted Tatge standing about 90 feet away from him and in front of a large tree; Tatge's hands were tied behind his back while his eyes were covered by a black bandana. A Viet Cong soldier held a knife to Tatge's throat, all the while keeping his head hidden behind the taller Tatge's neck and shoulders.

Joe hand signaled the rest of the team and then slowly lowered himself to one knee.

Each man recognized this as a textbook Viet Cong ambush with both the VC soldier and Tatge as bait. One-on-one or even three-on-one, Tatge probably could have taken the VC and alerted them to his situation. Because his hands were tied, that meant there had to be a group of at least a dozen VC that had somehow surprised him. The VC planned to draw them toward them, having several soldiers concealed in the bush in a V-shape pattern, to the right and left of the tree.

The VC platoon was aware that a **PBR** had gone upriver the day before and that some Americans had kidnapped one of their own the night before. The American's next move would be to head back down the river to one of two geographic choices large enough for a helo to land.

Therefore, the VC set an ambush at each location. What they did not know was that they were not regular Brown Water Navy. They were the "men with the green faces" as they called them, ghosts that appear when and where the VC least expected.

Joe slowly forced his body to melt down into the jungle undergrowth, his Stoner hidden by the brush, pointed in the direction of the VC. Slowly looking to his left, Proctor had spotted the VC and was crouched low and looking back at Joe.

Joe nodded and using hand signals, told him what he saw and to wait.

Knowing that Kaffar would be on his right, Joe turned and signaled him as to what he thought they had, and what he thought they should do. The final call was Kaffar's, but he quickly nodded in agreement and, to confirmed that he had the plan by pointing his submachine gun to their left, Tatge's right.

Joe looked back at Proctor and signaled that he would take-out the VC holding Tatge hostage, and then cover the area to Proctor's right, Tatge's left. Proctor knew how the ambush had been set, that their alignment would catch them by surprise, and the enemy would be caught in their crossfire.

Because all of them were trained to notice such things, when the jungle quiets down, an alarm goes off and their senses go on high alert. Therefore Tatge, while feeling anxious, knew that his brothers were close by.

It was up to Joe to start the ambush in motion. Knowing what was about to occur sent an adrenaline rush charging through his veins. Joe took a deep breath and gradually rose to a standing position, exposing his position to the VC holding Austin Tatge.

Joe stared at the VC; his eyes wide opened as he stared back at Joe's. The soldier knew he should do something, anything, to notify his comrades who were positioned low in the bushes to his left and right. The VC was so frightened that his body trembled from head to foot and, instead of notifying

217

his comrades, he froze; he could not move or talk, and barely able to breathe.

What the VC did not know was that Proctor had been watching his every move and had locked the sights of his Stoner 63 carbine on to the side of the VC's head. At the same moment that Tatge's captor opened his mouth to warn his comrades, Proctor squeezed off one round. The 5.56 mm round, traveling at a speed of 3,250 feet per second, entered the head of the enemy soldier, about a quarter inch over his right ear. Joe was the last person that the VC ever saw.

Joe watched the VC's head explode a split-second before he heard the report of Proctor's rifle. The impact of the bullet caused the upper part of the skull to fly five feet straight up in the air. A mass of jelled brains, bone, and blood flew out at 270 degrees, completely covering the back of Tatge's head, neck, and shoulders.

Austin Tatge immediately dropped to the ground, getting as small as possible, knowing that the other VC would assume he was dead. As Tatge fell to the ground, Joe opened fire, spraying the tree and foliage behind Tatge's position. After his burst of a dozen rounds, a group of six VC on Joe's left opened fire in his direction. Kaffar responded using his submachine gun, firing at 750 rounds a minute. That meant that in a 5-second burst, Brenden Kaffar fired 63 rounds, waist level or lower, at the six VC.

Joe dropped flat and pulled the Colt 45 from its holster, just as the VC on Joe's right thought that the time was right for them to advance. They stood and began firing wildly at both his and Kaffar's positions. Unfortunately for them, this was the move that Proctor had been expecting. Jimmy threw a grenade close behind their job, then fired an entire clip in their direction.

Kaffar threw a grenade behind the VC on his left.

Joe followed by getting to one knee and firing two sharp bursts from his Stoner. Afterward, he dropped to the ground and began crawling, his chest equipment scrapping along the ground, to get to Tatge. Kaffar and Proctor both sprayed dozens of rounds on the entire area, so many rounds that they cut down a couple of the small trees.

Then silence.

The firefight lasted 90-seconds, max.

Kaffar and Proctor got small and surveyed the jungle in every direction. Once everything stayed quiet for three or four minutes, Joe yelled, "CopperSun." This alerted Proctor, Kaffar that he had reached Tatge's position. Joe pulled the blindfold off Austin's eyes and cut the rope from his wrists.

Austin faked a yawn, acted bored, and said, "About time."

Joe yelled "clear" to let everyone know Tatge was safe, then handed Austin his Stoner and pulled the riot gun off his back. They both laid motionless as Proctor slowly crept his way to one side of them, checking and counting VC bodies along the way. Kaffar did the same with the now dead VC on his right. After they both finished, Tatge and Joe slowly and cautiously got to their feet.

Soon, all four were standing, albeit about ten feet apart from one another, just in-case any bad guys were still around. Kaffar and Proctor did a double-check of the dead enemy soldiers. A couple of times, either one or both put a VC soldier out of their misery. While this was going on Kaffar checked Presley.

Before heading back to the gunboat, Kaffar assured himself that no one on the team was injured. Kaffar and Tatge headed back to the boat. Part way back, Austin would split-off from Kaffar and hide along the path. Joe waited a short time, with Jimmy Proctor joining in about 25 feet behind him. When they got within sight of the gunboat, Procter would peel off behind them to guard their six while the other three were climbing aboard the PBR.

Because he had lent his carbine to Tatge, Joe held the riot gun in front of him as they began walking toward the PBR, both on high alert for any movement in the bush. When Joe got to where he thought Tatge would be positioned, he stopped, crouched down and very slowly, began turning in a 360-degree circle, studying the nearby foliage for anything out of place.

As he began turning to his right, a very slight movement on his left caught his attention. Joe quickly spun back to his left. As he was turning, a Viet Cong soldier broke from the bush, a long silvery bayonet in his right hand aimed in Joe's direction.

Joe pulled the trigger on his riot. The blast removed a portion of his attacker's left torso, spinning him and propelling what remained of the soldier's body backward.

The other squad members on the fireteam immediately dropped to the ground, their weapons pointed in the direction of the attack. Everyone stayed in position until after Tyler crawled forward, double checked the soldier's carcass, visually checked the area for additional Viet Cong soldiers, then called all clear.

What happened next blew everyone's mind.

CHAPTER TWENTY-THREE
January 1967

The four of them made it safely back to the PBR without further incident. As they boarded the gunboat, they pounded each other on the back like they had won the 1966 World Series.

Presley called in the bird, and they prepared to transfer their prisoner, the Vietnamese officer, and the CIA field agent. Meanwhile, Tatge jumped in the river to clean his captor's body-remains from his hair and clothing.

An Air Force helicopter arrived within five minutes, sand and water blowing: everyone covering their faces to ward off the stinging sand pellets and rocks. The two officers and CIA operator loaded their hostage, still tied and blindfolded, on the aircraft. Once all three were aboard, the helicopter rotors picked up the pace, and they lifted off.

Kaffar, the adrenaline having left his system, laid on his back on the gunboat's deck and asked Presley to take them home. While they were all happier than 5-year-olds on Christmas, they still knew they should be on the lookout for more VC lurking in the area.

Personally, Joe could not have been higher on adrenaline than if heroin was shooting straight into his veins. He wanted to yell, scream, laugh, jump up and down as he felt like the Warrior King of Vietnam. Proctor and Tatge were on their own adrenaline highs.

Especially Tatge. Getting trapped. Knowing his team would not leave him there and being used as bait and being freed. Wow!

As Presley maneuvered the boat to the middle of the river, all they wanted to do was talk about what recently happened; to relive what they had been through. Moment by moment, second by second, over, and over again.

Like the guy's head being blown off: What was Proctor thinking about when lining-up that shot? What did he feel when watching the VC's head disintegrate?

What about Tatge? How did he feel when he knew his team had found him? And, that they were going to blow those guys away? Or when he felt that guy's head exploding behind him?

How about when Proctor dropped that grenade on their asses? Bet the bad guys could have crapped their black pajamas when they saw that little green ball hit the ground behind them!

Or, how about Joe when he slowly stood up so that the little grease monkey holding Tatge could get a look at him? How cool was that? John Wayne was daring them to take the shot!

Then later, walking back to the gunboat and that gook jumped out of the bushes, and Joe ripped him apart with the riot gun? Oh, man, was this like the most wonderful day ever, or what?

◆◆◆

Just when they all thought the day could not get any stranger, they heard the helo returning, looked up, and, silently now, watched as the Air Force pilot maneuvered over the jungle, then hovered, suspended three or four hundred feet above the jungle floor. Each man became as quiet and as still as statutes; each trying to figure out what was happening or was about to happen.

Did the bird have a mechanical problem?

Why would it just hover over the jungle like that?

They remained standing there, watching in silence and awe. The jungle that had been abuzz with excitement also fell quiet. As the helicopter held steady in the air, a figure stood in the open doorway. As each man was staring skyward, everyone recognized him as the village bad guy they snatched.

Standing in the open frame of the bird, the prisoner looked down into the jungle, his hands tied behind him. Someone's hand was grasping the neckline of his jersey, pushing him forward while at the same time, preventing him from falling. The pilot was doing his best to keep the copter steady, but the wind kept bouncing the hovering machine as he fought to maintain his position.

The once jubilant SEAL Team could only stand there, silently watching; each assuming the impossible was about to happen. Each man was mesmerized by their thoughts and yet, unable to take their eyes off the sky.

The arm holding the prisoner slowly relaxed as it let go of the guy's jersey. A leg and foot behind the bad-guy and pushed hard into his back. While falling toward the treetops, the prisoner's legs kicked in a desperate attempt to slow his descent. They heard the body land, hard, not too far to the north of their position.

No one on the boat said a word. What the men had just witnessed was something they had never heard, nor ever dreamed of happening.

The unspoken question on everyone's mind was: How do they digest what they had just witnessed?

Joe never got over it. The vision stayed with him forever.

CHAPTER TWENTY-FOUR

January 6, 1967

They returned to Cam Ranh early the next morning. LCDR Wheeler had flown to MACV headquarters in Saigon and was not expected back in Cam Ranh Bay until the following day. As the Rat Catcher Fireteam leader, Kaffar suggested they gather at four that afternoon in the mess tent to complete the SitRep (Situation Report). Each man would review their own actions while on the mission, what they felt they did right, what went wrong, and what they could have done better. Kaffar followed each man's thoughts by coaching on what they could have done differently.

In the meantime, everyone welcomed having several hours to catch-up with much-needed rest.

Upon reaching his hooch, Joe stripped, cleaned, oiled, and reassembled his weapons. Satisfied they were operating smoothly, he reloaded each, then propped the long guns next to his bunk. This done, he took his soiled bush clothing to the river, rinsed them thoroughly, then hung them on the rope-line in his hooch.

Finally, he permitted himself a real shower with hot water and soap.

Later, laying on his cot, Joe expected to sleep until it was time to meet with the squad later that afternoon. Though both his body and his mind needed rest, sleep did not come as quickly as he had hoped for. Instead of shutting down and he began reliving the entire mission. His mind raced through the different events of the last three days, and once again, adrenaline began pumping through his nervous system.

◆ ◆ ◆

CCC = Contact. Confess. Correct.

During their post-mission meeting that afternoon, Tatge admitted that he had zoned out for a minute or two while walking to his position; he was not 100% focused on the task at hand. When he heard a twig snap behind him, Austin knew he was in trouble.

If something had gone wrong during a mission, you were seldom admonished. Instead, you and your team were expected to learn from the mistake, share it with others, and, most importantly, not repeat it. The honest sharing of your experience was received as continuing education for the rest of the team. This was especially true when they were in the bush. If you did something wrong and the situation was not working as planned, confess, and correct as soon as the opportunity presented itself.

Nothing more would become of it.

No one would write a memo into your military jacket.

No repercussion would be forthcoming.

Carbon copies of some report would not be distributed on different colors of paper to the powers-that-be. At their level of expertise, it was correct-the-problem and move forward.

Since the beginning of the UDT in WWII, the Navy continuously filtered out who could, or could not withstand unbelievable amounts of stress. Throughout their many months of training, the instructors would reinforce to each man that they were the best-of-the-best-warriors among all mankind.

During Qual-School and AWT, the Navy spent a lot of time, energy, and money training them on the strategic, tactical, and mechanical aspects of close-proximity combat. All day, every day, they were often reminded it was kill or be killed.

Their instructors emphasized the viciousness of their enemy's military actions with graphic color pictures and black & white movies of the North Vietnamese brutalizing their French captives during their failed attempt to control Vietnam.

Prospective Special Operations Warriors saw graphic slides of how the NVA, and Viet Cong tortured the men of villages, then raped captive's wives and daughters, and kidnapped their sons to work in labor camps.

Remember, too, that these American men were children of the 1950s. Beginning with elementary school, they were taught that communism was evil. They were always being reminded that the Russian and Chinese communist wanted to destroy America and the American democratic freedoms that they enjoyed. Per the politicians, if they allowed the Chinese-backed North Vietnamese to conquer South Vietnam, then all of

Indochina would become communists, each falling like so many dominoes. Eventually, New Zealand and Australia.

Each man was determined that the Communists were not going to overtake South Vietnam. Not this day. Not on their watch. Deeply entrenched within each man's were fundamental traits that Jeff Wheeler was looking for in their individual psychological profile: Loyal to a fault. Protectionism. Low tolerance for bullies. Defenders of the meek. A dislike of anyone that acted superior to them and/or talked down to them.

Due to their physical training and the Navy's subliminal brainwashing, each man got to Vietnam with psychological attitudes that overflowed with protectionism, and a sincere sense of brotherhood. Each would give his life for any other member of the team, for the Navy, and for their beloved country.

With the help of the right psychologist and the medication from psychiatrists experienced in working with combat veterans, Joe has begun to realize that, subconsciously, he has been searching to regain that solidarity every day for the past 50 years. He understands, too, that there is nothing his body could ever consume that could fill an emptiness that could not be measured in the first place.

Significant, too, is Joe's accepting that the exhilaration, and the adrenaline rush from being in combat will never happen again.

What Joe's doctors, and doctors of other retired Specials Ops men with PTSD need to comprehend, is that there is a peculiar conflict going on deep inside these men: Sometimes it hurts really bad. The pain goes deep in the core of their souls, when a man finally admits to himself that their days as elite warriors are gone forever and ever.

CHAPTER TWENTY-FIVE
January 11, 1967

Five days later they gathered in LCDR's tent in Quang Tri to meet the other people that made up the nucleus of their combined platoon squads. In addition to the 14 BUD/S trained guys, there were four other individuals, two radiomen and 2 corpsmen. As a group, the platoon spent the first hour getting to know one another.

Wheeler had them introduce themselves, present a short history of their Navy life and the name and population of the town where they grew up. Most of the men were born and raised in Small Town, USA. Because of this, the men who heralded from cities larger than 50,000 people got booed and harassed for being "big-city rich boys," "socialites," or "beatniks."

This was Joe's 20th month of military service. While he no longer felt like the greenie, no one, including him, doubted that he was still the youngster of the bunch.

Last to be introduced was their platoon leader, LTJG Frank J. Sallie. Talk about your military non-conformist, Sallie was it. Unlike any other officer Joe had ever encountered, Frank Sallie would have never been selected as the poster-officer for the United States Military.

Frank sprouted a thick, bushy mustache that balanced his face against equally thick, furry eyebrows. His haircut was equally non-military: thick, long and over his ears that sat above his six-foot, one-inch muscular frame. What struck Joe the most about him was his deep, dark brown eyes. They delivered a peculiar mixed message: one part mischievous and the other, a heavy dose of "you really don't want to mess with me."

LTJG Sallie was the last person to be introduced. Lieutenant Junior Grade arrived wearing shipboard, officer work khakis that appeared as if he had found them rolled-up in a ball in the back of an old wooden chest. His khaki officer's hat had grease stains and worn back away from his forehead. His trousers were cut-off just below his knees, and he came into the morning meeting wearing flip-flops and drinking a bottle of Budweiser.

Naturally, everyone liked Lieutenant Sallie from the start.

As far as these hard-ass, Navy SEALs sitting around the room were concerned, LCDR Wheeler had chosen the perfect leader for the group of enlisted men hand-chosen to gather that morning.

What each man there eventually learned was that Frank Sallie's façade was even more complicated as, hidden beneath the surface was a highly intelligent, down-to-earth guy.

The LCDR relayed Frank's story as graduating from MIT in 3 years with a degree in mechanical engineering. Then, "mostly to piss off his wealthy Ivy League parents," Frank was accepted for a two-year stint at Annapolis.

For reasons never revealed to the enlisted men present, this was Frank's second stint as an LT JG, having been a full Lieutenant a few months before joining SOG Team 19 in Quang Tri. Like all Navy frogmen, he graduated from BUD/S. Unlike some, Frank Sallie had spent time in the Rung-Sat Zone with SEAL Team 2, making him among the first combat SEALs in Vietnam.

As rumor had it, sometime during the summer of 1966, Frank promoted as a full Lieutenant and within a few short weeks, managed to upset someone really high-up in Washington DC. In addition to his demotion to Junior Grade, Frank received a transfer to SEAL Team One and came under the supervision of LCDR Wheeler.

Despite being polar-opposites, Jeff and Frank hit it off like peanut butter and jelly; an unnatural, natural fit.

To begin their noon meeting, LCDR Wheeler had commandeered a case of iced-down Budweiser which LTJG Sallie proceeded to hand out an ice-cold beer to each man in the platoon. When he got to Joe Tyler, the JG stopped. Frank stared at Joe for what seemed like several seconds. Not knowing what to expect but not worried about it either, Joe stared back into his eyes.

When he finally asked, "How old are you?" everyone got a big chuckle.

"Nineteen." Joe's reply, while honest, was delivered with a 'yeah, what's your point?' attitude.

"No. Seriously. Is this a joke that Wheler put you up to?"

Joe stared at him, said nothing, and held out his hand out for his beer.

"They let kids go through Coronado, now? What was it, Tyler? A boy scout weekend at the men's camp and they let you stay?"

Before the LTJG could blink, Joe snatched the beer from his hand. When Frank reached for it, Joe tossed it to Kaffar. Kaffar caught it in the air as he was standing-up from his seat.

Brenden was upset, which was more than apparent from his body language. He took six slow steps over to the JG and, while looking at him dead in the eye, handed him the bottle of beer.

"Tyler is our point, man. He has a history with this fireteam and even more time with the Lieutenant Commander. In the bush, he is the best point this man's Navy has ever produced. I do not care if he is twelve, or even ten for that matter. He drinks with the rest of us."

Everything became a little tense. All eyes focused on the two gladiators. Joe glanced at Wheeler, hoping he would step in and cool things down. Instead, he leaned back in his chair, put his feet up on his desk, smiling from ear to ear.

LTJG Sallie stepped into Kaffar's space and put his face within 3 inches of Kaffar's.

The veins in each man's face and neck stood out; muscles tensed.

For a long time, nothing was said.

Just. Very. Intense. Staring.

"I'm cool with that. Now sit down."

For a split-second, Kaffar looked at him quizzically. Then his whole body relaxed, shrugged his shoulders, replied, "Roger that, LT," smiled and sat down.

The tension left the room in a rush, and several nervous chuckles could be heard. Joe's included. "I read all your jackets. Theoretically, I know as much about each one of you as anyone else in the Navy. I know that Tyler recently earned a bronze star in Cam Ranh. I know what happened 3 days ago on the snatch and recovery. What I do not know is what makes each of you tick. So, when I get in your shorts, it's to squeeze your balls."

Frank Sallie paused for effect. "Get over it."

"Kaffar was right to stand up for his squad point man, Tyler."

Frank Sallie continued to take command of the meeting. "I expect each man here to do what Kaffar did – lay it all on the line for any man in this tent. Remember, we are the guys that put the 'special' in Special Warfare and Special Ops."

Frank paused and slowly looked around the room.

"On the B-side of the record, we're also the psychos of the Psychological Ops Group."

After delivering this last line, he looked at Psych Warfare guys with a big grin on his face. Before he continued, he chugged the entire bottle of beer.

"Each man here has passed numerous mental exams, lived through Hell Week, and survived Cavite. You have been hand-picked by Jeff Wheeler and field tested at least three times in actual combat situations just to get into this tent. Each man here has signed off, for all intent and purposes, to become forever invisible in military history. By agreeing never to tell anyone exactly what you do, and that, by the way, includes your brothers in this platoon, you will have to live a lie for the remainder of your life. Hooyah?"

"Hooyah!"

CHAPTER TWENTY-SIX
January 11, 1967

With that, LCDR Wheeler stood up at his desk. He began by reminding them, again, about all the training and extraordinary effort each had put in to get where they were headed, adding that everyone in the room was hand-picked by him. LCDR Wheeler paused before continuing. He looked at Frank, signaling him to hand-out the cards that had been sitting on the corner of the desk.

After each man received a card, LCDR Wheeler read the card aloud:

MILITARY ASSISTANCE COMMAND - VIETNAM STUDIES AND OBSERVATION GROUP APO SAN FRANCISCO

The bearer of this document is acting under the direct orders of the President of the United States.

DO NOT DETAIN OR QUESTION HIM!

He is authorized to wear civilian clothing, carry unusual personal weapons, transport, and possess prohibited items, including foreign currency, pass into restricted areas, and requisition equipment of all types, including weapons and vehicles.

IF HE IS KILLED OR INJURED,
DO NOT REMOVE THIS DOCUMENT.
ALERT YOUR
COMMANDING OFFICER IMMEDIATELY!

LCDR Wheeler paused to allow the information he had read to sink in.

"You will carry this card anytime you are in the Republic of South Vietnam," he added. "Should any person - any rank, no matter what branch of military service - give you any crap, tell them you work for me, and LTJG Sallie. Be very direct. Very stern.

"Do not provide them with any additional information, whatsoever. Under no circumstances shall you allow anyone other than yourself, to retain this card, no matter what their rank.

Should anyone other than myself, LTJG Sallie or any other credentialed senior officer from MACV, refuse to return your card immediately after reading it, you are hereby granted permission to recover the card, using physical force, if necessary."

"Hooyah?"

"Hooyah!"

That speech, but more particular, before receiving his card, Joe somehow assumed most everyone went through strict training to earn the right to do whatever they did while in the combat. Never, not even for the slightest of moments had he given any thought of himself as being exceptional.

Looking back, that specific meeting was the major turning point in his often-adolescent mind. And not just about his military training, but more to the point, life as he would forever see it.

Another round of beers got passed. This time, being the newest and youngest member of the platoon, he jumped up immediately to serve everyone. When he got to Kaffar, he looked him in the eye and slightly nodded his head to say thanks. When he got to the LTJG, Joe smiled and nodded the same thanks to him.

Once they all had fresh, cold brews, the LCDR went on to explain exactly who they were and what they would be doing while operating out of Quang Tri. "Okay men, some of you have heard the Six General Mission Orders of Special Ops before, but just to make sure, here they are again. If you have not done so already, you need to memorize them, forthwith."

Joe had memorized them from the first time he heard them and whispered them to himself as the LCDR read them aloud:

GMO 1: Abductions and/or extractions, or as they referred to them, Snatch and Grabs.

GMO 2: Search and Rescue Missions. Because of the nature of the entire platoon's training, any squad or fireteam from their Special Operations Group could be called upon for an immediate SAR mission for any allied personal, no matter where on the Planet Earth that it may take them.

(For Team 19, these missions almost always took place outside the borders of South Vietnam.)

GMO 3: Also, about SAR Missions: modified for their MACV-SOG platoon, specifically covered American Prisoners of War that intelligence suspected of being held within North Vietnam. This was also covered by Joe's fireteam, under GMO One.

GMO 4: Psychological Warfare within North Vietnam, aka Psy-ops. Within their platoon, a squad of six men who also trained in Cavite specialized in planting seeds of discontent toward the Hanoi government throughout the civilian population that lived within the lower geographic third of North Vietnam.

GMO 5: Intelligence Reconnaissance. These missions were always performed by the platoon's 8-member Recon squad. Joe's fireteam referred to them as the Ghost Squad. Wherever they went, no one saw them arrive, saw them do their job, nor knew when they had left. Yet, they were so good at what they did, that General Westmoreland, MACV's Commanding Officer, and his staff, all too often disbelieved what they reported, because no other branch of the service could verify their information.

GMO 6: Find the enemy. Kill the enemy. Come back alive.

Without provocation, they all yelled "Hooyah!" in unison.

As if on cue, LTJG Sallie stepped forward and took over the discussion.

"We are all members of SEAL Team One, Combat MACV-SOG Team 19, is currently the only platoon of Frogmen operating this far north in South Vietnam. We are comprised of 23 enlisted men and two officers. Some of you trained in Virginia, others, California. Regardless, all frogmen present today went through Cavite.

And, fortunately for this Team, Cavite was the brainchild of our boss, Lieutenant Commander Wheeler."

Upon hearing this, they all stood, cheered, and applauded.

"Let's start with the basics. MACV: Military Assistance Command Vietnam. Now the tricky one: SOG."

With that, LTJG Sallie went silent and began searching the faces of each man in the room. Brendon Kaffar and several others yelled out, "Special Ops Guys!"

"Wrong, but thanks for playing. According to the General's organizational chart, not to mention the minds of the US Congress, SOG ONLY stands for Special Observation Group. Which, by the way, is the Number One of many reasons that, as of this moment, you no longer exist."

Jimmy Proctor, the only black-skinned person in the room, spoke-up.

"Shit. Ain't no big deal. You white-folks been telling me that I shouldn't be existing my whole life!"

The whole room broke out laughing then began tossing their empty cans in his direction. Proctor laughed harder than anyone, stood up, announced that it was his turn to get the beer. Obviously, that resulted in everyone to stand and applaud. Having grown up in a multi-cultural neighborhood, the only person in the room not understanding the joke was Joe Tyler.

Growing up on the Southwest side of Warren, Ohio meant that everyone, no matter race, color, or ethnic group was the same. Oh sure, the Greeks and Italians were always competitive and never seemed to get along. And everyone had ethnic jokes about the Irish and the Polish. But in the end, everyone knew every member of every family for a mile in any direction.

As a boy, Joe Tyler played sandlot sports, shared water and pop from the same bottles or glasses and ate meals at other's homes. In the heat of the summer, the boys often ended up sleeping on the front porch of each other's homes as no one owned air conditioning.

The only discrimination Joe was aware of was that kids from the southwest side seldom made any of the high-school teams; especially those living south of the railroad tracks, regardless of race or color.

There were exceptions. A great example would be the great NFL Hall of Famer Paul Warfield. The Warfield's grew up only a few blocks away on Second Street. He was a nationally recognized professional football player, first for the Cleveland Browns and then for the Miami Dolphins.

Other than that, people with last names like Tyler, Nicopolis, Mariano, Svenson, McCleod, Smith and Johnson all lived within a quarter to half-mile of one another.

◆ ◆ ◆

"The intel/recon squad has eight men attached. Later today, your squad, along with the radiomen and corpsmen, will transfer to CCN at Phu Bai FOB. Psy-ops and Fire-Team Rat Catcher will remain here.

"When you leave this tent, you are to gather all your personal belongings, and put them in special satchels that you will find in your hooch. By all, I mean everything and anything that will connect you as being an American.

That includes letters, trinkets, pictures, your ID cards, dog-tags. Anything and everything that foreign agents can connect you the United States! Failure to do so will end your career; not to mention a provide you a minimum of 10 years in solitary confinement.

"Starting a week ago, all of your outgoing and incoming mail will be censored. Your mailing address will be a post-office in San Francisco. Hence forth, official paperwork and communications will demonstrate that you are out to sea on various ships in the Seventh Fleet.

"Should you be killed or taken prisoner while in the bush, your family will be notified you are MIA, but your hometown newspaper will never get an acknowledgement that you ever existed.

"From this moment forward, your government will disavow any knowledge of your existence. Your military records have been cleansed. Assuming that you survive until the end of your enlistment or, better yet, until the end of the war, the cover story about your military life will have been fabricated and memorized by you, before you are allowed to receive your separation papers."

With that he paused, looked around the room that was now dead silent and, saw everyman there staring in his direction, not blinking and very trance-like.

"We also have four new bodies that have volunteered to join us. While not BUD/S graduates, they have extensive training in Special Operations. Each has a minimum of 13 months humping the bush with either Green Beret units or Marine Recon teams."

LTJG Sallie finished by introducing two radiomen and two corpsmen. Other things they learned that day included that occasionally, they would have other people joining their squads, possibly some combination of a corpsman, radio-operator, platoon officer, Vietnamese translator, or CIA field officer.

Upon hearing the words CIA Field Officer, all the enlisted men shared a quick 'aha' look. Even though they had guessed that Team 19 was under the direction of the

Central Intelligence Agency, this was the first confirmation from a Navy Officer.

The LTJG allowed them to digest the information before bringing them back to the many issues at hand. Frank Sallie began by reiterating that they had all been sworn to a lifetime of secrecy, re-emphasized the words lifetime and secrecy.

Lifetime meant 100 years from that day in January 1967 or untilled they died, whichever came first.

Secrecy meant you cannot tell another soul. No one in your current family, no one in your future family; no one included discussions with their fellow warriors in the other two squads.

Any violation of those orders, no matter how trite, would result in a court-martial for treason and imprisonment in solitary confinement for the remainder of their lives.

Why?

Because the Military Assistance Command - Vietnam was forbidden by the U.S. Congress to operate combat units beyond the borders of South Vietnam. That meant from that moment forward, they did not legally exist. (To wit, someone who violated their oath could quickly disappear).

To emphasize this point, he explained that they were so secret that only a handful of people in the CIA, the Joint Chiefs of Staff and the White House knew of their existence. Upon hearing this, everyone in the room sat tall – all the humor of the morning had vanished.

Then LCDR Jeff Wheeler got even more specific. Each man would affirm that they understood what they had been told, by individually repeating back, in their own words, what they had just heard. Each man stood and shared that should he be caught or killed, he understood that the U.S. government would disavow any knowledge that he existed.

Each of them further affirmed that they were aware that their current military jackets had been sent by private carrier to the Langley Headquarters in Virginia. Their individual service records would be cleaned, sanitized, and held until such time that the Central Intelligence Agency, in coordination with the Department of Defense, decided to make said information public. The amount of sanitation and the degree of information contained depended upon whether they were killed, or captured, and if they had returned to their forward operating base.

After the last person spoke, the tent became very still. Naturally, being the youngster of the group, Joe had to raise his hand with a question. Wheeler paused, stared at him, took a deep breath, and then, with a somber look across his face, nodded for him to continue.

"This is all well and good, sir, but what's the downside of volunteering?"

The tension was immediately replaced with laughter and several people threw empty, or nearly empty beer bottles at him. Kaffar reached over and smacked Joe hard on the back of the head.

When everyone settled down, Frank Sallie handed out the additional documents for their signatures. Each document was labeled Top Secret, Restricted, Limited Circulation. The contracts had been prepared with their names, rank, service numbers, place of birth, and social security numbers. Each man had to read and initial every paragraph, then place their signature at the bottom of each page.

When they had finished, Stevenson collected the documents and placed them in a large security envelope. Both the Recon and Psy-ops squads were dismissed, along with Stevenson, the two corpsmen and the radio operators.

All that remained were LCDR Jeffrey Wheeler, LTJG Frank Sallie, and the four-man fireteam: Petty Officer First Class Kaffar, Petty Officers Second Class Proctor and Tatge, and Petty Officer Third Class Joseph E. Tyler.

The fireteam squad remained sitting. Once again, tension began to build inside the tent slowly.

CHAPTER TWENTY-SEVEN
January - February 1967

Frank Sallie stood, then made individual eye contact with each of them, after which he somewhat leaned, but mostly half-sat, on the corner of LDCR Wheeler's desk. As Frank continued to look them over, LCDR Wheeler reached into the cooler, produced another six-pack of beer, and personally handed each person their own bottle. Once each had a fresh bottle, LTJG Sallie raised his bottle to present a toast. The four enlisted men, along with Jeff Wheeler, stood and formed a semi-circle in front of Frank Sallie and raised their bottles.

"Here's to Rat Catcher. May you never have to walk home."

After the men tapped their bottles together, LTJG Sallie asked everyone to grab a chair and form a circle. The officers sat opposite one another with two enlisted men to either side. Before he sat down, LCDR Wheeler went to the front of the tent, and Joe could see him talking to several Marines. Whatever he told them they nodded in the affirmative, and then their Sergeant began directing the others. Wheeler stepped back inside, nodded to Sallie, and took his seat.

Sallie began by saying there was another, unwritten Special Mission Order, for the ears of Rat Team only. They were not to discuss their missions, even with one another, anywhere on the camp. There were only two places where the discussion would be permitted - inside the LCDR tent when their senior officers were present or while they were in the bush on their mission.

The fireteam's covert CIA orchestrated missions were coded OP34-Alpha and came under the jurisdiction of Department of Defense's Operation Foot Boy. Each mission would come to them directly from the White House and personally sanctified by the President of the United States. Thus, the extraordinary sensitivity to keeping everything lipped.

The penalty for divulging sensitive information concerning their missions was life-imprisonment in solitary confinement within a military prison.

The top-line overview of each mission followed the same structure: There would be a meeting with the Field Officer, LCDR Wheeler, LTJG Sallie, and the Rat Catcher Team. Everyone in attendance had equal input on the general execution of the plan. Other than arranging the alternate pick-up locations, specific details would be finalized once Rat Catcher connected with the CIA Field Officer, who was always known as Mr. Jones.

Likewise, the Rat Catcher team members were CopperSun, Crossbow, Raider, and Cowboy.

Rat Catcher would escort the Field Officer to the coordinates, and, for security purposes, would do so without knowing the name of the nearby city. Likewise, the Vietnamese on the CIA payroll would not be aware that he, she, or they were about to be kidnapped by an American SEAL team.

Getting to the grab site could take anywhere from three to five days. Not because of the distance they had to walk; more because of the circuitous journey required to check and recheck everything happening within a designated radius of the individual snatch.

After understanding everything that they could about the ingress and egress, Kaffar would meet with the Field Officers, and together they would determine how the mission would go down.

The person or persons they were there to get out of North Vietnam were always called Grab 1, Grab 2, etc.

The exact routes to and from the target would initially be determined by Tyler, then approved by Kaffar. The Field Officer would review to point-out areas of concern. Once confirmed, all five individuals would determine the picks, and pops for their exit route.

(Picks were SOG slang for temporary sniper positions; Pops would be the explosives set by Proctor to eliminate anyone following them.)

Grab target abductions had a maximum four-minute-apprehension window and only occurred during moonless nights.

The physical grab would be directed by the CIA Field Officer and executed by Kaffar and Tatge. As soon as they exited, Proctor and Tyler would guarantee that the beginning of the escape route was free of both barking dogs and anyone who may have witnessed their departure. Once they had the target secured, the fireteam would escort the group to the Alpha pick-up point.

It was Tyler's job to get everyone to Alpha ahead of time. In coordination with their Air Force counterparts, they only had a fifteen-minute window at the exact spot. If the fireteam was not there, the Air Force helo would disappear from the area. Once missed, the fireteam immediately headed to the Bravo coordinates. A delay usually meant they had to not only stay in North Vietnam for another three days but also move further inland, in the opposite direction of any body of water and South Vietnam.

If the team and their guests missed the Bravo pick-up, the only alternative was to walk home South Vietnam and find an American outfit to get them back to Quang Tri. In the meantime, the Navy listed them as Missing in Action (MIA). If they were not back in thirty days, they were presumed dead; no further action would be taken to find them. After all, only their two senior officers knew they had even left the base camp. And even they did not know where they went.

There was only one of their missions that would be considered a failure. One of the Rat Catcher team members and the two grab targets failed to make it back to the rendezvous pick-up.

CHAPTER TWENTY-EIGHT
September 1967

Late in 1967, having already participated in four uneventful and successful CIA-sanctioned grabs, Rat Catcher had just successfully grabbed a two-member spy team, both medical doctors, in a town located 90-to-100 miles north of Quang Tri.

Several miles out of town, they came across four farmers about a half-an-hour before the sun had fully risen in the east. One of the two doctors said he knew one of the farmers, approached the group, and asked if he or his friends knew somewhere where the doctor and his friends could get something to eat.

Obviously, this came as a shock to Joe, Brenden, and the CIA officer. Fortunately, Tatge and Proctor were far enough back that they were able to take cover and not be seen.

The farmer was polite and asked them to come with him to his farmhouse. The doctors readily agreed and began walking with their friend. Caught completely off guard, Kaffar and Tyler could only accept, albeit with their collective intuitions on high alert. In the meantime, the other three farmers split-off, saying they had to go to their respective fields to tend to their cows.

As the three American reached the farm, Joe whispered to Kaffar that his intuition was super-active, and that they should be on high alert for danger. Kaffar easily agreed as by now, he was aware of his point-man's uncanny ability to predict things.

Before entering the farmhouse, Kaffar told Tyler to stand guard outside, while CIA agent, the two doctors, and Brenden followed the farmer inside. Before entering the house, Kaffar took the safety off his Stoner 63, chambered a round in the breech and unsnapped the SK22 pistol on his chest.

As the doctors and the farmers spoke to one another, Kaffar alerted the CIA agent. The American agent, armed only with Colt 45, nonchalantly unsnapped the holster.

Meanwhile, Tatge and Proctor stayed hidden in the trees away from the house. Tatge tried to keep his eyes on the other three farmers in their adjacent fields but found the effort to be virtually impossible. Proctor, as normal, kept his eyes out behind them. The last thought Jimmy would ever have, was that he should have set tripwires, just in case. At that same exact moment, a single rifle shot rang out from the farmhouse, and Proctor instinctively turned his head in the direction of the sound.

As he was doing so, another shot rang out from the opposite direction; but Jimmy never heard it.

About 25% of Proctor's skull flew off as the enemy's bullet struck the back corner of his head. Jimmy's body collapsed upon itself, blood and brain tissue flying in every direction.

Meanwhile, Tatge, who also turned toward the farmhouse when he heard the first shot, instinctively fell to the ground, facing Jimmy's position just as Jimmy's now lifeless body had collapsed to the ground.

Inside the farmhouse, three more shots rang out. One of the doctors, the one that that knew the farmer, was bent over, holding his left side. The other doctor fell to the floor in a fetal position. Kaffar got off two shots, and the CIA agent, one. The CIA agent's shot ended up high and into the wall, while both of Kaffar's rounds found their mark; the first in the farmer's heart, the second in the farmer's head.

Not knowing what happened inside the home, Joe threw his body prone against the lower part of an outside wall, pulled his SK22 pistol from the chest holster, and aimed it at the doorway.

Twenty seconds later, the CIA agent came out the door with his weapon drawn and, after taking several steps, dropped to one knee with his weapon pointed toward the tree-line a hundred yards away.

Kaffar came out thirty-seconds later, glanced at Joe lying against the house, nodded, turned back toward the door, and called to the doctors to leave the house. Brenden turned back to the woods and began moving quickly toward his left. In doing so, he told the CIA Agent to go right. In the meantime, the doctors left the house, each supporting one another.

Meanwhile, Tatge had arrived at the tree line. When he glanced over his shoulder, saw the doctor's leaving the farmhouse and moving in the opposite direction of his position. Tatge moved to his right, which placed him in a better, defensive position.

Tyler got up from the ground and ran at a full sprint to the tree to Tatge's left. Kaffar called to the CIA agent to follow him and bolted low and fast to Austin Tatge's right.

Once Kaffar and the agent reached the trees, he told him the agent to lay flat on the tree roots, point his pistol straight ahead, but not to fire his weapon unless one of the Special Ops team told him to.

Six North Vietnamese men who were obviously untrained militia began jumping sideways from tree to tree as they advanced toward the American team. The three SEALS waited for just the right moment and then, following Kaffar's first shot, Tyler and Tatge squeezed off two rounds each.

All six American bullets hit their intended human targets. Each SEAL put had put one round into the heart of two different militia. After the all six of the militiamen fell, the CIA Field Agent fired off a round in the general direction of one of the now-dead wannabe North Vietnam soldiers.

Kaffar looked down at the agent, a question-marked stare covering his face. Then said: "You'd be better off saving your ammunition."

Kaffar, Tatge, Tyler, and the CIA Agent gathered to figure out their options.

Brendan, as the team leader, began asking the questions.

"Tyler. What are our options to get to Alpha?" "The closest route would be 9 miles to the southwest. That would take us directly over top of the hill west of us, passing a few farms and skirting two villages."

Joe Tyler paused and looked at his watch. "We have six hours and seven minutes."

"If it were just the three of us, I'd say we had enough time to stop for dinner," Tatge chimed in sarcastically. After a short pause, he added, "One: We've gotta get Jimmy home. Second, we have two civilians that are injured, one seriously. And C, ain't no way Mr. Spook here is going to be able to keep up."

When Austin finished stating the obvious, the other two members of the Rat Catcher team nodded in agreement, their minds racing with the alternatives.

Kaffar again looked at Tyler. "Bravo?"

Tyler sat back, closed his eyes, and did some calculations.

"Twenty-seven to thirty miles. Fifty-two-hour window."

Kaffar spoke-up again, "If we miss both pick-ups, I'm guessing 88-100 miles to the FOB?"

"Sounds about right," Tyler confirmed while remembering the geography between their current position and Quang Tri.

"Probably add another 12-15 miles considering all the villages, towns, unknown NVA bases, camps, and patrols that we would have to skirt."

Never one to be left out, Tatge offered another bit of advice, "At least they won't be expecting us at the base, so we won't have to explain why we were AWOL."

The CIA Field Agent excused himself to go the farmhouse and talk to the doctors. When he left, the remaining three members of Rat Catcher walked over to where Jimmy Proctor's body was lying. They used his shirt to cover what remained of his head. Kaffar positioned the body over his shoulders in a fireman's carry, and the three of them made their way back to the farmhouse.

As they reached the doorway, the CIA Agent and the two doctors were coming out. Brendan Kaffar eased Jimmy's body against the side of the house, and the six men stood off to the side in a loose circle.

The CIA Agent spoke-up, "Both the doctors are injured and need medical attention. There is no way they can walk any real distance. There is a small town about two "klicks" east of here. I'll escort them to the edge of the town."

"And what about you?" Kaffar asked.

"I'm good," he replied matter-of-factly. "I've spent most of the last six years taking care of myself over here. I think I'm good for another week or so. Once I get to the coast, I'm golden."

Everyone shook hands, and then the CIA Agent and the doctors turned to the east and set off.

The unwritten creed of the Special Operation warrior, whether it be working underwater as a frogman or as member of a SEAL team was "No man left behind."

The fireteam set-off in the direction of the pickup area. They took turns carrying Jimmy's body, switching off every 30 minutes; each man proud that they adhered to the Navy Frogman's creed. Jimmy was much more than a fellow member of Rat Catcher. In every way possible, he was their brother.

In the end, the three surviving frogmen took 30-minute shifts of carrying Jimmy Proctor's body nearly 20 miles to the Bravo pickup point. By skirting the Alpha pick-up, they arrived a full day before the Air Force bird was scheduled to arrive.

On the last day, the bird and its small crew arrived precisely on time. Tatge was the first man aboard the aircraft and advised the Air Force crew of Proctor's body needing a stretcher.

The pilot lifted away from the pick-up zone, did a 360 of the pickup area's surroundings to look for any enemy movement. When he felt certain that there were no enemy soldiers nearby, he went back to the pick-up point, hovered at tree-top level, and dropped the basket along with a black body bag. Tyler and Kaffar quickly zipped Jimmy's body into the bag, strapped him onto the bucket and signaled the helicopter that was steadily hovering above them.

As the basket was pulled upward, Tyler hand signaled the crew that he and Kaffar were changing positions as hovering a noisy American helicopter for any length of time, especially behind enemy lines, was extremely dangerous.

Through use of hand signals, the pilot and Kaffar agreed to meet 300 yards to the south in 30 minutes. The door gunner gave a thumbs up, told his pilot who slowly began to gain altitude. Once the body was on board, the pilot banked the bird into a 180-degree turn as he continued to gain altitude.

The two remaining frogmen gathered their gear, policed the area, and then headed off in a 90-degree angle to where they were next headed. Tyler led, followed by Kaffar. Tatge did his best to keep visual tabs on them from the helicopter.

About 120 yards down the hill, Tyler stopped and stood inside thick foliage that was on his right. Within 30 seconds Kaffar stood alongside him, but purposely facing in the opposite direction.

Technically, Kaffar was in charge. In reality, he would have followed his point man anywhere, trusting him implicitly to get them precisely when they needed to be there.

Once again, Kaffar's trust was well-founded. At precisely the right time, the Air Force Bird came overhead at tree-top level and dropped a rope ladder that drug across the ground. Tyler broke from the dense underbrush, grabbed hold of the rope, and began to scramble upward. Not more than 30 seconds later, Kaffar quickly followed his actions.

In 2015, with help from the Department of Defense, Joe Tyler was able to review several CIA documents that memorialized the many different clandestine efforts that occurred under the Operation Footboy umbrella. On two pages of the 750 pages document, Joe Tyler found the CIA accounting of the only failed Snatch and Grab mission in 1967.

At the end of the review, it noted that the two doctors were subsequently captured by North Vietnamese Rangers who had been assigned to find and eliminate them. Both men were tortured for over a year before being finally executed.

CHAPTER TWENTY-NINE
February 1968

February 1968 became the month when the SEAL slogan: "Yesterday Was Easy" took on a new, accelerated and extremely intense meaning.

This was when the NVA launched the now infamous Tet Offensive of 1968. The Tet Offensive was so named because it began on the Tet Holiday, the Vietnamese New Year. Forces from the Viet Cong and North Vietnam Army launched a series of surprise attacks against military and civilian targets throughout I and II Corps Tactical Zones of South Vietnam during the late hours of January 30, 1968.

The powers-that-be in Saigon did not understand the need to accelerate defensive measures throughout South Vietnam immediately. The next morning, things really picked up as over 80,000 NVA, and VC soldiers began attacking more than 100 towns throughout most of South Vietnam, including several dozen provincial capitals, among them Saigon, Hue, and others.

Because the military leaders never believed the reports from the SEAL recon teams, nor similar stories from the Army 101st Airborne recon teams, the attacks caught the embedded American, South Korean, Australian, and South Vietnamese armies off guard.

During the Battle of Hue, intense, around-the-clock fighting lasted for a month. During this time, the NVA took control of the city, rounded up several thousand people, and executed them. The city and its ancient relics ended up in ruins. A lot of the destruction was at the direction of the NVA. However, most of the damage was caused by American Marines trying to get significant strategic positions back under allied control.

It was during the 1968 Tet Offensive that Joe earned his Purple Heart and a nightmare he eventually called "The Hotel," that remained with him most of his life.

A week into the Tet assault on the capital city of Hue, Lt. Sallie said volunteered SOG Team 19 to make some runs to Hue, which was about 30 miles away. With the consistently bad weather throughout the entire region and the Capital City of Hue surrounded by several thousand NVA soldiers, the Marines desperately needed supplies and getting their wounded out to the hospital ship USS Hope.

"By the way," Sallie added, "at least half the bridges they would pass under were controlled by the Viet Cong. The other half have been destroyed by American bombers. Therefore, as they made their way down the Perfume River toward Hue, everyone should be on the lookout for submerged pieces and parts that could rip their boats to shreds.

"One last point: once they reach the MACV compound at Hue, everyone should be on full alert that both sides of the river were controlled by the North Vietnamese Army."

He ended by asking, what could possibly go wrong?
Their answer? "Hooyah!"

The men topped their fuel tanks then overloaded their boats with 50- and 35-caliber ammunition. The plan was for the boats to dock alongside supply ships that were anchored miles off the coast, race the 17 miles of Perfume River, dock outside the MACV Compound, unload their supplies, pick up wounded Marines and ferry them to the hospital ship, USS Hope which was also anchored off the coast.

Once the wounded were on board the hospital ship, the boats would return to the supply ship and then do everything all over again. It was not long before they were back on the Perfume River, their gunboats looking like overloaded kayaks with weapons sticking out at every angle.

The Alpha boat, with LTJG Sallie, took the Delta boat a hundred yards behind them. For most of the run, they would travel at half-throttle, about 18 miles per hour. This would enable their front gunner, in this case, Tatge, to sit high on the back part of his turret to look for objects in the water that they needed to avoid.

His signals to the coxswain were simple. If he pointed right, the coxswain turned the boat to the right and continued their journey. If he pointed left, he cut to the left. Very scientific.

As they began the first half of their journey toward Hue, everything seemed normal enough, including the occasional potshot that always missed by several dozen yards. What was missing were the kids playing by the riverbanks, the women doing laundry and the merchandise laden sampans boat traffic clogging up the center of the river. The smell from the beautiful flowers that lined the riverbanks contrasted sharply with the occasional whiff of military grade cordite.

They passed under bridges that were obviously under enemy control as they could plainly see the Viet Cong machine gun placements at either end. Each man prepared to do battle only to be disappointed. After a few of their trips, the SEALs would sometimes taunt them by waving at them. Joe swore one VC waved back.

Miraculously, no one fired a shot at them the entire way to the MACV compound in Hue and back. To be sure, the boats did indeed encounter enemy fighters. The closer they got to Hue, the more fighting and heard a tremendous amount of gunfire, explosions, M80s, and artillery from both sides of the battle.

All the Team 19 men could figure out was that the VC had not expected them to run the rivers in the rain. On their third trip to Hue, both boats pulled up to the MACV boat ramp.

LTJG Sallie ordered the nearby Marines to clear the supplies and the SEAL crews to secure the gunboat's weapons. Once done, Sallie told them to follow him to the MACV compound, which was typically reserved for officers. Inside the war-room, the SEALs got a firsthand look at how bad the situation surrounding them was.

Despite its importance and size, Hue had relatively few defenders within its limits. On the Eve of Tet, the greater metropolitan area contained fewer than a thousand South Vietnamese troops on active duty. Most of these troops were on holiday leave with their families to celebrate Tet, either at nearby homes within the city or in one of the neighboring districts.

The headquarters of the South Vietnamese 1st Infantry Division made its home in the Mang Ca compound, a mini fortress that occupied the northern corner of the Citadel. Apart from the MACV headquarters staff and a handful of support people, the only combat units in the Citadel were South Vietnams 36-man Reconnaissance Platoon and their elite Black Panther Company.

The American military presence in the city was minimal, about 200 troops. Approximately 100 U.S. Army advisers and administrative personnel, as well as a few Marine guards, were headquartered in a lightly defended compound, two blocks south of the Perfume River. A small detachment of regular U.S. Navy personnel was stationed at the MACV-SOG compound where LTJG Sallie had just arrived.

The War Room at the MACV compound had a map that showed where the various enemy forces had attacked every side of the Citadel and Triangle. At this point, the NVA controlled most of the metropolitan area. Due to bad weather and the continuing attacks going on everywhere in South Vietnam, the prospects for getting reinforcements, supplies, and ammunition to support the relatively small group of American and ARVN soldiers did not look good.

The Navy's part was going to be especially vital if the weather continued to be low-hanging clouds and plenty of rain. Their ships were gathering at the eastern point where the Perfume River emptied into the Gulf of Tonkin. They were loaded with everything from rifles, machine guns, and ammunition to light artillery, armored personnel carriers and even a couple of tanks. In addition, there was plenty of food to go along with much needed medical supplies and equipment.

Riverine personnel and equipment were a rare commodity, but the boat crews were volunteering as often as they could. Tugboats and barges were also employed, but carried little, if any, weaponry to defend themselves. In addition to their runs up and down the river with wounded soldiers and small portions of supplies, their boats would escort the barges and tugs to the Citadel and Triangle areas.

For the next couple of weeks, their platoon ran up and down the rivers with as many trips as their ammunition, gas and minimal amounts of sleep would allow.

It was always a mystery as to where and when they would encounter the NVA or VC. One day a section of the river would be held by friendly troops, the next day by enemy forces. At other times one side of the river was friendly and the other side held by the NVA.

The bridges were the most frightening part. When they were held by the NVA, it meant they had to get support from friendly forces or run under the bridges while they fired directly at them from above. Whenever possible, their Seawolves helicopters would be there to make swooping runs at the bridges to scatter the bad guys. Because they could not use their rockets for fear of destroying the structures that would soon be needed by the good guys. That meant these birds had to fly in with minimal stationary machine guns and some super-brave door gunners hanging out of each side, sans any type of protection from incoming rounds.

When they got to Hue, one or two of them would make their way through the various hot combat zones to a medevac area renamed Hell Zone. Whenever there was the tiniest break in the weather, the medevac helicopter teams would risk their own lives to load injured soldiers and carry them to safe medical sites.

Sometimes Joe, or another squad member, would escort their corpsman and the walking wounded to their boat. Other times, the Marines would load up the injured on a half-track or armored personnel carrier, and together, they would fight their way back to the boat.

Whenever Joe's turn came up, he mostly carried a Stoner 60 lite machine gun. Every trip, he effortlessly went through the 200-round clip by the time he made it back to the boat. On February 22, about 11:00 in the morning, Joe's luck dodging enemy bullets to help evacuate the wounded, ran out.

After three weeks of fighting, reinforcements had arrived to support the Marines. Because of the rapid changes in retreating enemy soldiers, Joe had to take a different route to

Hell Zone. The enemy soldiers who remained in the area were holed up in various buildings, popping up every so often to take quick shots at American and South Vietnamese Marines. After firing a few rounds, the NVA soldiers would disappear only to reappear several minutes later from another window, or even another building.

Joe took one last look around, and even though there was the usual amount of combat going on, he made a dash to the safety of the bunkers. About halfway across, something akin to a two-by-four piece of lumber hit his upper back and slammed him to the ground. Just as Joe was hit, his beloved Stoner carbine flew from his grip and was then hit by another rifle round, destroying the weapon.

CHAPTER THIRTY
February 22, 1968

As Joe lay there stunned, his immediate thought was "Did someone hit me in the back with a two-by-four?"

He laid still for several minutes as he struggled to clear both is brain and his eyes. As his mind began to clear, Joe realized that his mouth was full of dirt and mud. As he lifted his face out of the muck, several rounds from an enemy machine gun hit the ground around him. The Marines returned a huge volley in the general direction of the enemy position.

His mind suddenly cleared, and the cacophony of war returned. Because he remained wearing the flak-vest from the gunboat, the searing pain in his upper, left shoulder surprised him. Slowly, trying not to draw too much attention, Joe reached over the back of his neck with his right hand, feeling along the upper rim of the vest. Just a few inches left of his spine, he felt something warm and wet.

He brought his bloodied hand near his face and, somewhat mesmerized, stared at it for a second or so. He had two thoughts. First, he had to admit that he had been hit. Second, he needed to find out if there was an exit hole in his upper chest cavity.

Without wanting to move too fast and draw additional attention to himself, he brought his right hand and slid-it between the ground and the front of his body.

Good news - no blood.

From Joe's experience in combat, he guessed that he had been hit by a ricochet; a bullet from a machine gun would, at the very least, gone through and through. And more than likely would have ripped his entire shoulder off.

In addition to the wound in his back, when he got hit by what-ever-it-was, he landed face-first into the sand and rocks, Joe cut his lip open and had blood flowing slowly from his nose. That brought back memories of one of the no-so-friendly fights he had as a kid at Quinby Park. And like those school-boy altercations, whatever hit him really made him mad and wanting to get even.

Slowly, Joe turned his head and looked behind him, to his right and then slowly turned his head to the left. The building where the shot came from stood about 45 yards behind him and to his right.

Wondering what he should do next, Joe raised his head toward the nearest medevac bunker and realized it was four times further away than the building behind him. He also figured he would be a harder target to hit by running directly under the machine gun placement.

He took another deep breath, raised his head, and looked forward, toward Marine emplacement. A Marine Sergeant got his attention, pointed to the building behind Joe, held up three fingers, and then pointed upward. Joe assumed that he meant the shots that were occasionally hitting all around him were fired from the third floor of that building.

Not caring about his movements any further, he got to his hands and knees, and shook the stars from his head. Crouching, he feigned one step toward the Americans, did a one-eighty, and ran as fast as he could to the building behind him. Remarkably, none of the enemy soldiers that had been firing at them seemed took an interest in him.

Joe retrieved the Hushpuppy from his chest holster and began sliding along the poured-concrete wall, searching for an opening adjacent to a stairway. He moved slowly and cautiously, stopping to check his surroundings every third or fourth step.

As he moved along the building, two thoughts bothered him: First, that some reckless, hyped up Marine private would mistake him for an enemy soldier and unload his M-1 in his direction. Second, he would pass out from loss of blood.

Joe found his opening and easily made it up the three flights of stairs. Before reaching the top steps on the third floor, he crouched and listened. Hearing nothing, he walked with his back along the wall, the flak jacket started rubbing the wound on his back, so he took it off.

He consciously wished he was in the bush, instead of a city, as this kind of combat sucked.

He eased along the wall, stopping every few steps to listen. Every door along the hallway was missing, as were all the windows. For that matter, about a quarter of the walls were missing, too.

As he approached each doorway, he would stop for two minutes to listen for movement, voices, or the sound of weapons being readied. The first four doorways were quiet, and he pushed by them quickly, his MK22 sweeping the empty rooms.

As he approached the fifth door, he heard the rapid, whiny, high pitched cadence of Vietnamese voices. At least two people were talking and not making any effort to keep their voices low. Joe rechecked that he had a round chambered in his pistol and the safety was off. Quickly, he jumped through the doorway, his back against the closest wall, both body and weapon at a 45-degree angle to his targets.

It was immediately apparent that his entry into their hideaway completely surprised them. The three NVA soldiers spun around, surprised looks covering each of their faces. Their surprise was quickly replaced with confusion, and then terror, as collectively they stared at the end of the pistol barrel in his right hand.

Anger manifested itself into Joe's whole being: He knew one of these three men had just tried to kill him. His anger intensified and raised the adrenaline rush developing throughout his body. For Joe, the rush, as always, caused everything to move in slow motion.

Joe's rage escalated to hate. His mind called out for the revenge of JJ's death and an incessant need to balance the score for Jimmy Proctor being killed.

The three Vietnamese men in front of him were frozen with fear. To Joe's mind, their dark eyes began to glow, each fearing their death was at hand: Each man understood that they were about to die.

The only thought in running through Joe's mind was that this was going to be the biggest adrenaline rush of his life: Joe was going to be the last human being they would ever see in their miserable lifetime.

He did not want to just kill enemy soldiers: This time, he wanted to execute them.

It took several seconds to complete the deed. Joe took his time, looked into each person's eyes, felt their fear, then slowly squeezed the trigger. With great anticipation, he witnessed a neat, circular hole form in each man's forehead.

One. Pause.

Two.

Pause.

Now you, you lousy bastard! Three.

Pause.

Joe stood over the collapsed bundle of bodies. He lowered the pistol and emptied the remaining contents of the pistol's clip into the bodies before him.

And then exhaustion began to overcome every other emotion. Emotionally drained and realizing that the loss of blood was going to cause him to black-out, Joe staggered the two or three steps necessary to lean his back into a corner of the room.

Feeling his strength slipping away, Joe leaned back and wedged himself into the corner in a kind of worthless defensive posture. Despite his best efforts, his legs weakened, and his torso slowly began to slide downward. Gradually, even somewhat gracefully, he slid down to his butt, leaving a blood-stained streak on the wall behind him.

With his last bit of will power, Joe brought his knees toward his chest. He rested his hand holding the pistol with the emptied clip at the lifeless bodies before him.

The now-empty Mk22 remained locked in his right hand. Both arms laid resting over his knees; his left hand was trying hard to support his right wrist. His breathing became heavy and labored; his body feeling like he had just finished a ten-mile run in the surf at Coronado.

He felt no pity for the dead people lying across the bullet-riddled, dusty room.

What he did feel was utter exhaustion.

Slowly, it became completely apparent that he was tired of fighting.

Tired of hunting for downed pilots.

Tired of having North Vietnam professional trackers trying to kill him after each CIA spy snatch, like they did to Jimmy Proctor.

Joe's effort of hold the weight of his head become too much of a struggle.

Mumbling incoherently to himself, he lowered his head onto his arms, allowed himself to drop his beloved Hushpuppy and slowly, easily drift off to sleep.

His last thought before becoming unconscious was: "Please Lord, just let everything stop. Right. Here. Right. Now......"

CHAPTER THIRTY-ONE
March 1968

Joe stayed in the Quang Tri medical area for four days before rejoining his fireteam. Once released from the medical care unit, Joe Tyler was given another week to recuperate. This meant he hung around the LT's tent with Frank Sallie and their new second in command, LTJG Daniel Sisler.

When Joe shook hands with Frank Sallie, he noticed that he was wearing Lieutenant bars. He congratulated his new LT, promotion. Lt. Sallie in return, commended Joe on his new rank of Petty Officer Second Class.

Joe thanked him but added that he did not remember taking his E-5 exam. Frank Sallie smiled and said Joe had to have taken it because the citation said he scored 100%. They both began to laugh, and Joe again thanked him for his support.

One day while Joe sat next to the command radio listening to battles going on all over northern South Vietnam, Lt. Sallie called him into his office. Frank told him that because he had more than 13 months in-country, he should expect transfer orders soon to another duty station. Where he was headed, no one knew.

Objecting was futile as the Navy could care less about what Joe wanted.

What he did not want was to get transferred out of MACV-SOG. So, he put in a request asking that he serve another 13 months in-country. To his surprise, LT Sallie turned him down.

At first, Joe was upset but, after talking it over with Frank Sallie, they concluded that he needed to approach the request from a different angle. So, he put in another request chit, this time asking to be reassigned to a different position within MACV-SOG, possibly in one of the three South Vietnam Command Centers. His requested that he be permitted to stay with MACV in a non-direct combatant position until mid-January 1969, thus providing enough time in-country that he be credited with a second combat tour.

After talking about it with Lt. Sallie, he recommended Joe ask for an enlisted liaison position and that he explicitly not be reassigned to another Special Ops Platoon.

Joe added that a second tour would provide him leverage for a better billet when he left the MACV. One thing that did bother Lt. Sallie was Joe's revenge-oriented side trip in Hue. Wanting revenge went against the grain of their training. He did not talk to Joe about it but started making inquiries with his peers to see what non-direct combat positions might be available.

Frank Sallie reminded Joe that the MACV headquarters had plenty of other things to deal with; therefore, it would be a while before they let them know.

Until they heard anything, Frank suggested Joe got off his lazy butt and got back to earning the extra $50 a month combat pay that the benevolent U.S. Navy was generously paying him.

"And remember, you are officially NOT a short-timer," Solley yelled to Joe as he left his tent. That news caused Joe to perk-up and wear a smile going back to his hooch. Not being a designated short timer was huge in Vietnam combat vernacular.

Being "short" was like wearing a big target on your back. Each man in Vietnam knew someone that made it through nearly 13 months of surviving in the abyss, then killed within the final couple weeks or days of being rotated out. Some guys would plead to stay in camp, preferably in an underground bunker, until they got "short enough to slide under a dime."

Other platoon members would avoid being anywhere near a short timer; afraid they would get killed by mistake if Charlie missed his designated target.

There was another phobia about getting killed: the dreaded "threes." Remembering what the gruff old boatswain's mate who did not care what his name was or where he was from when Joe jumped aboard Swift boat?

Basically, every man in Vietnam took it as gospel that as a newbie, the odds were high that you would get killed on your third day in-country, or within the third week, or that you would most certainly be in a black body bag by the end of the third month. Surviving "the threes" meant the odds were in your favor to survive the next 10 months. When you got your rotation-out date, you officially became short. As a short timer, your chances of getting killed rose exponentially. That is why Joe was smiling when he left the LT's tent.

What no warrior could conceive of then, was that for most of them, going home was when the real torment began.

A week later, Lt. Sallie called him into his tent.

"Good news. You got your transfer."

Joe pulled the orders from the envelope, looked at them, and then looked up at Sallie.

"Where's Phan Thiet?" "South of Cam Ranh, the bottom of II Corps."

CHAPTER THIRTY-TWO
April 1968

A week later, in mid-afternoon, Joe found himself walking down the back ramp of a Chinook helicopter at Landing Zone (LZ) Betty, a large airfield and military base built on a plateau that overlooked a large fishing bay. In the northwest corner of the bay, and a few miles north of the base was the city of Phan Thiet. He threw his empty sea bag over his left shoulder and made his way to the MACV-SOG compound.

Like Hue, but unlike Quang Tri, LZ Betty was itself a small city with several dozen permanent buildings. The fortifications and overall feel of the place indicated high security. While the VC would occasionally fire rockets into the base, attempting an actual full-scale assault would take several thousand men, artillery, and supportive air power. Which, by the way, is what the NVA attempted during Tet.

After making his way to the Commander's office, he handed the yeoman his orders. The yeoman was dressed in Navy dungarees and chambray shirt, both of which had recently been cleaned, starched, and pressed! His deck boots were polished; the toes of each boot sported mirror-like finishes. His pristine, starched, enlisted-man's white hat sat on top of a corner cabinet.

What the hell? What happened to his war?

In complete contrast, Joe wore ragged blue jeans, black, worn-out Converse tennis shoes, an oil-stained, Army-issued tee-shirt, topped by his ever-present camo-bandana, that had seen better days.

He could not remember the last time a real barber had cut his hair.

And yes, he wore both K-bars, one belted behind his right hip, the other strapped to his right calf. The Mk22 Hushpuppy with silencer attached, rested in his makeshift chest holster.

Prissy, (as Joe referred to him) after reading where Petty Officer Second Class Joseph E. Tyler was to report forthwith to Prissy's boss, LCDR Jack Gallagher, outwardly showed his disapproval. Prissy, (as Joe referred to him) reviewed Joe's orders and reading where he was to report forthwith to Prissy's boss, LCDR Jack Gallagher, outwardly showed his disapproval.

With Joe's apparent disregard for hygiene and wearing proper Navy apparel, Prissy reluctantly asked him to take a seat while he updated his documentation and prepared a neat little folder with his name on it.

If Joe had not been enjoying Prissy's discomfort and attitude so much, he might have broken his bony fingers as he hit the keys on his typewriter. Instead, he remained standing in front of his gray metal desk, staring, and smirking at him.

"Lieutenant Commander Jack Gallagher won't be back until tomorrow morning," he said without looking up. You're assigned to building Sierra Oscar One."

While remaining seated, Prissy turned, looked out a window and held Joe's paperwork up in the air for Joe to take. After Joe stood and stared at him for a several seconds, Prissy threw-out, "I assume you're qualified to find it on your own."

He did. Joe also found an empty bunk, threw his gear on it, then headed to the supply depot to draw out fresh, Navy-issued t-shirts, underwear, and socks. As soon as he returned to the barracks, he took his first hot shower in several months. Afterward, feeling clean and wearing new underwear, not to mention a complete set of new tiger-stripes, he found the chow hall.

Before going in, he stopped and got a real haircut, which took two, maybe three minutes.

"Will that be close, really close or peach fuzz?" Got to love military barbers.

The next morning, he went back to the MACV compound, groomed, dressed in newly acquired tiger stripes and carried his carefully folded, new 27 by 27-inch bandana in his left hand.

Petty Officer Mr. Prissy glanced at him; he may have even gestured his approval, but Joe could not be sure.

He told Joe that the XO was in a meeting and he was to sit and wait. XO was short for Executive Officer, which made him the second-highest ranked officer in the Compound. Joe thought it strange that he would be meeting with someone of such high rank.

While sitting there, it also occurred to Joe that because Prissy was stationed in South Vietnam, he got paid the same $55 a month as Joe for being in a combat zone.

After the Lieutenant Commander's meeting ended, Prissy instructed him to go in. Joe had a sudden flashback of being called to the Captain's wardroom aboard the USS Henderson. Except now, he was 20 years old, had 18 months of combat behind him, had killed more people than he remembered, and had not truly smiled in two years; not to mention he had a bad attitude and a permanent chip on his shoulder.

Jack Gallagher stood, and Joe was immediately impressed. Like Prissy, his uniform was neatly starched. Unlike Prissy, he was six feet, well-muscled, neatly trimmed military haircut, and wore a gold Underwater Demolition Badge over his left breast pocket.

"Petty Officer Tyler," Gallagher said coming around his desk to shake his hand. "Jack Gallagher. Welcome aboard. Relax, sit down. Water, Coke, beer?"

"With all your experience, I expected someone older," Gallagher said after Prissy delivered two cans of ice-cold Coke, then strutted out of the office. Gallagher looked again through his paperwork, reread Joe's birth date, and shrugged his massive shoulders.

"No, I just didn't read the birth year," he added. "You're 20."

"Before Quang Tri, I used to get asked my age every other week, sir," he replied.

Gallagher gave him a nod. "Well, now you look 20. Living in the bush changes everyone. Combat changes your attitude and view of all life in general. Your whole demeanor changes, along with the addition of that thousand-yard glare you are wearing but trying to hide.

"Your Lieutenant called looking for a slot for you. I have known Sallie for several years and was impressed with what Frank had to say. Getting high praise from him is rare. After reading your jacket, I knew you would fit in with what I needed.

"I was most impressed to read you were personally hand-chosen, fresh out of Boot, by Jeffrey Wheeler. Whatever you said and did talking to the shrinks, it must have impressed the hell out of him."

Upon hearing that, Joe's mind raced as he never recalled meeting Wheeler before Cavite. Then he remembered the exam rooms each had a two-way mirror on one wall. He always assumed that other doctor were the only people behind them. He made a mental note to ask Master Chief Glenn when he got back to the States.

Gallagher finished their meeting by talking about his need for a fourth guy as part of a liaison squad. He would be embedded with three Green Berets. They would be training and acting as advisors for an ARVN Special Operations team near Cat Tien, which was southwest of Phan Thiet. For the most part, they would be living off the land, which meant his

24 hours of enjoying the Good Life was about to come to an end.

Before they finished talking, LCDR Gallagher asked to see the Smith and Wesson MK22 on Joe's chest. Joe removed it from the holster, dropped the clip, and discharged the 9mm round from the chamber.

"What is this?" Gallagher grinned like he had just handed him the Royal Crown of Scotland. He knew exactly what the weapon was but had never held one in his hands. He tested the weight and balance, then unscrewed the suppressor.

Once removed, he frowned a bit at the shorter barrel length and raised sights created an unbalanced, seven-and-a-half-inch weapon. He looked at Joe, quizzically.

"Hushpuppy."

"Hushpuppy," Jack Gallagher echoed and smiled again.

"I suppose they had to raise the sights to see over the silencer. The shortened barrel probably helps reduce the noise. What are you using?"

"Nine-by-nineteens, but, because of the four-inch barrel, the FPS (feet per second) is limited to 995. Accuracy is limited with the silencer and non-existent without."

"Wish I could have you around for a week so we could talk shop," Gallagher said with a twinge of regret in his voice, "but then again Tango Charlie (Team California)

284

needed you a week ago. By the way, the team of advisors you're joining are all seasoned Army Special Forces."

With that, he came around his desk, put his big meat paw on Joe's shoulder, and walked him passed Prissy and down the hallway.

"The war is a little different where you're headed than what you had up north, but I have no doubt you'll adapt quickly. Gather whatever gear you'll need in the bush and meet me at my bird in an hour."

They shook hands and went on their separate ways. On Joe's way back to the barracks, he stopped by the supply tent and got another six pair of socks, and two then walked over to the armory, showed them his credentials, and requisitioned a Stoner 63A light machine gun.

Once back at barracks, Joe broke down and thoroughly cleaned and oiled the new weapon. Afterward, he took another long, hot shower, packed his gear, and went to the helo pad to meet with LCDR Gallagher.

When he arrived at Helo-port, the pilot came out, said Gallagher could not make it but he would take him to the Green Beret base.

Team California was camped-out in the hills, a dozen miles northeast of Cat Tien. Meeting with his new partners was refreshing; five seasoned, Army Green Berets. Joe could tell they were experts from their initial handshakes. All three were on their second, 13-month tour in-country and reminded him of the Army Special Forces guys he worked within Cavite.

Joe was not real sure what to expect, but these men were impressive.

While he had been on snatch and grabs or some SAR adventure, these five had spent the last four months living in the bush and training a platoon of 22 ARVN Special Forces. The Vietnamese national special forces guys were well-armed, from M16s to rocket-propelled grenades, and very well trained. They were true patriots and, from what Joe gathered, most had lost part or all their family to the Viet Cong.

Their life in the bush had only one goal. It was what his former Team 19 bothers referred to as General Mission Order Number 6: Find the enemy. Kill the enemy. Come back alive.

Their previous point man, also a Green Beret, had been killed a month ago when one of his trainees snapped a tripwire on a VC boobie-trap. The wire was connected to double grenades that sat on opposite sides of the trial. The ARVN and the Green Beret were killed instantly.

From their initial gratitude of having him there, plus the apparent warm friendship between the ARVN's and their Army trainers made happy and willing to share his knowledge with them. They always stayed out in the hills with them for a month, taking a slow, winding route back toward Phan Thiet.

They had a group of soldiers from the elite South Korean Tiger Division join them for a week or 10 days. As a Navy SEAL, Joe always felt he was one of the warriors at the top of the food chain.

Admittedly, the Korean Tigers were a bit on the scary side. A couple of them wore long leather necklaces around their necks, made from human ears - souvenirs from various nightly missions.

CHAPTER THIRTY-THREE
August 1968

In mid-August, they separated from the ARVN and began hitching rides with convoys back to LZ Betty. Eventually, as the truck convoy approached the coastline turn-off near Xã Thuần Quy, the American advisors were told to depart the convoy. They were 12 miles south of the base, and when they called for a helo pick-up, they were informed that the entire area between their current position and LZ Betty was hot; meaning that enemy activity was extremely active, and all available helicopters were high demand.

The Green Beret First Sergeant thought about it for a brief second than decided it would be easier, safer, and quicker simply to walk back. Because they were close to the ocean, if they followed the shoreline north there would be a lower probability of running into enemy units.

A couple of hours into their hike North, a firefight broke out a few hundred yards ahead of them. Almost immediately they heard the launching of Viet Cong M30 mortar rounds. They closed in near the tree line and hurriedly moved toward the activity. As they progressed, the men first heard and then saw several more rounds explode just inside the dense foliage ahead of them.

When they got less than a quarter mile away, they saw that a squad of Marines had managed to get themselves pinned down ahead of them. Two Green Berets split to the south and west of the Marine platoon to set up a flanking position. The Sergeant and the radioman moved into the center of the Marine platoon to help direct the counterattack. Meanwhile, Joe and the last Green Beret followed the edge of the jungle and moved into a flanking position on the east side of the attack.

Joe, along with his Green Beret counterpart, had no sooner established a strong offensive position when a black-pajamaed VC soldier suddenly broke from the dense jungle underbrush. The enemy soldier began running hard away from the American's location and appeared to be carrying several mortar rounds against his chest.

Pushing the Stoner 63 tight against his shoulder, Joe centered the gun's sights between the shoulder blades of the fleeing figure. Slowing his breathing, he gently squeezed the trigger. Twice. The first bullet struck the enemy soldier in the back of the neck, precisely where the spinal cord and brain attached; the Viet Cong's body momentarily locked in an upright position. A quarter-second later, Joe's second-round penetrated the middle of the enemy soldier's back, causing the now lifeless body to tumble into the sandy beach.

A few minutes, with the assistance of a Navy destroyer's four cannons, the enemy attack came to a quick conclusion. The warship's first barrage dissipated the Viet Cong's central assault. Any enemy soldiers not killed or severely wounded, quickly disappeared into the hillside.

Once the all-clear signal sounded, he cautiously walked down the white sandy beach to secure the enemy mortar rounds. Holding his pistol in his right hand, he slowly approached the enemy soldier's body.

Because his first-round had entered at the back of the soldier's skull, Joe assumed that the VC's facial features would have been obliterated. The Navy SEALs Stoner 63A was infamous for making a small hole when the bullet penetrated a human body, leaving a cavity the size of a man's fist when it exited.

The second round had entered the middle of soldier's back, several inches below the first shot. Using the heel of his left foot, Joe gently pulled the body onto its back and discovered the black-clad soldier was female. Having been aware that thousands of women were combat soldiers in both the Viet Cong and North Vietnamese Army, Joe was only mildly surprised by the discovery.

His carbine had lived up to its reputation. Where the lady's face should have been was now a jelled mass of blood, bone, and brain matter. Having seen dozens of mutilated bodies over the past 20 months, he was not the least bit bothered by the sight in front of him.

However, what he saw next overwhelmed his senses. The horrifying sight caused bile to fill his throat, forcing Joe to drop on his hands and knees and began to vomit.

The female soldier was not carrying mortar rounds. Instead, she was carrying a child, a baby girl. The girl's tiny body was nearly ripped in half by Joe's second shot.

◆◆◆

Over the next two weeks, Joe saw a psychologist, a psychiatrist, and the base Protestant minister. All three came to the same conclusion:

After 20 months and 15 days of combat, Petty Officer Second Class Joseph E. Tyler needed to be sent back to the United States for further evaluation.

CHAPTER THIRTY-FOUR
End of August 1968

It was the end of the month. Joe was sitting aboard a Northwest Orient passenger jet. The big plane moves slowly on the taxiway as they prepare to launch down the runway. A couple of hundred military guys are on board, representing every branch of service, all having been in Vietnam only a day or two before. Soon they would be airborne and heading to Tacoma, Washington. Back to civilization. Back to the World, as they always called it.

The jet full of Vietnam warriors arrived at the Seattle-Tacoma International Airport in the late afternoon. Everything was wet from a warm August rain. Instead of joining the other planes at the terminal, they sat off the runway on an empty spot of the tarmac.

After traveling a long period of time, finally getting back to USA soil, and then forced to stay cooped-up was not well received.

About the time the men were getting too noisy, the plane's captain announced that, as a military flight, they would be disembarking at a different area of the airport. The pilot added that the reason for the delay was that they had caught a favorable jet stream and landed well ahead of their scheduled time. He apologized but added they had no choice other than to sit and wait.

As seasoned military people, they all understood the "hurry up and wait" routine. Another hour past before the pilot announced that the plane would be moving to another area, where they would disembark. They were told that buses would be taking them to their final destinations and the coaches would meet the plane near the exit ramp.

The flight attendant making the announcements added that a couple dozen people would deplane first and board the first bus. In a few minutes, the buses arrived beside the ramp near the front of the plane. Joe's name was called as part of the group to board the first bus.

Further back in the aircraft someone yelled out that the buses had Walla Walla Prison stenciled on the sides and had bars on the windows. Everyone crowded the small windows to look. Others started cracking jokes about their next duty stations have been chosen for them.

When Joe left home in June of 1965, he had dreamt of returning from the war to people celebrating, waving American flags. As the caravan of soldiers passed by, the people applauded and shouting their gratitude.

After all six buses were loaded, they drove in a convoy toward a nondescript gate, far away from the main terminal.

But this was three-years later - August of 1968.

Joe's dream was about to be replaced by stark reality.

Twenty-five yards before reaching the gate, the buses were met by police in riot gear. Police officers came on-board each bus and told shield their faces in case of broken glass.

Other police gathered at the gate a few yards ahead of them just as two fire trucks pulled up on either side of them.

As the gates opened, the riot police, several on rather large horses, began physically pushing back aa massive mob of angry people. There were people waving flags all right - but the flags were upside down.

It seemed to Joe that most of the people held posters and pictures of dead Vietnamese women and children. Many of those not carrying placards began throwing rocks, tomatoes, eggs, feces, and red paint against each of the bus's windows

Every human being outside and not in uniform was screaming obscenities calling the American warriors all sorts of vicious, spiteful, and degenerate names.

Everyone on the bus stayed dead silent, bewildered as to how their beloved country had turned against them.

One specific poster hurt Joe to his very core, caused tears to swell in his eyes and brought physical pain to his chest.

The poster had the word "BABY" written in black ink across the top. Along the bottom was the word "KILLERS" in replicated, red blood dripping across the bottom.

Between the header and footer was a color photograph of three American GI's standing semi-circle around the bodies of infants and young children.

CHAPTER THIRTY-FIVE
August - September 1968

Joe found out later there had been rumors of a massacre in the Mi Lai, South Vietnam. The news was that American soldiers had entered the village and killed every man, woman, and child.

Just when he thought things could not get any more bizarre, their bus pulled up to a hospital. A nurse with a clipboard came on board. She called out names, and when the person acknowledged their presence, she announced which wing of the hospital they had been assigned.

They entered through a side door where another nurse met them and escorted to their specialized areas. Six other guys and Joe had been assigned to a sizeable dorm-type room with about a dozen beds. The nurse checked her chart and assigned each of them to a numbered bed.

There were open shelves between each bed where they could store their personal belongings. On each bed were pajama tops, bottoms, and slippers. That was all the invitation Joe needed. He grabbed his new clothes, found the head, took a shower, and climbed into bed. The other guys were still chattering when he fell into a deep sleep.

At 6:00 the next morning, two nurses came in pushing small carts. They checked their blood pressure, pulse, weight, and height. Later another nurse came in and drew a couple of vials of blood from each of them. She told each of them their respective doctor's name and said that they would be in to examine them later that morning, according to each doctor's schedule.

Joe had been out of the ward, exploring the hospital. His doctor came in, just as he returned to the room. The doctor introduced himself, and they shook hands. He grabbed Joe's chart and scribbled something.

Joe sat toward the end of the bed and awaited his examination.

The doctor pulled up a chair, sat down, and then propped his feet on his bed. He looked up over thin reading glasses and asked him two questions: When was the last time he took any bennies? (aka Navy vitamin pills – two days ago.)

What was the most bennies he had ever taken in any 24 hours? Joe told him eight, which was four times the original prescribed amount. The doctor added a few scribbled notes, flipped the chart closed, and stood up.

"See you tomorrow morning."

So much for the medical exam. For the life of him, he could never remember this doctor's name. But he always remembered enjoying their morning visits. After the doctor left, Joe laid back in the bed. To his amazement, he slept until four or five o'clock when they woke him for supper. After supper, he did another recon of the hospital, tried to watch some television with the other guys and then slept all night; this became his routine for the next several days.

One day his doctor came in wearing slacks and a dress shirt, sans clinician gown with embroidered name.

"Get dressed. We're going for a walk." he put on the only clothes he had -- tiger-striped pants, a tan T-shirt, jungle boots and a Navy-issued short-sleeved fatigue shirt. It had originally belonged to someone else, but he had crossed out his stenciled name and printed his name above his with a black marker.

"That's it?" he asked, somewhat bewildered. "You don't have any civvies?"

"No, sir. They plucked me out of the jungle, put me on a variety of aircraft and then the bus dropped me off here."

"If you're going to be walking around outside, I suggest you get some jeans and other shirts."

"I don't have any money," Joe said, somewhat embarrassed. "I've been in the bush for the last few years and only kept $10 a month. Where we were, how we dressed and all, there just was not much use for having any money around. So, I sent the rest to the bank back home. My mom co-signed with the bank so she could get money out to pay the bills."

They continued to walk down the street in silence until they entered a Woolworth store. Over his objections, the doctor bought him jeans, underwear, socks, tennis shoes and some shirts.

Joe thanked him several times over. They walked back to the hospital, this time through using the front entrance.

"Okay, here's the deal," the doctor said as they stepped into the lobby. "After I see you each morning, you are to put on civilian clothes. "After a good, protein-packed lunch, I want you to spend the rest of the day exploring Tacoma and Seattle. I do not care where you go or what you do, but I want you to walk almost everywhere.

"Be back for bed check by eight. When I come in the next morning, I want you to tell me what you did, what you saw, who you talked to, and what you talked about."

After a short pause, he held out his hand and said, "Deal?"

They solidified the deal with a handshake. For the next several days, that's the way his life went. Every day after lunch, he would leave the hospital. Although he rode the bus to Seattle twice, mostly he went everywhere on foot. Judging by the amount of time he spent moving, he probably averaged 12 miles a day.

Nothing was off-limits. Joe might walk into a museum, wander along Puget Sound, or walk through the seediest neighborhood he could find. On another day, he might hang around the Space Needle and watch the hippies hustle money from the tourists.

The next morning after the blood tests, pulse, blood pressure readings, and finally breakfast, Joe would sit and waited for the doctor to show up.

Everything was grand except that he really was broke.

He related the top view of his call home to tell his mother where he was and asked her to wire $100 from his savings account. He received another shock. She began crying and sobbing, then told him that his dad had gotten into his bank account and drank all the money he had saved.

Every two weeks, his father pretty much wiped out whatever the Navy had paid him. Joe told her to calm down, that he was not upset with her and that he was at fault, not her, as he should have expected him to do something like that.

Joe and the doctor had a reasonably long discussion about that call the next day. The paymaster stopped the deposits and agreed to hold his pay until he stopped by again. It took half a day, but Joe finally tracked down his older brother at the Army's Monterey Language School.

Bill agreed to wire the $100, which Joe got the next day. After he repaid the doctor (against his strong objections), he still had about $40. That was more than enough to hold him until he got his regular pay flowing again.

Finally, after three weeks in the hospital, he was the only one left in the ward. And then one morning the doctor did not show up. After lunch, he just sat on his bed, waiting for him. Joe questioned a couple of the nurses, but no one had an explanation.

About an hour after lunch, a young Marine corporal arrived with a large manila envelope in his hand.

"Petty Officer Tyler?"

"No one else here but me, so I guess I'm him."

"I still need to see your ID."

After he showed him his military credentials, he had Joe sign several pieces of paper. Immediately after he signed the last document, the Marine turned and began to walk away.

"Hey," he shouted, "what the hell is this?" "You're going home. Enjoy the rest of your life."

In the envelope were his discharge papers from active military duty, along with instructions to report to the Naval Reserve Center in Youngstown, Ohio, within the next 90 days, and $3,500 in $100 bills.

CHAPTER THIRTY-SIX
September 1968

When he left Tacoma, Joe took a bus down to Monterey to visit his brother Bill and repaid the money he had wired him a few weeks earlier. He had joined the Army after he left for the Navy boot camp and, other than calling him last week, he had not seen, nor barely heard from him the past couple of years.

A word about his older brother -- Bill had a knack for picking up new languages like regular people might learn how to perform essential math functions. He says this because Monterey is home to the world-renowned Defense Language Institute Foreign Language Center, which is run by the Department of Defense. The DLIFLC is where the government trains people from a variety of military and intelligence organizations on how they will be using their new language skills in their chosen occupations. They were brothers who grew up together, but differently.

Bill was the Brainiac.

Joe was - was what?

His sister, Karen, always called him "The Hood," which Joe had thought of as a reference to the guys he hung out with at Quimby Park. He found out later that it was actually because of how often he needed his father, uncles, or cousins to give him a ride home from the police station.

Bill was always studying and never really had time for neighborhood sports. He would not play football with them until they goaded him into it. Then he would make them pay: Whenever he ran the football, Bill would obliterate whoever was dumb enough to attempt a tackle. He would not just run over someone; he would run through them. After scoring a touchdown, he would turn around, smile at them, and say something to the effect that they were all too weak to play at his level. Bill would follow-up by throwing the ball at him, extremely hard, nearly knocking him over.

Joe would always catch it if only to prove he could take it. The next day, he would have a bruise on his torso where the ball had hit. As a kid, Joe always thought Bill wasted a chance to be a high-school football superstar.

Then again, Joe was probably thinking more about himself. After all, who wants to lose bragging rights to having a brother who could have been the star running back.

After Joe joined the military, he was deployed in dangerous environments. Bill, on the other hand, with his love of languages, was afforded a different path.

After the service, or even during his service tenure, Joe's brother could attend college on the GI Bill and earn a variety of language degrees.

By enlisting in the Army and going to the Language Skills to read, write and speak Russian, French and German on the government's dime also excluded Bill from having to go to Vietnam as part of the enlisted Army infantry.

Joe arrived at Bill's base, thinking about the guys they had escorted on Grab missions. It was a good bet they had attended classes here in Monterey. In the end, Bill and he had more in common than he would ever realize. The Marine guard took his information and made a few phone calls.

Joe sat there in the little guard shack, found a spot on the wall to focus on and waited about 45 minutes. Bill and a couple of his bookish friends, none of whom had been born in America, met him at the front gate.

For a second, Bill did not recognize him. He cocked his head to one side, and then a smile spread across his face. They were never a demonstrative family, so he was surprised when Bill greeted his younger brother with a big, bear hug.

Then he held him back at arm's length, looked him up and down, causing a huge smile to overtake his face.

"My little brother finally grew up! Look at you! You're big. Muscled. Tan. You even got older. I barely recognized you!"

Bill introduced Joe to his buddies, and they all went out for burgers and beers. It was great to relax, hang out with him and his friends, and laugh about mundane things.

When the subject about what he did in Vietnam arose, he answered truthfully, saying he was not allowed to talk about it, even to them. Bill offered that these guys obviously had high-security clearance levels.

Bill, with deep furrows in his brow, just stared at him.

Joe knew what he was thinking: Is he kidding me or what?

"Mom said you were sailing around the Pacific aboard a Navy destroyer," he finally said.

Joe stared at him for a few seconds and, using his eyes, pleaded with him to not take it any further. Communication through eye contact was something they did as far back as he could remember.

"Good," Bill replied. "We should just leave it at that."

All too soon, the guys needed to head back to the base. Even though they were attending classes, they were still in the military. Their day began at 0530.

When they got to the gate, Joe waited as his brother, and his buddies tried to get him on base. Sure enough, the Marines on duty would not allow him to pass.

Joe asked the Jarhead (military slang for a Marine) if there was a "visitors' pamphlet" for the base. Before the Marine could answer, one of his brother's friends reached beside the gate, took a pamphlet, and handed Joe one, "For when you visit tomorrow."

Joe looked inside and found what he had hoped for: The Army had provided a complete diagram of the base, including perimeter fences.

After taking Bill aside and asking him a few questions about the layout, Joe told his brother he would see him within the hour.

Bill's parting words were, "Don't call me from the brig. These aren't the Warren cops."

Forty minutes later, he was knocking on their dorm room door. Joe stayed with them for two or three days.

Free food, a place to sleep and, once again, if he looked like he belonged on the base, no one bothered to ask for any credentials.

They were having dinner at one of the base restaurants the first night when he mentioned he was thinking about driving back home.

Bill spread the word to see if anyone had a vehicle to sell. As luck would have it, one of the instructors was selling his low mileage 1963 Triumph Bonneville motorcycle. The next day Joe bought the bike for $300 cash.

Just before Joe left, he mentioned to his brother that on Navy bases, they always had Marines guarding the gates. And, on Army bases, he saw Army personnel and guard dogs.

Joe wondered why that was. Without skipping a beat, Bill replied, "It was because the Army had the first choice."

Laughing, Joe said his goodbyes, promised to stay in touch and began a circuitous ride home.

CHAPTER THIRTY-SEVEN
Mid-September 1968

Before heading east, Joe decided to visit Coronado, which was some 450 miles to the south. He took the coastal highway, often stopping to enjoy the ocean and other scenery. While riding, he thought a lot about the guys on the MACV-SOG teams. Their missions in the bush had changed a lot after the Tet Offensive. Everything everywhere got a lot more intense.

He wondered exactly how the bush assignments had changed. Were the teams getting more Recon missions in the hill country? But mostly, he wondered if - 'hoped' would be a better word - that his brother-warriors were safe without him there as their point man.

Because Joe wanted to experience America and needed to get in touch with the way American life had changed, it took three-and-a-half days to get down to Coronado. Joe purposely stayed off the freeways the entire trip, referring to witness the good, the bad, the strange.

He bought a sleeping bag and some light camping gear at a surplus store just after leaving Monterey. He thought finding spots to bed down along the ocean would be easy, and he was right.

However, once he reached the greater Los Angeles area, he had to ride east and through the city streets of Los

Angeles to find some eastern-area foothills and possible places to camp.

Joe ended up camping near a small lake called Elsinore.

Before he got to the camping area, the evening temperatures were so warm, he rode with his shirt off through Watts and Compton areas before heading southeast toward the foothills. Even when he was in boot camp in San Diego in 1965, he had heard a lot about the riots in Watts, the looting, the burning of vehicles and buildings, and the National Guard having been called.

To him, these areas were a part of American history, and he wanted to see what they were like, today. As his psychologist said to him fifty years later, at least that was the reason he gave himself.

Later in life, he learned that most likely, the actual reason he chose to ride a motorcycle through these extremely volatile neighborhoods, (at night, and being a shirtless white boy), was to invite confrontation so Joe could once again feel the adrenaline rush he loved so much.

As his sister Karen always remarked, Joe was never said to be the brightest lightbulb on the Christmas tree.

When he finally got down to Coronado, Joe went directly to the Master Chief's home, hoping to find him or Marsha. When no one came to the door, Joe looked in the living room window and found their house vacated.

Because his ID was now red (military inactive) rather than green, Joe was having trouble getting past the Marine guards. He started name-dropping until he hit one that rang a bell with the Marine Corporal on duty. After rolling his eyes then stepping back inside the guard shack, he made a phone call. Whoever he spoke to give the guard the okay to let him pass. After handed Joe his visitor pass, he instructed him to report to the base administration offices.

When he got to the admin offices, he was asked to sit and wait, and told someone would be coming to get him.

Hurry up and wait: Some things never change.

Joe waited over an hour when he heard someone say his call sign.

"CopperSun? Hey CopperSun, is that really you?" Joe looked up, and there was CWO Presley. They had not seen each other since they parted company in Cam Ranh Bay.

Presley looked impressive, standing there in a starched tan uniform. He also appeared in better physical condition than Joe remembered. He stood up and walked over to shake his hand. Presley would have none of that and immediately gave him a big bear hug.

"Man, I lost track of you after July. Thought Charlie finally found you but couldn't find where your name had been attached to a black-bag."

With that, Presley placed two big meat paws on either shoulder and, for a second, Joe thought another bear hug was on the way. Presley face glowed with genuine enthusiasm of finding that a long-lost friend was still alive. His eyes were sincere, whereas Joe's must have revealed confusion.

"Hungry?" he asked while spinning him toward the door. "Let's grab some chow. Barry Glenn is going to be glad to hear you popped up on the radar."

"Speaking of Barry," Joe asked as they walked toward the officer's mess, "how is the big guy? Better yet, where is he?"

"You missed him by two weeks. The short version is he replaced me in Saigon for a 13-month stint and a bunch more medals for his parade uniform. Marsha moved back to Eugene to be near her family. My wife and I are moving into their old place the first of the month. Stop by if you get a chance."

They arrived at the officer's mess and sat down at a regular square dining table with a tablecloth, linen napkins, and real silverware.

Joe was awestruck. Considering all the time he spent in Coronado, he never knew this restaurant existed. A sailor who appeared to be a Philippine native, brought over water, then took their orders. They both ordered their favorite meal: cheeseburgers with mustard and a quarter-inch slice of raw Vidalia onion, fries, and Cokes.

Presley explained that one of his functions in Saigon was to keep tabs on the guys who were fast-tracked into MACV-SOG teams. That part of his job was frustrating and made worse due to communications problems. Trying to get written documentation from a dozen different MACV-SOG platoons comprised of Green Berets, Marine Recons and Frogmen, all running secret operations in three different countries, was challenging at best.

Adding to this difficulty was that the information they did receive was limited to the numbers of operations, close geographic area, enemy KIA, and confirmation of U.S. and coalition MIA/KIA. For security reasons, the names of those involved were omitted.

Joe told him about his bizarre discharge experience. In fact, the whole trip from the bush to Tacoma was surreal.

In a matter of 30 hours, he had gone from being actively involved on a search and destroy mission, to jumping from plane to plane to plane, flying in a first class seat to the State of Washington that ended with them riding a bus sent in from Walla Walla Prison to Tacoma, where he ended up in a psych ward.

The entire trip was accomplished with little notice, direction, nor any conversation as to what to expect once he left 'Nam. When he arrived at the hospital, they explained his visit was designed to wean him off his daily ration of bennies.

When Joe told Prescott that he had to talk to a shrink a couple of times a day, Prescott's eyebrows wrinkled as he cocked his head to one side. He took out a small notebook and began scribbling. Presley asked to see Joe's DD-214 (discharge documentation), and he told him he had never received it. All he had been given was a letter instructing him to see a Naval Reserve Recruiter and $3,500 in cash. He gave him the letter which Prescott read during their late lunch. Afterward, he said he could sleep on the base that night, promising to track down his information the next day.

After nearly an entire day of phone calls, the final answer, unfortunately, was incomplete. His current designation was JFW. Even Prescott had to look it up: it was the Navy's secret separation code which meant: Incomplete Information. In other words, officially, the Navy had no clue why it was letting him out of his active enlistment.

Presley was also told to get Joe's signature on another document stating he would never talk about the Military Assistance Command, Vietnam – Studies and Operations Group, nor his relationship, functions or duties within the various teams, for the rest of his life or until the information became part of the public domain.

All this came as an addendum to what he had signed nearly two years earlier with Master Chief Glenn. Presley concluded by stating someone from either the Pentagon or Langley, advised Presley to Charlie Delta (Cease and Desist) and not make further inquiries on his behalf. They concluded by stating someone would soon be in touch with them both.

As Presley related his tale, both men smiled, shrugged their shoulders, stood, and said their goodbyes. At this point in their lives, and even though Presley was 12 to 15 years his senior, they had a lot in common. They were both BUD/S Special Operation Warfare-trained.

They had both finished nearly two years of in-country military duty within a highly classified, multi-service unit that conducted covert, unconventional warfare operations within the boundaries of an enemy country.

Joe, as a designated Fence Jumper (a term given to those who often operated north of the DMZ in North Vietnam), and Presley, working at the MACV-SOG Central Command, both knew there was nothing more that should be said. Nor could be said, for that matter. Everything they had learned, heard, witnessed, knew about, or done over the past couple of years may as well have never happened.

Now that they were no longer in-country, they were not permitted to ever talk about their experiences, even among themselves. The more he thought about it, the more he felt that he might as well forget about it. There would never be any official acknowledgment of a Navy Special Operations Group. Not to mention, in 1968 (nor for the next 40 years) was there any government information nor military evidence saying that the MACV-SOG ever existed.

Even if he mentioned to other Vietnam vets that he had been to Cam Ranh Bay, Quang Tri, Da Nang, or Phan Thiet, he could not prove it. When he finally got his original DD-214 discharge papers, all they mentioned was "two tours of duty in Vietnam," various medals and citations, and 20 months and 15 days of combat.

For him personally, there would never be an official, relevant document saying where he was assigned, how long he was there, where he fought nor what he did. In BUD/S, he learned how to control his mind.

Especially, how to shove the pain back so he could move forward.

CHAPTER THIRTY-EIGHT
September 1968

Riding east from Coronado, Joe would often stop to admire the hills or just stare out over the desert. It was then, just as he had crossed into Arizona, that he got the idea to find JJ Smith's mother in Oklahoma and Jimmy Proctor's family in Florida.

For some unknown reason that rattles around in the back of his brain, Joe needed to sit, and get to know their families. It was important to Joe that they knew what brave sons they had. Without breaking his government oath, he would do his best to let them know how and where their sons died.

Once again, because he wanted to see the American landscape, the 1,500-mile ride from Coronado to Bartlesville, Oklahoma, took four days and nearly 2,000 miles. Joe took a southern route through Tucson, proceeded to Las Cruces, New Mexico, traveled north through Socorro and then east again until he arrived at Cannon Air Force Base outside of Clovis, New Mexico.

He saw many F-100 Super Sabre's in Vietnam camouflage flying overhead as he crossed the state. It turned out that Cannon was being used as a training base for Vietnam pilots. While the Super Sabre lacked the superior technology of the Air Force F-105 Thunderchief and the Navy/Marine F-4 Phantoms, the Super Sabre was the plane they wanted to see on the horizon when it came to close-in air support.

These pilots were trained to bomb close and tight to Army units in the bush. More times than not, they flew at treetop level at 350 mph over a terrain of hills and valleys.

Most impressive.

Joe decided to try to get on yet another military base. He sat on the Triumph alongside the road that led to the base. One of the more seasoned pilots stopped to check on him and, after swapping a couple of war stories to check out each man's creds, Joe was able to get a tour of the base and two free meals.

On the advice of one of the line Master Sergeants, Joe stayed the night in a small motel across the Texas border in Muleshoe, population 2,800. Muleshoe was an old western town with a lot of the original early 1900s buildings still intact.

The town was founded in 1913 when the Pecos and Northern Texas Railway built an 88-mile line from Farwell, Texas, to Lubbock.

When he left Muleshoe, Joe first headed north to Amarillo, then northeast into Oklahoma. The first night in Oklahoma, he stayed just south of Broken Arrow because he liked the name of the town. When he left Broken Arrow, he rode around the city of Tulsa and still ended up in Bartlesville an hour-and-a-half, later.

After asking around town, he finally found JJ Smith's mother and younger brother living in the adjacent town of Dewey, just a few miles further north of downtown Bartlesville.

JJ's mom had been married to a guy who worked on the oil rigs and, for whatever reason, they were no longer together. She worked two different part-time jobs. In the morning and evening, she worked as a waitress at a local diner and, during the middle of the day, at the neighborhood Fresh Cut Meat market.

JJ's brother, Robert, was a senior in high school. Robert's immediate goal in life was to become a Navy SEAL and avenge his brother's death.

Joe had dinner at the cafe where Jerry's mom worked. It was chicken-fried steak with a side of mashed potatoes, smothered in a thick grey gravy. He always remembered that meal because, until then, he had never heard of chicken-fried steak before.

And not being from that area of America, he did not realize that all three meals of the day regularly came smothered in gravy.

Later that evening, Jerry's mom and Joe sat outside on the front stoop of the trailer home, under a star-filled sky. She brought them each a cold beer. Meanwhile, Bobby sat in the kitchen, doing his homework. Whereas Jerry was strong and an inch shorter than Joe, both his mother and brother were tall and wiry.

After several minutes of saying nothing, Jerry's mother broke the silence by asking about her son's death. While leaving out the horrendous specifics, Joe was as honest as possible. He emphasized that her son died when their gunboat came to the aid of a small Army company that was overwhelmed by a large company of Viet Cong.

As she sat listening, she held herself and rocked back and forth as Joe spoke, never interrupting, never asking a single question. Tears formed in her eyes, and occasionally, one would escape and roll down her cheek.

She never once looked at Joe after handing him his beer. When Joe spoke about Jerry, she looked the other way. They finished their beer and sat there in silence for quite a spell. After a while, she stood up and, looking out in the distance, thanked him for coming by. Without looking at him, she turned and went inside, saying something along the lines that she had to get up early the next morning to go to work.

Having been quietly dismissed, Joe got on the Triumph motorcycle and headed south. At the edge of Bartlesville, he headed east and slept under the stars just a short distance from Nowata, near the banks of Oologah Lake, Oklahoma.

That night Joe had a nightmare about Jerry getting killed. He awoke in a panic, sweating and panting like he had just run a 100-meter sprint in full combat gear. Looking back, that was probably the first of the many wartime nightmares he would endure over the next several decades.

When he awoke, it was about 3:30 in the morning. Deciding that he was too geared-up to sleep, he stretched, gathered his gear and set-out for Lacoochee, Florida to meet Jimmy Proctor's family.

As often as possible, he stayed to the back roads. Cutting first through Arkansas, then committing to a winding southeastern journey through Mississippi and Alabama, meaning that most of Joe's travels took him on dirt roads. In doing so, he witnessed some of the poorest, loneliest geography that he could have ever imagined.

Joe spent the next night in Florida, near the small town of Chipley, just west of Tallahassee. The next day, it took a couple of stops at some wonderfully old-fashioned services stations, to find out exactly how to get to Lacoochee. As usual, his perseverance paid off.

Lacoochee was a small town about 50 to 60 miles northeast of Tampa and sat another 55 miles due west of Orlando. By the way, remembering the name of Jimmy's hometown was easy: One of Joe's favorite pitchers for the Cleveland Indians was Jim "Mudcat" Grant, who, like Jimmy, was born and raised in.

Once Joe got into town, it took only one mention of the Proctor name, and the lady owner and lead mechanic of a small Sinclair gas station gave him precise instructions on how to find their home.

As Joe was about to discover, while Jerry Smith's mother had been stoic, Jimmy Proctor's family would greet him with something that felt like a family homecoming. It took him less than five minutes to get to the Proctor's house. When he turned off the dirt road into their driveway, he looked up to find Jimmy's parents standing side-by-side, holding hands on their front porch waiting for him.

You got to love small town America. In the short amount of time it took him to get to their home, they were alerted that he was coming and stood on their front porch, holding hands, awaiting his arrival.

Their house was a beautifully kept, immaculate white ranch home surrounded by some of the prettiest flowers Joe had ever seen. Joe got off the bike and walked up to within five feet of the three wooden porch steps.

"Mr. and Mrs. Proctor? My name is Joe Tyler and ..."

Before he could finish talking, Jimmy's dad bounded off the porch, grabbed his right hand in his and began slapping his shoulders with this huge left meat paw.

"You're Joe Tyler? We know who you are! You served with our boy, Jimmy John! Come on in. Come on in."

Mr. Proctor turned to his wife, who was still standing on the porch, apparently looking out to nowhere.

"Mother? This here is Mr. Tyler, Jimmy John's best friend from The United States Navy."

As Mr. Proctor spoke to her, it occurred to Joe that she was blind. As she turned her head in the direction of their voices, a huge smile lit up her face. Joe walked up to the steps to where she stood.

Joe took both her hands in his, then, without thinking, pulled her into a hug.

"Mother Proctor," he said softly in her ear, "it sure is wonderful to finally meet you."

He slowly backed away as she raised her weathered hands, then softly caressed every feature of his face.

"Why, you're a white boy! Jimmy John never said!" She stammered a bit, but through her tears, she managed to get out what she was trying to say.

"I just assumed you were colored, Jimmy John always saying how close you two being and all."

She turned her head to one side and in the direction of where her husband was standing.

"Big Jim, please bring our guest some of that fresh lemonade I made this morning. And while you are in the kitchen, maybe a plate of those delicious lemon cookies I baked yesterday. They would be in the pantry."

After a short pause, she added, "Get you and me some, too. Then come on out and sit with us a spell, as Mr. Tyler and us gots a lot to talk about."

"Yes, Mother, I think that would be rather nice," he said before moving away. "Mr. Tyler, Mother Proctor would be quite pleased if you would escort her to that porch swing over there. Mother, you and he could sit there since I like to sit in that big spring chair over next to you."

Joe spent two days and nights with Jimmy's family. He offered to find a place in town, but they would not hear of it. No one had been in Jimmy's room since he had left for his last duty station, and they felt he should have the honor of "transitioning-it," as they called it.

That evening, Joe got to hear about the other five siblings, how Jimmy, err, Jimmy John, was the baby and had spent three years in the Navy before finally getting accepted to BUD/S. Two of his sisters and one brother had graduated from medical universities, while another brother was an attorney. The youngest sister was a special education teacher at a middle school.

They did ask about Jimmy's death, just the one time, but they had more questions about his life, what he did, what he talked about, and how he reacted to different situations. They wanted to remember their son as he lived, not as he died. Naturally, Joe structured his conversations in such a way as to not jeopardize his agreement with the U.S. Government.

Joe told Jimmy's parents about how he and Jimmy ended up sharing the same hooch in Quang Tri. How they became good friends from when they first said hello to one another, and how they became closer friends when Joe told Jimmy that he had met Mudcat Grant after one of the Cleveland Indians baseball games.

When Big Jim heard that, he got up out of his chair, went in the house and came back out with a shoebox full of his son's letters home.

"About when did you and Jimmy John first meet?" he asked, holding the box on his lap. While his wife and Joe sat on the porch swing sipping their drinks, Big Jim began going through the envelopes. He had arranged them by date, and it took only a minute to find what he was looking for.

"I found it, Mother Proctor. Do you remember when he wrote this?" As he asked, a tear rolled down her cheek.

"I surely do," she replied and then began quoting the date of the letter and what her son had written. "Jimmy John said he had been in Quang Tri for about a week now, and he and this kid from Ohio have become good friends. He said "he's a lot younger than me and I suppose I will have to teach him some, but already we are getting pretty close. The word is he single-handed broke up a surprise attack by an entire company of Mr. Charlie down in Cam Ranh."

Saying that Mother Proctor slowly reached out for Joe's hand. Seeing that, he put his hand in hers. When he did, she squeezed his hand tightly.

Joe looked into her face as tears began rolling down both cheeks. His own tears soon followed. Once Big Jim regained his own composure, he began reading from where she had left off.

"Joe had made Charlie figure they had just walked into a big trap. The Viet Cong would have been twice as surprised had they had seen it was just some white boy throwing rocks and grenades at them. Ha. Ha.

"I just found out Tyler, that's his name, was a big Mudcat Grant fan! Can you believe that? He even met him once. He did not believe me when I told him that me and Mudcat would see each almost every day. Used to play catch with the baseball with him. Had to show him our address on this envelope afore he believed me. You know what he said? That we was like two brothers that got separated in heaven before we was born!!!"

With that, Big Jim finished reading, folded the letter back into the envelope and, keeping his head bent down, shook it slowly from side to side. Joe noticed Big Jim's eyes were a little moist, same as his. He leaned over and squeezed Mother Proctors hand a little tighter. They just sat there for several minutes, holding hands.

Joe remembering his good friend Jimmy Proctor in his way, and his parents missing their youngest son, in the only way two loving, proud American parents could.

Big Jim stood up and quietly mumbled something about time he got dinner going, and Mother Proctor said she would go with him to cook up some fried chicken. After dinner that evening, they again sat out on the porch, and Joe got to hear all about Jimmy's brothers and sisters.

He also learned that he and Jimmy had a lot of things in common.

Both their older siblings were bookworms, while Jimmy and Joe preferred hanging out with their buddies, playing ball, or going over to a nearby fishing pond. The difference being that Jimmy was able to catch bass while Joe was reduced to only catching small bluegills or, occasionally, 15" carps. Neither of them felt the need to study, as both wanted to join the Navy and become underwater demolition guys.

Joe stayed at their home for two nights. On the second day, Joe went with Big Jim into town where he owned the local hardware store. In the morning, Big Jim attended to business while Joe wandered about town. Everyone Joe talked to had already known he was Jimmy Proctor's best friend from "THE United States Navy."

When it came time for lunch, Big Jim and Joe went back to the house to where Mother Proctor had sandwiches and sweet tea waiting for them. Joe offered to stay at the house that afternoon and do a couple of chores. Mother Proctor quickly pointed out that he was not welcome and that she did not need some man bothering her while she had things to do.

Big Jim just laughed and said he would put Joe to work in the store.

Instead, when they got back to town, together they walked through town visiting Big Jim's friends (everyone in town). Joe heard stories about Jimmy as a youngster and all the trouble he would get into. In turn, Joe got to tell some "war" stories, more to brag about his opportunity to serve with such a great American hero like Jimmy Proctor.

Looking back, staying with them was the closest feeling of being "at home" that he had in several years. And while he promised to keep in touch, he would be the first to tell anyone that asked, he regretted never getting back in contact with them.

CHAPTER THIRTY-NINE
2018

Joe Tyler spent the next fifty years, moving from job to job, to job.

Most of his life centered around broadcast and sports marketing. To be sure, he was a very, reliable worker. Everywhere Joe had been employed, his superiors enjoyed and benefited from him being there. He did his best work when his direct-report-to simply pointed out that "this mountain needed to be crossed" and left him alone to figure it out.

From 1987 to 1992 he worked for the Cleveland Cavaliers. New owners came in, and the bean counters told them that his sales staff was "over-indexing" on their commission pay when measured against the other teams in the NBA.

Joe explained that his staff was one-third the size of the major market teams. And, they out billed every other salesperson in the NBA. The bean counters reply was, regardless, their income per market size did not meet NBA standards. Therefore, Joe was to lower their base pay by 25% and their commissions by 50%.

Joe said: "Not in this lifetime."

To wit, they replied: "Your services are no longer needed."

Several years later, Joe worked as a trainer/consultant for the Arbitron Radio Rating Company. Several years into his career with them, he was an hour late meeting with a significant client. On Joe's behalf, he always hid his military background from every employer. Unfortunately, his Post Traumatic Stress Syndrome problems were increasing. For whatever reason, when Joe arrived for the meeting, he had a severe anxiety attack.

Without asking either "why" or "what happened" his junior, rookie boss fired him.

◆◆◆

Today, Joe is an entirely different person than he was just one year ago.

Why?

Dr. Rene Mack, PTSD Psychologist. Dr. Keri Fate, Internal Medicine. Dr. Stacy Walker, PTSD Psychiatry.

In 2018, this trio of specialist helped Joe get his health, his medications, and most importantly, his brain back in balance. In Joe's opinion, the critical factor was the EMDR treatments: Eye Movement Desensitization and Reprocessing by Dr. Mack.

During his EMDR therapy, Joe was introduced to emotionally disturbing material in brief sequential doses while he simultaneously focused on an external stimulus. For Joe's treatment, lateral eye movements were used as the external stimulus, but a variety of other stimuli, including hand-tapping and audio stimulation, are also often used.

In short, too many Vietnam Veterans still needlessly suffer from PTSD – nearly 200,000 according to the Veterans Administration. Likewise, hundreds of thousands of recent combat veterans also suffer needlessly.

Why? Ego and pride. Joe Tyler's advice?

Get over yourself. The help you need is nearby.

**

Note: EMDR - Eye Movement Desensitization and Reprocessing is a psychotherapy treatment that was initially designed to alleviate the distress associated with traumatic memories. Shapiro's (2001) Adaptive Information Processing model posits that EMDR therapy facilitates the accessing and processing of traumatic memories and other adverse life experience to bring these to an adaptive resolution. After successful treatment with EMDR therapy, affective distress is relieved, negative beliefs are reformulated, and physiological arousal is reduced. (Source: EMDR Institute, Inc.)

ACKNOWLEDGEMENTS

Marcia Chicoine
Maury Forsyth (USAF Retired)
Shelley Sandbulte, Psychologist, Clinical
Kimberly Tyler
Donna Wodianka

Ms. Kristi Tornquist
Chief University Librarian/Professor
Hilton M. Briggs Library
South Dakota State University

A special thanks to the "Ask the Librarians" staff
The Department of Defense
Washington DC

And the
SOUTH DAKOTA HUMANITIES COUNCIL

Please consider an annual donation to:

The Navy SEAL Foundation
Virginia Beach, VA

Comments? Questions?
Contact Joe Walker, via Email:
Coppersun265@yahoo.com

Made in the USA
Lexington, KY
06 November 2019